THE BETRAYAL

By

E. PHILLIPS OPPENHEIM

The Betrayal

by E. Phillips Oppenheim

ISBN: 978-93-57272-56-8

Published by

DOUBLE 9 BOOKS

2/13-B, Ansari Road, Daryaganj
New Delhi – 110002
info@double9books.com
www.double9books.com
Tel. 011-40042856

This book is under public domain

ABOUT THE AUTHOR

E. Phillips Oppenheim was born on October 22, 1866, in Tohhenham, London, England, to Henrietta Susannah Temperley Budd and Edward John Oppenheim, a leather retailer. After leaving school at age 17, he helped his father in his leather business and used to write in his extra time. His first novel, Expiration (1886), and subsequent thrillers piqued the interest of a wealthy New York businessman who eventually bought out the leather business and made Oppenheim a high-paid director. He is more focused on dedicating most of his time to writing. The novels, volumes of short stories, and plays that followed, numbering more than 150, were about humans with modern heroes, fearless spies, and stylish noblemen. The Long Arm of Mannister (1910), The Moving Finger (1911), and The Great Impersonation (1920) are three of his most famous essays.

CONTENTS

CHAPTER I
THE FACE AT THE WINDOW

Like a clap of thunder, the north wind, rushing seawards, seemed suddenly to threaten the ancient little building with destruction. The window sashes rattled, the beams which supported the roof creaked and groaned, the oil lamps by which alone the place was lit swung perilously in their chains. A row of maps designed for the instruction of the young—the place was a schoolhouse—commenced a devil's dance against the wall. In the street without we heard the crash of a fallen chimneypot. My audience of four rose timorously to its feet, and I, glad of the excuse, folded my notes and stepped from the slightly raised platform on to the floor.

"I am much obliged to you for coming," I said, "but I think that it is quite useless to continue, for I can scarcely make you hear, and I am not at all sure that the place is safe."

I spoke hastily, my one desire being to escape from the scene of my humiliation unaccosted. One of my little audience, however, was of a different mind. Rising quickly from one of the back seats, she barred the way. Her broad comely face was full of mingled contrition and sympathy.

"I am so sorry, Mr. Ducaine," she exclaimed. "It does seem a cruel pity, doesn't it?—and such a beautiful lecture! I tried so hard to persuade dad and the others to come, but you know how they all love hearing anything about the war, and—"

"My dear Miss Moyat," I interrupted, "I am only sorry that a mistaken sense of kindness should have brought you here. With one less in the audience I think I should have ventured to suggest that we all went round to hear Colonel Ray. I should like to have gone myself immensely."

Blanche Moyat looked at me doubtfully.

"That's all very well," she declared, "but I think it's jolly mean of the Duke to bring him down here the very night you were giving your lecture."

"I do not suppose he knew anything about that," I answered. "In any case, I can give my lecture again any time, but none of us may ever have another opportunity of hearing Colonel Ray. Allow me—"

I opened the door, and a storm of sleet and spray stung our faces. Old Pegg, who had been there to sell and collect tickets, shouted to us.

"Shut the door quick, master, or it'll be blown to smithereens. It's a real nor'easter, and a bad 'un at that. Why, the missie'll hardly stand. I'll see to the lights and lock up, Master Ducaine. Better be getting hoam while thee can, for the creeks'll run full to-night."

Once out in the village street I was spared the embarrassment of conversation. We had to battle the way step by step. We were drenched with spray and the driving rain. The wind kept us breathless, mocking any attempt at speech. We passed the village hall, brilliantly lit; the shadowy forms of a closely packed crowd of people were dimly visible through the uncurtained windows. I fancied that my companion's clutch upon my arm tightened as we hurried past.

We reached a large grey stone house fronting the street. Miss Moyat laid her hand upon the handle of the door and motioned to me to enter.

I shook my head.

"Not to-night," I shouted. "I am drenched."

She endeavoured to persuade me.

"For a few moments, at any rate," she pleaded. "The others will not be home yet, and I will make you something hot. Father is expecting you to supper."

I shook my head and staggered on. At the corner of the street I looked behind. She was holding on to the door handle, still watching me, her skirts blowing about her in strange confusion. For a moment I had half a mind to turn back. The dead loneliness before me seemed imbued with fresh horrors—the loneliness, my fireless grate and empty larder. Moyat was at least hospitable. There would be a big fire, plenty to eat and drink. Then I remembered the man's coarse hints, his unveiled references to his daughters and his wish to see them settled in life, his superabundance of whisky and his only half-veiled tone of patronage. The man was within his rights. He was the rich man of the neighbourhood, corn dealer, farmer, and horse breeder. I was an unknown and practically destitute stranger, come from Heaven knew where, and staying on—because it took a little less to keep body and soul together here than in the town. But my nerves were all raw that night, and the thought of John Moyat with his hearty voice and slap on the shoulder was unbearable. I set my face homewards.

From the village to my cottage stretched a perfectly straight road, with dykes on either side. No sooner had I passed the last house, and set my foot upon the road, than I saw strange things. The marshland, which on the right reached to the sea, was hung here and there with sheets of mist driven along the ground like clouds before an April tempest. White flakes of spray, salt and luminous, were dashed into my face. The sea, indriven up the creeks, swept the road in many places. The cattle, trembling with fear, had left the marshland, and were coming, lowing, along the high path which bordered the dyke. And all the time an undernote of terror, the thunder of the sea rushing in upon the land, came like a deep monotonous refrain to the roaring of the wind.

Through it all I battled my way, hatless, soaked to the skin, yet finding a certain wild pleasure in the storm. By the time I had reached my little dwelling I was exhausted. My hair and clothes were in wild disorder, my boots were like pulp upon my feet. My remaining strength was expended in closing the door. The fire was out, the place struck cold. I staggered towards the easy chair, but the floor seemed suddenly to heave beneath my feet. I was conscious of the fact that for two days I had had little to eat, and that my larder was empty. My limbs were giving way, a mist was before my eyes, and the roar of the sea seemed to be in my ears, even in my brain. My hands went out like a blind man's, and I suppose broke my fall. There was rest at least in the unconsciousness which came down like a black pall upon my senses.

It could only have been a short time before I opened my eyes. Some one was knocking at the door. Outside I could hear the low panting of a motor-car, the flashing of brilliant lamps threw a gleam of light across the floor of my room. Again there came a sharp rapping upon the door. I raised myself upon my elbow, but I made no attempt at speech. The motor was the Rowchester Daimler omnibus. What did these people want with me? I was horribly afraid of being found in such straits. I lay quite still, and prayed that they might go away.

But my visitor, whoever he was, had apparently no idea of doing anything of the sort. I heard the latch lifted, and the tall bulky form of a man filled the threshold. With him came the wind, playing havoc about my room, sending papers and ornaments flying around in wild confusion. He closed the door quickly with a little imprecation. I heard the scratching of a match, saw it carefully shielded in the hollow of the man's hand. Then it burned clearly, and I knew that I was discovered.

The man was wrapped from head to foot in a huge ulster. He was so tall that his cap almost brushed my ceiling. I raised myself upon my elbow and looked at him, looked for the first time at Mostyn Ray. He had the blackest and the heaviest eyebrows I had ever seen, very piercing eyes, and a finely shaped mouth, firm even to cruelty. I should have known him anywhere from the pictures which were filling the newspapers and magazines. My first impression, I think, was that they had done him but scanty justice.

As for me, there is no doubt but that I was a pitiful object. Of colour I had never very much, and my fainting fit could scarcely have improved matters. My cheeks, I had noticed that morning when shaving, were hollow, and there were black rims under my eyes. With my disordered clothing and hair, I must indeed have presented a strange appearance as I struggled to gain my feet.

He looked at me, as well he might, in amazement.

"I would ask you," he said, "to excuse my unceremonious entrance, but that it seems to have been providential. You have met with an accident, I am afraid. Allow me."

He helped me to stagger to my feet, and pushed me gently into the easy chair. The match burnt out, and he quietly struck another and looked around the room for a candle or lamp. It was a vain search, for I had neither.

"I am afraid," I said, "that I am out of candles—and oil. I got a little overtired walking here, and my foot slipped in the dark. Did I understand that you wished to see me?"

"I did," he answered gravely. "My name is Mostyn Ray—but I think that we had better have some light. I am going to get one of the motor lamps."

"If you could call—in the morning," I began desperately, but he had already opened and closed the door. I looked around my room, and I could have sobbed with mortification. The omnibus was lit inside as well as out, and I knew very well who was there. Already he was talking with the occupants. I saw a girl lean forward and listen to him. Then my worst fears were verified. I saw her descend, and they both stood for a moment by the side of the man who was tugging at one of the huge lamps. I closed my eyes in despair.

Once more the wind swept into my room, the door was quickly opened and closed. A man-servant in his long coat, and cockaded hat tied round his head with a piece of string, set down the lamp upon my table. Behind, the girl and Mostyn Ray were talking.

"The man had better stop," he whispered. "There is the fire to be made."

For the first time I heard her voice, very slow and soft, almost languid, yet very pleasant to listen to.

"No!" she said firmly. "It will look so much like taking him by storm. I can assure you that I am by no means a helpless person."

"And I," he answered, "am a campaigner."

— "Get back as quickly as you can, Richards," she directed, "and get the things I told you from Mrs. Brown. Jean must bring you back in the motor."

Once more the door opened and shut. I heard the swish of her skirts as she came over towards me.

"Poor fellow!" she murmured. "I'm afraid that he is very ill."

I opened my eyes and made an attempt to rise. She laid her hand upon my shoulder and smiled,

"Please don't move," she said, "and do forgive us for this intrusion. Colonel Ray wanted to call and apologize about this evening, and I am so glad that he did. We are going to take no end of liberties, but you must remember that we are neighbours, and therefore have privileges."

What could I say in answer to such a speech as this? As a matter of fact speech of any sort was denied me; a great sob had stuck in my throat. They did what was kindest. They left me alone.

I heard them rummaging about in my back room, and soon I heard the chopping of sticks. Presently I heard the crackling of flames, and I knew that a fire had been lit. A dreamy partial unconsciousness destitute of all pain, and not in itself unpleasant, stole over me. I felt my boots cut from my feet. I was gently lifted up. Some of my outer garments were removed. Every now and then I heard their voices, I heard her shocked exclamation as she examined my larder, I heard the words "starvation," "exhaustion," scarcely applying them to myself. Then I heard her call to him softly. She was standing by my bookcase.

"Do you see this?" she murmured. "'Guy Ducaine, Magdalen,' and the college coat of arms. They must belong to him, for that is his name."

I did not hear his answer, but directly afterwards a little exclamation escaped him.

"By Jove, what luck! I have my flask with me, after all. Is there a spoon there, Lady Angela?"

She brought him one directly. He stooped down, and I felt the metal strike my teeth. The brandy seemed to set all my blood flowing once more warmly in my veins. The heat of the fire, too, was delicious.

And then the strangest thing of all happened. I opened my eyes. My chair was drawn sideways to the fire and immediately facing the window. The first thing that I saw was this. Pressed against it, peering into the room, was the white face of a man, an entire stranger to me.

CHAPTER II
GOOD SAMARITANS

They both hurried to my side. I was sitting up in my chair, pointing, my eyes fixed with surprise. I do not know even now why the incident should so much have alarmed me, but it is a fact that for the moment I was palsied with fear. There had been murder in the man's eyes, loathsome things in his white unkempt face. My tongue clove to the roof of my mouth. They gave me more brandy, and then I spoke.

"There was a man—looking in. A man's face there, at the window!"

Ray took up the lamp and strode to the door. When he returned he exchanged a significant glance with Lady Angela.

"There is no one there now, at any rate," he said. "I dare say it was fancy."

"It was not," I answered. "It was a man's face—a horrible face."

"The omnibus is coming back," he said quietly. "The servants shall have a good look round."

"I would not worry about it," Lady Angela said, soothingly. "It is easy to fancy things when one is not well."

So they meant to treat me like a child. I said nothing, but it was a long time before my limbs ceased to shake. The tall servant reappeared with a huge luncheon basket—all manner of delicacies were emptied out upon my table. Lady Angela was making something in a clip, Ray was undoing a gold-foiled bottle. Soon I found myself eating and drinking, and the blood once more was mashing through my veins. I was my own man again, rescued by charity. And of all the women in the world, fate had sent this one to play the Lady Bountiful.

"You are looking better, my young friend," Colonel Ray said presently.

"I feel-quite all right again, thank you," I answered. "I wish I could thank you and Lady Angela."

"You must not attempt anything of the sort," she declared. "My father, by-the-bye, Mr. Ducaine, wished me to express his great regret that he should have interfered in any way with your arrangements for this evening. You know, there are so many stupid people around here who have never understood anything at all about the war, and he was very anxious to get Colonel Ray to talk to them. He had no idea, however, that it was the night fixed for your lecture, and he hopes that you will accept the loan of the village hall from him any night you like, and we should so much like all of us to come."

"His Grace is very kind," I murmured. "I fear, however, that the people are not very much interested in lectures, even about their own neighbourhood."

"I am, at any rate," Lady Angela answered, smiling, "and I think we can promise you an audience."

Colonel Ray, who had been standing at the window, came back to us.

"If I may be permitted to make a suggestion, Lady Angela," he said, "I think it would be well if you returned home now, and I will follow shortly on foot."

"Indeed," I said, "there is no need for you, Colonel Ray, to remain. I am absolutely recovered now, and the old woman who looks after me will be here in the morning."

He seemed scarcely to have heard me. Afterwards, when I knew him better, I understood his apparent unconcern of any suggestion counter to his own. He thought slowly and he spoke seldom, but when he had once spoken the matter, so far as he was concerned, was done with. Lady Angela apparently was used to him, for she rose at once. She did not shake hands, but she nodded to me pleasantly. Colonel Ray handed her into the wagonette, and I heard the quicker throbbing of the engine as it glided off into the darkness.

It was several minutes before he returned. I began to wonder whether he had changed his mind, and returned to Rowchester with Lady Angela. Then the door handle suddenly turned, and he stepped in. His hair was tossed with the wind, his shoes were wet and covered with mud, and he was breathing rather fast, as though he had been running. I looked at him inquiringly. He offered me no explanation. But on his way to the chair, which he presently drew up to the fire, he paused for a full minute by the window, and shading the carriage lamp which he still carried, with his hand, he looked steadily out into the darkness. A thought struck me.

"You have seen him!" I exclaimed.

He set down the lamp upon the table, and deliberately seated himself.

"Seen whom?" he asked, producing a pipe and tobacco.

"The man who looked in — whose face I saw at the window."

He struck a match and lit his pipe.

"I have seen no one," he answered quietly. "The face was probably a fancy of yours. I should recommend you to forget it."

I looked down at his marsh-stained shoes. One foot was wet to the ankle, and a thin strip of green seaweed had wound itself around his trousers. To any other man I should have had more to say. Yet even in those first few hours of our acquaintance I had become, like all the others, to some extent the servant of his will, spoken or unspoken. So I held my peace and looked away into the fire. I felt he had something to say to me, and I waited.

He moved his head slowly towards the bookcase.

"Those books," he asked, "are yours?"

"Yes," I answered.

"Your name then is Guy Ducaine?"

"Yes."

"Did you ever know your father?"

It was a singular question. I looked at him quickly. His face was sphinxlike.

"No. Why do you ask? Did you?"

He ignored me absolutely for several moments. His whole attention seemed fixed upon the curling wreath of blue smoke which hung between us.

"He died, I suppose," he continued, "when you were about twelve years old."

I nodded.

"My uncle," I said, "gave me a holiday and a sovereign to spend. He told me that a great piece of good fortune had happened to me."

Colonel Ray smiled grimly.

"That was like old Stephen Ducaine," he remarked. "He died himself a few years afterwards."

"Three years."

"He left you ten thousand pounds. What have you done with it?"

"Mr. Heathcote, of Heathcote, Sons, and Vyse, was my solicitor."

"Well?"

I remembered that he had been away from England for several years.

"The firm failed," I told him, "for a quarter of a million. Mr. Heathcote shot himself. I am told that there is a probable dividend of sixpence-half-penny in the pound to come some day."

Colonel Ray smoked on in silence. This was evidently news to him.

"Awkward for you," he remarked at last.

I laughed a little bitterly. I knew quite well that he was expecting me to continue, and I did so.

"I sold my things at Magdalen, and paid my debts. I was promised two pupils if I would take a house somewhere on this coast. I took one and got ready for them with my last few pounds. Their father died suddenly — and they did not come. I got rid of the house, at a sacrifice, and came to this cottage."

"You took your degree?"

"With honours."

He blew out more smoke.

"You are young," he said, "a gentleman by birth, and I should imagine a moderate athlete. You have an exceptional degree, and I presume a fair knowledge of the world. Yet you appear to be deliberately settling down here to starve."

"I can assure you," I answered, "that the deliberation is lacking. I have no fear of anything of the sort. I expect to get some pupils in the neighbourhood, and also some literary work. For the moment I am a little hard up, and I thought perhaps that I might make a few shillings by a lecture."

"Of the proceeds of which," he remarked, with a dry little smile, "I appear to have robbed you."

I shrugged my shoulders.

"I hoped for little but a meal or two from it," I answered. "The only loss is to my self-respect. I owe to charity what I might have earned."

He took his pipe from his mouth and looked at me with a thin derisive smile.

"You talk," he said, "like a very young man. If you had knocked about in all corners of the world as I have you would have learnt a greater lesson from a greater book. When a man meets brother man in the wilds, who talks of charity? They divide goods and pass on. Even the savages do this."

"These," I ventured to remark, "are not the wilds."

He sighed and replaced his pipe in his mouth.

"You are young, very young," he remarked, thoughtfully. "You have that beastly hothouse education, big ideas on thin stalks, orchids instead of roses, the stove instead of the sun. The wilds are everywhere—on the Thames Embankment, even in this God-forsaken corner of the world. The wilds are wherever men meet men."

I was silent. Who was I to argue with Ray, whose fame was in every one's mouth—soldier, traveller, and diplomatist? For many years he had been living hand and glove with life and death. There were many who spoke well of him, and many ill—many to whom he was a hero, many to whom his very name was like poison. But he was emphatically not a man to contradict. In my little cottage he seemed like a giant, six-foot-two, broad, and swart with the burning fire of tropical suns. He seemed to fill the place, to dominate me and my paltry surroundings, even as in later years I saw him, the master spirit in a great assembly, eagle-eyed, strenuous, omnipotent. There was something about him which made other men seem like pygmies.

There was force in the stern self-repression of his speech, in the curve of his lips, the clear lightning of his eyes.

My silence did not seem altogether to satisfy him. I felt his eyes challenge mine, and I was forced to meet his darkly questioning gaze.

"Come," he said, "I trust that I have said enough. You have buried the thought of that hateful word."

"You have stricken it mortally," I answered, "but I can scarcely promise so speedy a funeral. However, what more I feel," I added, "I will keep to myself."

"It would be better," he answered curtly.

"You have asked me," I said, "many questions. I am emboldened to ask you one. You have spoken of my father."

The look he threw upon me was little short of terrible.

"Ay," he answered, "I have spoken of him. Let me tell you this, young man. If I believed that you were a creature of his breed, if I believed that a drop of his black blood ran in your veins, I would take you by the neck now and throw you into the nearest creek where the water was deep enough to drown."

I rose to my feet, trembling.

"If those are your feelings, sir," I declared, "I have no wish to claim your kindness."

"Sit down, boy," he answered coldly. "I have no fear of you. Nature does not pay us so evil a trick as to send us two such as he in successive generations."

He rose and looked out of the window. The storm had abated but little. The roar of the sea and wind was still like thunder in the air. Black clouds were driven furiously across the sky, torrents of rain and spray beat every now and then upon the window. He turned back and examined the carriage lamp.

"It is an awful night," I said. "I cannot offer you a bed unless you will take mine, but I can bring rugs and a pillow to the fire if you will lie there."

Then for the only time in my life I saw him hesitate. He looked out of my uncurtained window into the night. Very often have I wondered what thought it was that passed then through his brain.

"I thank you," he said; "the walk is nothing, and they will expect me at Rowchester. You have pencil and paper. Write down what I tell you. — Colonel Mostyn Ray, No. 17, Sussex Square. You have that? Good! It is my address. Presently I think you will get tired of your life here. Come then to me. I may be able to show you the way — "

"Out of the conservatory," I interrupted, smiling.

He nodded, and took up the lantern. To my surprise, he did not offer to shake hands. Without another word he passed out into the darkness.

In my dreams that night I fancied that a strange cry came ringing to my ears from the marshes — a long-drawn-out cry of terror, ending in a sob. I was weary, and I turned on my side again and slept.

CHAPTER III
THE CRY IN THE NIGHT

"You'd be having company last night, sir?" Mrs. Hollings remarked inquisitively. Mrs. Hollings was an elderly widow, who devoted two hours of her morning to cleaning my rooms and preparing my breakfast.

"Some friends did call," I answered, pouring out the coffee.

"Friends! Good Samaritans I should call 'em," Mrs. Hollings declared, "if so be as they left all the things I found here this morning. Why, there's a whole chicken, to say nothing of tongue and biscuits, and butter, and relishes, and savouries, the names of which isn't often heard in this part of the world. There's wine, too, with gold paper round the top, champagne wine, I do believe."

"Is the tide up this morning?" I asked.

"None to speak of," Mrs. Hollings answered, "though the road's been washed dry, and the creeks are brimming. I've scarcely set foot in the village this morning, but they're all a-talking about the soldier gentleman the Duke brought down to the village hall last night. Might you have seen him, sir?"

"Yes, I saw him," I answered.

"A sad shame as it was the night of your lecture, sir," the woman babbled on, "for they were all crazy to hear him. My! the hall was packed."

"Would you mind seeing to my room now, Mrs. Hollings?" I asked. "I am going out early this morning."

Mrs. Hollings ascended my frail little staircase. I finished my breakfast in haste, and catching up my hat escaped out of doors.

I shall never forget the glory of that morning. The sky was blue and cloudless, the sun was as hot as though this were indeed a midsummer morning. The whole land, saturated still with the fast receding sea, seemed to gleam and glitter with a strange iridescence. Great pools in unaccustomed places shone like burnished silver, the wet sands were sparkling and brilliant, the creeks had become swollen rivers full of huge masses of emerald seaweed, running far up into the marshland and spreading themselves out over the meadows beyond. There was salt in the very atmosphere. I felt it on my tongue, and my cheeks were rough with it. Overhead the seagulls in great flocks were returning from shelter, screaming as though with joy as they dived down to the sea. It was a wonderful morning.

About two hundred yards past my cottage the road, which from the village ran perfectly straight, took a sharp turn inland, leaving the coast abruptly on account of the greater stretch of marshland beyond. It was towards this bend that I walked, and curiously enough, with every step I took some inexplicable sense of nervous excitement grew stronger and stronger within me. The fresh morning air and the sunlight seemed powerless to dissipate for a moment the haunting terror of last night. It was a real face which I had seen pressed against the window, and where had Ray been when he returned with sand-clogged boots and the telltale seaweed upon his trousers? And later on, had I dreamed it, or had there really been a cry? It came back to me with horrible distinctness. It was a real cry, the cry of a man in terror for his life. I stopped short in the road and wiped my damp forehead. What a fool I was! The night was over. Here in the garish day there was surely nothing to fear? Nevertheless, I, who had started out thirsting only to breathe the fresh salt air, now walked along with stealthy nervous footsteps, looking all the time from left to right, starting at the sight of a dark log on the sands, terrified at a broken buoy which had floated up one of the creeks. Some fear had come over me which I could not shake off. I was afraid of what I might see.

So I walked to the bend of the road. Here, in case the turn might be too sharp for some to see at night, a dozen yards or so of white posts and railings bordered the marshes. I leaned over them for a moment, telling myself that I paused only to admire the strange colours drawn by the sunlight from the sea-soaked wilderness, the deep brown, the strange purple, the faint pink of the distant sands. But it was none of these which my eyes sought with such fierce eagerness. It was none of the artist's fervour which turned my limbs into dead weights, which drew the colour even from my lips, and set my heart beating with fierce quick throbs. Half in the creek and half out, not a dozen yards from the road, was the figure of a man. His head and shoulders were beneath the water, his body and legs and outstretched arms were upon the marsh. And although never before had I looked upon death, I knew very well that I was face to face with it now.

How long it was before I moved I cannot tell. At last, however, I climbed the palings, jumped at its narrowest point a smaller creek, and with slow footsteps approached the dead man. Even when I stood by his side I dared not touch him, I dared not turn him round to see his face. I saw that he was of middle size, fairly well dressed, and as some blown sand had drifted over his boots and ankles I knew that he had been there for some hours. There was blood upon his collar, and the fingers of his right hand were tightly clenched. I told myself that I was a coward, and I set my teeth. I must lift his head from the water, and cover him up with my own coat while I fetched help. But when I stooped down a deadly faintness came over me. My fingers were palsied with horror. I had a sudden irresistible conviction I could not touch him. It was a sheer impossibility. There was something between us more potent than the dread of a dead man — something inimical between us two, the dead and the living. I staggered away and ran reeling to the road, plunging blindly through the creek.

About two hundred yards further down the road was a small lodge at one of the entrances of Rowchester. It was towards this I turned and ran. The door was closed, and I beat upon it fiercely with clenched fists. The woman who answered it stared at me strangely. I suppose that I was a wild-looking object.

"It's Mr. Ducaine, isn't it?" she exclaimed. "Why, sakes alive! what's wrong, sir?"

"A dead man in the marshes," I faltered.

She was interested enough, but her comely weather-hardened face reflected none of the horror which she must have seen on mine.

"Lordy me! whereabouts, sir?" she inquired.

I pointed with a trembling forefinger. She stood by my side on the threshold of the cottage and shaded her eyes with her hand, for the glare of the sun was dazzling.

"Well, I never did!" she remarked. "But I said to John last night that I pitied them at sea. He's been washed up by the tide, I suppose, and I count there'll be more before the day's out. A year come next September there was six of 'em, gentlefolk, too, who'd been yachting. Eh, but it's a cruel thing is the sea."

"Where is your husband?" I asked.

"Up chopping wood in Fernham Spinney," she answered. "I'd best send one of the children for him. He'll have a cart with him. Will you step inside, sir?"

I shook my head and answered her vaguely. She sent a boy with a message, and brought me out a chair, dusting it carefully with her apron.

"You'd best sit down, sir. You look all struck of a heap, so to speak. Maybe you came upon it sudden."

I was glad enough to sit down, but I answered her at random. She re-entered the cottage and continued some household duties. I sat quite still, with my eyes steadily fixed upon a dark object a little to the left of those white palings. Above my head a starling in a wicker cage was making an insane cackling, on the green patch in front a couple of tame rabbits sat and watched me, pink-eyed, imperturbable. Inside I could hear the slow ticking of an eight-day clock. The woman was humming to herself as she worked. All these things, which my senses took quick note of and retained, seemed to me to belong to another world. I myself was under some sort of spell. My brain was numb with terror, the fire of life had left my veins, so that I sat there in the warm sunshine and shivered until my teeth chattered. Inside, the woman was singing over her work.

And then the spell developed. A nameless but loathsome fascination drew me from my seat, drew me with uneven and reluctant footsteps out of the gate and down the narrow straight road. There was still not a soul in sight. I drew nearer and nearer to the spot. Once more I essayed to move him. It was utterly in vain. Such nerve as I possessed had left me wholly and altogether. A sense of repulsion, nauseating, invincible, made a child of me. I stood up and looked around wildly. It was then for the first time I saw what my right foot had trodden into the sand.

I picked it up, and a little cry, unheard save by the sea-birds which circled about my head, broke from my lips. It was a man's signet ring, thin and worn smooth with age. It was quaintly shaped, and in the centre was set a small jet-black stone. The device was a bird, and underneath the motto — "Vinco!"

My hand closed suddenly upon it, and again I looked searchingly around. There was not a soul in sight. I slipped the ring into my waistcoat pocket and moved back to the white railings. I leaned against them, and, taking a pipe and tobacco from my pocket, began to smoke.

Strangely enough, I had now recovered my nerve. I was able to think and reason calmly. The woman at the lodge had taken it for granted that this man's body had been thrown up by the sea. Was that a possible conclusion? There was a line all down the sands where the tide had reached, a straggling uneven line marked with huge masses of wet seaweeds, fragments of timber, the flotsam and jetsam of the sea. The creek where the man's body was lying was forty yards above this. Yet on such a night who could say where those great breakers, driven in by the wind as well as by their own mighty force, might not have cast their prey? Within a few yards of him was a jagged mass of timber. The cause of those wounds would be obvious enough. I felt the ring in my waistcoat pocket — it was there, safely enough hidden, and I looked toward the lodge. As yet there were no signs of John or the cart.

But behind me, coming from the village, I heard the sound of light and rapid footsteps. I turned my head. It was Blanche Moyat, short-skirted, a stick in her hand, a feather stuck through her Tam-o'-Shanter.

"Good-morning," she cried out heartily; "I've been to call at your cottage."

"Very kind of you," I answered, hesitatingly. Miss Moyat was good-hearted, but a little overpowering — and in certain moods she reminded me of her father.

"Oh, I had an errand," she explained, laughing. "Father said if I saw you I was to say that he has to call on the Duke this afternoon, and, if you liked, he would explain about your lecture last night, and try and get the village hall for you for nothing. The Duke is very good-natured, and if he knows that he spoilt your evening, father thinks he might let you have it for nothing."

"It is very kind of your father," I answered. "I do not think that I shall ever give that lecture again."

"Why not?" she protested. "I am sure I thought it a beautiful lecture, and I'm not keen on churches and ruins myself," she added, with a laugh which somehow grated upon me. "What are you doing here?"

"Watching the dead," I answered grimly.

She looked at me for an explanation. I pointed to the dark object by the side of the creek. She gave a violent start. Then she screamed and caught hold of my arm.

"Mr. Ducaine!" she cried. "What is it?"

"A dead man!" I answered.

Her face was a strange study. There was fear mingled with unwholesome curiosity, the heritage of her natural lack of refinement. She leaned over the palings.

"Oh, how horrible!" she exclaimed. "I don't know whether I want to look or not. I've never seen any one dead."

"I should advise you," I said, "to go away."

It was apparently the last thing she desired to do. Of the various emotions which had possessed her, curiosity was the one which survived.

"You are sure he is dead?" she asked.

"Quite," I answered.

"Was he drowned, then?"

"I think," I replied, "that he has been washed up by the tide. There has probably been a shipwreck."

"Gracious!" she exclaimed. "It is just a sailor, then?"

"I have not looked at his face," I answered, "and I should not advise you to. He has been tossed about and injured. His clothes, though, are not a seaman's."

She passed through a gap in the palings.

"I must look just a little closer," she exclaimed. "Do come with me, Mr. Ducaine. I'm horribly afraid."

"Then don't go near him," I advised. "A dead man is surely not a pleasant spectacle for you. Come away, Miss Moyat."

But she had advanced to within a couple of yards of him. Then she stopped short, and a little exclamation escaped from her lips.

"Why, Mr. Ducaine," she cried out, "this is the very man who stopped me last night outside our house, and asked the way to your cottage."

CHAPTER IV
MISS MOYAT'S PROMISE

We stood looking at one another on the edge of the marsh. In the clear morning sunlight I had no chance of escape or subterfuge. There was terror in my face, and she could see it.

"You — you cannot be sure!" I exclaimed. "It may not be the same man."

"It is the same man," she answered confidently. "He stopped me and asked if I could direct him to your house. It was about half an hour after you had gone. He spoke very softly and almost like a foreigner. I told him exactly where your cottage was. Didn't he come to you?"

"No," I answered. "I have never seen him before in my life."

"Why do you look — so terrified?" she asked. "You are as pale as a ghost."

I clutched hold of the railings. She came over to my side. Up the road I heard in the distance the crunching of heavy wheels. A wagon was passing through the lodge gates. John, the woodman, was walking with unaccustomed briskness by the horses' heads, cracking his whip as he came. I looked into the girl's face by my side.

"Miss Moyat," I said hoarsely, "can't you forget that you saw this man?"

"Why?" she asked bewildered.

"I don't want to be dragged into it," I answered, glancing nervously over my shoulder along the road. "Don't you see that if he is just found here with his head and shoulders in the creek, and nothing is known about him, they will take it that he has been washed up by the sea in the storm last night? But if it is known that he came from the land, that he was seen in the village asking for me — then there will be many things said."

"I don't see as it matters," she answered, puzzled. "He didn't come, and you don't know anything about him. But, of course, if you want me to say nothing—"

She paused. I clutched her arm.

"Miss Moyat," I said, "I have strong reasons for not wishing to be brought into this."

"All right," she said, dropping her voice. "I will do—as you ask."

There was an absurd meaning in her little side-glance, which at another time would have put me on my guard. But just then I was engrossed with my own vague fears. I forgot even to remove my hand from her arm. So we were standing, when a moment later the silence was broken by the sound of a galloping horse coming fast across the marshes. We started aside. Lady Angela reined in a great bay mare a few yards away from us. Her habit was all bespattered with mud. She had evidently ridden across country from one of the private entrances to the Park.

"What is this terrible story, Mr. Ducaine?" she exclaimed. "Is there really a shipwreck? I can see no signs of it."

"No shipwreck that I know of, Lady Angela," I answered. "There is a dead man here—one only. I have heard of nothing else."

Her eyes followed my outstretched hand, and she saw the body half on the sands, half on the marsh. She shivered a little.

"Poor fellow!" she exclaimed. "Is it any one from the village, Mr. Ducaine?"

"It is a stranger, Lady Angela," I answered. "We think that his body must have been washed in from the sea."

She measured the distance from high-water mark with a glance, and shook her head.

"Too far away," she declared.

"There was a wild sea last night," I answered, "and such a tide as I have never seen here before."

"What are you doing with it?" she asked, pointing with her whip.

"John Hefford is bringing a wagon," I answered. "I suppose he had better take it to the police station."

She wheeled her horse round.

"I am glad that it is no worse," she said. "There are reports going about of a terrible shipwreck. I trust that you are feeling better, Mr. Ducaine?"

"I am quite recovered—thanks to your kindness and Colonel Ray's," I answered.

She nodded.

"You will hear from my father during the day," she said. "He is quite anxious to come to your lecture. Good-morning."

"Good-morning, Lady Angela."

She galloped away. Miss Moyat turned towards me eagerly.

"Why, Mr. Ducaine," she exclaimed, "I had no idea that you knew Lady
Angela."

"Nor do I," I answered shortly. "Our acquaintance is of the slightest."

"What did she mean about the lecture?"

I affected not to hear. John the wagoner had pulled up his team by the side of the palings, and was touching his hat respectfully.

"Another job for the dead 'ouse, sir, my missis tells me."

"There is the body of a dead man here, John," I answered, "washed up by the tide, I suppose. It isn't an uncommon occurrence here, is it?"

"Lor bless you, no, sir," the man answered, stepping over the palings. "I had three of them here in one month last year. If you'll just give me a hand, sir, we'll take him down to the police station."

I set my teeth and advanced towards the dead man. John Hefford proved at once that he was superior to all such trifles as nerves. He lifted the body up and laid it for the first time flat upon the sands.

"My! he's had a nasty smash on the head," John remarked, looking down at him with simple curiosity. "Quite the gent too, I should say. Will you give me a hand, sir, and we'll have him in the wagon."

So I was forced to touch him after all. Nevertheless I kept my eyes as far as possible from the ghastly face with the long hideous wound across it. I saw now, however, in one swift unwilling glance, what manner of man this was. He had thin features, a high forehead, deep-set eyes too close together, a thin iron-grey moustache. Whatever his station in life may have been, he was not of the labouring classes, for his hands were soft and his nails well cared for. We laid him in the bottom of the wagon, and covered him over with a couple of sacks. John cracked the whip and strode along by the side of the horses. Blanche Moyat and I followed behind.

She was unusually silent, and once or twice I caught her glancing curiously at me, as though she had something which it was in her mind to say, but needed encouragement. As we neared my cottage she asked me a question.

"Why don't you want me to say that I saw this man in the village last night, and that he asked for you, Mr. Ducaine? I can't understand what difference it makes. He may have spoken to others besides me, and then it is bound to be known. What harm can it do you?"

"I cannot explain how I feel about it," I answered. "I am not sure that I know myself. Only you must see that if it were known that he set out from the village last night to call upon me, people might say unpleasant things."

She lowered her voice.

"You mean — that they might suspect you of killing him?"

"Why not? Nobody knows much about me here, and it would seem suspicious. It was I who found him, and only a few hundred yards from my cottage. If it were known that he had left the village last night to see me, don't you think that it would occur to any one to wonder if we had met — and quarrelled? There could be no proof, of course, but the mere suggestion is unpleasant enough." We were in the middle of the open road, and the wagon was several yards in front. Nevertheless she drew a little closer to me, and almost whispered in my ear —

"Do you know who he is, what he wanted to see you about?"

"I have no idea," I answered. "I am quite sure that I never saw him before in my life."

"Did you see him last night?" she asked.

"Not to speak to," I answered. "I did catch just a glimpse of him, I believe, in rather a strange way. But that was all."

"What do you mean

"I saw him looking in through my window, but he came no nearer. Lady
Angela and Colonel Ray were in the room."

"In your room?"

"Yes. Colonel Ray called to say that he was sorry to have spoilt my lecture."

"And Lady Angela?"

"Yes."

"She came in too?"

The girl's open-mouthed curiosity irritated me.

"I happened to be ill when Colonel Ray came. They were both very kind to me."

"This man, then," she continued, "he looked in and went away?"

"I suppose so," I answered. "I saw no more of him."

She turned towards me breathlessly.

"I don't see how a fall could have killed him, or how he could have wandered off into the marshes just there. The creek isn't nearly deep enough to have drowned him unless he had walked deliberately in and lain down. He was quite sober, too, when he spoke to me. Mr. Ducaine, how did he die? What killed him?"

I shook my head.

"If I could answer you these questions," I said, "I should feel much easier in my own mind. But I cannot. I know no more about it than you do."

We were both silent for a time, but I saw that there was a new look in her face. It was a welcome relief when a groom from Rowchester overtook us and pulled up his horse by our side.

"Are you Mr. Ducaine, sir?" he asked, touching his hat.

"Yes," I answered.

"I have a note for you from his Grace, sir," he said. "I was to take back an answer if I found you at home."

He handed it to me, and I tore it open. It contained only a few lines, in a large sprawling hand-writing.

"ROWCHESTER, Wednesday Morning.

"The Duke of Rowchester presents his compliments to Mr. Ducaine, and would be much obliged if he could make it convenient to call upon him at Rowchester between three and four o'clock this afternoon."

I folded the note up and turned to the groom.

"Will you tell his Grace," I said, "that you found me on the road, and I was unable, therefore, to write my answer, but I will call at the time he mentions?"

The man touched his hat and rode away. Blanche Moyat, who had been standing a few yards off, rejoined me.

"Has the Duke sent for you to go there?" she asked, with obvious curiosity.

"Yes. He has offered to lend me the village hall," I told her. "I expect that is what he wants to see me about."

She tossed her head.

"You didn't tell me so just now when I told you that father had offered to speak about it," she remarked.

"I am afraid," I said, gravely, "my mind was full of more serious matters."

She said no more until we reached the front of the Moyats' house. Then she did not offer me her hand, but she stood quite close to me, and spoke in an unnaturally low tone.

"You wish me, then," she said, "not to mention about that man — his asking the way to your cottage?"

"It seems quite unnecessary," I answered, "and it would only mean that I should be bothered with questions which I could not answer."

"Very well," she said, "Good-bye!"

I shuddered to myself as I followed the wagon down the narrow street towards the police station. A strange reserve had crept into her manner during the latter portion of our walk. There was something in her mind which she shrank from putting into words. Did she believe that I was responsible for this grim tragedy which had so suddenly thrown its shadow over my humdrum little life?

CHAPTER V
THE GRACIOUSNESS OF THE DUKE

At a quarter-past three that afternoon I was ushered into the presence of the Duke of Rowchester. I had never seen him before, and his personality at once interested me. He was a small man, grey-haired, keen-eyed, clean shaven. He received me in a somewhat bare apartment, which he alluded to as his workroom, and I found him seated before a desk strewn with papers. He rose immediately at my entrance, and I could feel that he was taking more than usual note of my appearance.

"You are Mr. Ducaine," he said, holding out his hand. "I am very glad to see you."

He motioned me to a chair facing the window, a great uncurtained affair, through which the north light came flooding in, whilst he himself sat in the shadows.

"I trust," he said, "that you have quite recovered from your last night's indisposition. My daughter has been telling me about it."

"Quite, thank you," I answered. "Lady Angela and Colonel Ray were very kind to me."

He nodded, and then glanced at the papers on his desk.

"I have been going through several matters connected with the estate, Mr. Ducaine," he said, "and I have come across one which concerns you."

"The proposed lease of the Grange," I remarked.

"Exactly. It seems that you arranged a three years' tenancy with Mr. Hulshaw, my agent, and were then not prepared to carry it out."

"It was scarcely my own fault," I interposed. "I explained the circumstances to Mr. Hulshaw. I was promised two pupils if I took a suitable house in this neighbourhood, but, after all my plans were concluded, their father died unexpectedly, and their new guardian made other arrangements."

"Exactly," the Duke remarked. "The only reason why I have alluded to the matter is that I disapprove of the course adopted by my agent, who, I believe, enforced the payment of a year's rent from you."

"He was within his rights, your Grace," I said.

"He may have been," the Duke admitted, "but I consider his action arbitrary. Not only that, but it was unnecessary, for he has already found another tenant for the place. I have instructed him, therefore, to send you a cheque for the amount you paid him, less the actual cost of preparing the lease."

Now my entire capital at that moment was something under three shillings. A gift of fifty pounds, therefore, which after all was not a gift but only the just return of my own money, was more than opportune—it was Heaven-sent. If I could have given way to my feelings I should have sprung up and wrung the little man's hands. As it was, however, I expect my face betrayed my joy. "Your Grace is exceedingly kind," I told him. "The money will be invaluable to me just now."

The Duke inclined his head.

"I am only sorry," he said, "that Hulshaw should have exacted it. It shows how impossible it is to leave the conduct of one's affairs wholly in the hands of another person. Now there is a further matter, Mr. Ducaine, concerning which I desired to speak to you. I refer to your projected lecture last night."

"I beg that your Grace will not allude to it," I said, hastily. "It is really of very little importance." The Duke had a habit which I began at this time to observe. He appeared to enter into all discussions with his mind wholly made up upon the subject, and any interruptions and interpolations he simply endured with patience, and then continued on his way without the slightest reference to them. He sat during my remark with half-closed eyes, and when I had finished he went on, wholly ignoring it—

"This is a strange little corner of the world," he said, "and the minds of the people here are for the most part like the minds of little children; they need forming. I have heard some remarks concerning the war from one or two of my tenants which have not pleased me. Accordingly, while Colonel Ray was here, I thought it an excellent opportunity to endeavour to instruct them as to the real facts of the case. It was not until after the affair was arranged — not, indeed, until I was actually in the hall — that I heard of our misfortune in selecting the evening which you had already reserved for your own lecture. I trust that you will allow me to offer you the free use of the hall for any other date which you may select. My people here, and I myself, shall esteem it a pleasure to be amongst your audience."

I was quite overwhelmed. I could only murmur my thanks. The Duke went on to speak for a while on general matters, and then skilfully brought the conversation back again to myself and my own affairs. Before I knew where I was I found myself subjected to a close and merciless cross-examination. My youth, my college career, my subsequent adventures seemed all to be subjects of interest to him, and I, although every moment my bewilderment increased, answered him with the obedience of a schoolboy.

It came to an end at last. I found myself confronted with a question which, if I had answered it truthfully, must have disclosed my penniless condition. I rose instead to my feet.

"Your Grace will excuse me," I said, "but I am taking up too much of your time. It is not possible that these small personal details can be of any interest to you."

He waved me back to my chair, which I did not, however, immediately resume. I was not in the least offended. The Duke's manner throughout, and the framing of his questions, had been too tactful to awaken any resentment. But I had no fancy for exposing my ill-luck and friendless state to any one. I was democrat enough to feel that a cross-examination which would have been impertinent in anybody else was becoming a little too personal even from the Duke of Rowchester.

"Sit down, Mr. Ducaine," he said. "I do not blame you for resenting what seems to be curiosity, but you must take my word for it that it is nothing of the sort. I can perhaps explain myself better by asking you still another sort of question. Are you in a position to accept a post of some importance?"

I looked at him in surprise, as well I might.

"Sit down, Mr. Ducaine," he repeated. "I have said enough, I hope, to prove that I am not trifling with you."

"You have managed, at any rate, to surprise me very much, your Grace," I said. "I am eager to receive employment of any sort. May I ask what it was that you had in view?"

He shook his head slowly.

"I cannot tell you to-day," he said. "It is a matter upon which I should have to consult others."

A sudden thought struck me.

"May I ask at whose suggestion you thought of me?" I asked.

"It was Colonel Ray who pointed out certain necessary qualifications which you possess," the Duke answered. "I shall report to him, and to some others, the result of our conversation, and I presume you have no objection to my making such inquiries as I think necessary concerning you?"

"None whatever," I answered.

The Duke rose to his feet. I took up my cap.

"If Colonel Ray is in," I said, "and it is not inconvenient, I should be glad to see him for a moment."

"Colonel Ray left unexpectedly by the first train this morning," the Duke answered, looking at me keenly.

I gave no sign, but my heart sank.

"If it is anything important I can give you his address," he remarked.

"Thank you," I answered, "it is of no consequence."

There was a moment's silence. It seemed to me that the Duke was watching me with peculiar intentness.

"Ray stayed with you late last night," he remarked.

"Colonel Ray was very kind," I answered.

"By-the-bye," he said, "I hear that some stranger lost his life in the storm last night. You found the body, did you not?"

"Yes," I answered. "There was a great deal of wreckage on the shore this morning."

The Duke nodded.

"It was no one belonging to the neighbourhood, I understand?" he asked.

"The man was a stranger to all of us," I answered.

The Duke stood with knitted brows. He seemed on the point of asking me some other question, but apparently he abandoned the idea. He nodded again and rang the bell. I was dismissed.

CHAPTER VI
LADY ANGELA GIVES ME SOME ADVICE

Rowchester was a curious medley of a house, a mixture of farmhouse, mansion, and castle, added to apparently in every generation by men with varying ideas of architecture. The front was low and irregular, and a grey stone terrace ran the entire length, with several rows of steps leading down into the garden. On one of these, as I emerged from the house, Lady Angela was standing talking to a gardener. She turned round at the sound of my footsteps, and came at once towards me.

She was bareheaded, and looked as straight and slim as a dart. I fancied that she could be no more than eighteen, her figure and face were so girlish. The quiet composure of her manner, however, and the subdued yet graceful ease of her movements, were so suggestive of the "great lady," that it was hard to believe that she was indeed little more than a schoolgirl.

"I hope that you are better, Mr. Ducaine," she said.

"Thank you, Lady Angela, I have quite recovered," I answered.

She looked at me critically.

"I can assure you," she said, "that you look a very different person. You gave us quite a fright last night."

"I am ashamed to have been so much trouble," I answered. "Such a thing has never happened to me before."

"You must take more care of yourself," she said gravely. "I hope that my father has expressed himself properly about the lecture."

"His Grace has been very kind," I answered. "He has promised me the free use of the hall at any time."

"Of course," she said. "I hope that you will give your lecture soon. I am looking forward very much to hearing it. This always seems to me such a quaint, fascinating corner of the world that I love to read and hear all that people have to say about it."

"You are very kind," I said; "but if you come I am afraid you will be bored. The notes which I have put together are prepared for the comprehension of the village people."

"So much the better," she declared. "I prefer anything which does not make too great a strain upon the intellect. Besides, it is the very simplicity of this country which makes it so beautiful."

"Yet it is a land," I remarked, "of elusive charms."

"Sometimes, unless they are pointed out," she replied, "by one who has the eye and ear for nature, these are the hardest to appreciate. Only the other evening I was standing upon the cliffs, and I thought what a dreary waste of marshes and sands the place was, and then a single gleam of late sunshine seemed to transform everything. There is hidden colour everywhere if one looks closely enough, and I suppose it is true that the most beautiful things in the world are those which remain just below the surface—a little invisible until one searches for them. By-the-bye, Mr. Ducaine," she added, "if you are on your way home I can show you a path which will save you nearly half the distance."

"You are very kind, Lady Angela," I answered. "Cannot I find it, though, without taking you out of your way?"

She smiled.

"You might," she said, "but I walk down to the cliffs every afternoon. I was just starting when you came. It is quite a regular pilgrimage with me. All day long we hear the sea, but except from the upper windows we have no clear view of it. This is the path."

We crossed the Park together. All the while she talked to me easily and naturally of the country around, the great antiquity of its landmarks, the survival of many ancient customs and almost obsolete forms of speech. At last we came to a small plantation, through which we emerged on to the cliffs. Here, to my surprise, we came upon a quaintly shaped grey stone cottage almost hidden by the trees. I had passed on the sands below many times without seeing it.

"Rather a strange situation for a house, is it not?" Lady Angela remarked. "My grandfather built it for an old pensioner, but I do not think that it has been occupied for some time."

"It is marvellously hidden," I said. "I never had the least idea that there was a house here at all."

We stood now on the edge of the cliff, and she pointed downwards.

"There is a little path there, you see, leading to the sands," she said. "It saves you quite half the distance to your cottage if you do not mind a scramble. You must take care just at first. So many of the stones are loose."

I understood that I was dismissed, and I thanked her and turned away. But she almost immediately called me back.

"Mr. Ducaine!"

"Lady Angela?"

Her dark eyes were fixed curiously upon my face. She seemed to be weighing something in her mind. I had a fancy that when she spoke again it would be without that deliberation — almost restraint — which seemed to accord a little strangely with the girlishness of her appearance and actual years. She stood on the extreme edge of the cliff, her slim straight figure outlined to angularity against the sky. She remained so long without speech that I had time to note all these things. The sunshine, breaking through the thin-topped pine trees, lay everywhere about us; a little brown feathered bird, scarcely a dozen yards away, sang to us so lustily that the soft feathers around his throat stood out like a ruff. Down below the sea came rushing on to the shingles.

"Mr. Ducaine," she said at last, "did my father make you any offer of employment this afternoon?"

It was a direct, almost a blunt question. I was taken by surprise, but I answered her without hesitation.

"He made me no definite offer," I said. "At the same time he asked me a great many questions, for which he must have had some reason, and he gave me the idea that, subject to the approval of some others, he was thinking of me in connection with some post."

"Colonel Ray was telling me," she said, "how unfortunate you have been with your pupils. I wonder — don't you think perhaps that you might get some others?"

"I have tried," I answered. "So far I have not been lucky. At present, too, I scarcely see how I could expect to get any, for I have nowhere to put them. I had to give up the lease of the Grange, and there is no house round here which I could afford to take."

Some portion of her delicate assurance had certainly deserted her. Her manner was almost nervous.

"If you could possibly find the pupils," she said, hesitatingly, "I should like to ask you a favour. The Manor Farm on the other side of the village is my own, and I should so like it occupied. I would let it to you furnished for ten pounds a year. There is a man and his wife living there now as caretakers. They would be able to look after you."

"You are very kind," I said again, "but I am afraid that I could not take advantage of such an offer."

"Why not?"

"I have no claim upon you or your father," I answered. "We are almost strangers, are we not? I might accept and be grateful for employment, but this is charity."

"A very conventional reply, Mr. Ducaine," she remarked, with faint sarcasm. "I gave you credit for a larger view of things."

I found her still inexplicable. She was evidently annoyed, and yet she did not seem to wish me to be. There was a cloud upon her face and a nervousness in her manner which I wholly failed to understand.

"If I were to tell you," she said, raising her eyes suddenly to mine, "that your acceptance of my offer would be a favour—would put me under a real obligation to you?"

"I should still have to remind you," I declared, "that as yet I have no pupils, and it takes time to get them. Further, I have arrived at that position when immediate employment, if it is only as a breaker of stones upon the road, is a necessity to me."

She sighed.

"My father will offer you a post," she said slowly.

"Now you are a real Samaritan, Lady Angela," I declared. "I only hope that it may be so."

Her face reflected none of my enthusiasm.

"You jump at conclusions," she said, coldly. "How do you know that the post will be one which you will be able to fill?"

"If your father offers it to me," I answered, confidently, "he must take the risk of that."

I was surprised at her speech-perhaps a little nettled. I was an "Honours" man, an exceptional linguist, and twenty-five. It did not seem likely to me that there was any post which the Duke might offer which, on the score of ability, at any rate, I should not be competent to fill.

"He will offer it you," she said, looking steadily downwards on to the sands below, "and you will accept it. I am sorry!"

"Sorry!" I exclaimed.

"Very. If I could find you those pupils I would," she continued. "If I could persuade you to lay aside for once the pride which a man seems to think a part of his natural equipment, it would make me very happy. I—"

"Stop," I interrupted. "You must explain this, Lady Angela."

She shook her head.

"Explain is just what I cannot," she said, sadly. "That is what I can never do."

I was completely bewildered now. She was looking seaward, her face steadily averted from mine. As to her attitude towards me, I could make nothing of it. I could not even decide whether it was friendly or inimical. Did she want this post for some one else? If so, surely her influence with her father would be strong enough to secure it. She had spoken to me kindly enough. The faint air of reserve that she seemed to carry with her everywhere, which, coupled with a certain quietness of deportment, appeared to most of the people around to indicate pride, had for these few minutes, at any rate, been lifted. She had come down from the clouds, and spoken to me as any other woman to any other man. And now she had wound up by throwing me into a state of hopeless bewilderment.

"Lady Angela," I said, "I think that you owe me some explanation. If you can assure me that it is in any way against your wishes, if you will give me the shadow of a reason why I should refuse what has not yet been offered to me—well, I will do it. I will do it even if I must starve."

A little forced smile parted her lips. She looked at me kindly.

"I have said a great deal more than I meant to, Mr. Ducaine. I think that it would have been better if I had left most of it unsaid. You must go your own way. I only wanted to guard you against disappointment."

"Disappointment! You think, after all, then — "

"No, that is not what I meant," she interrupted. "I am sure that you will be offered the post, and I am sure that you will not hesitate to accept it. But nevertheless I think that it will bring with it great disappointments. I will tell you this. Already three young men whom I knew very well have held this post, and each in turn has been dismissed. They have lost the confidence of their employers, and though each, I believe, was ambitious and meant to make a career, they have now a black mark against their name."

"You are very mysterious, Lady Angela," I said, doubtfully.

"It is of necessity," she answered. "Perhaps I take rather a morbid view of things, but one of them was the brother of a great friend of mine, and they fear that he has lost his reason. There are peculiar and painful difficulties in connection with this post, Mr. Ducaine, and I think it only fair to give you this warning."

"You are very kind," I said. "I only wish that the whole thing was clearer to me."

She smiled a little sadly.

"At least," she said, "let me give you one word of advice. You will be brought into contact with many people whose integrity will seem to you a positive and certain thing. Nevertheless, treat every one alike. Trust no one. Absolutely no one, Mr. Ducaine. It is your only chance. Now go."

Her gesture of dismissal was almost imperative. I scrambled down the path and gained the sands. When I looked up she was still standing there. The wind blew her skirts around her slim young limbs, and her hair was streaming behind her. Her face seemed like a piece of delicate oval statuary, her steady eyes seemed fixed upon some point where the clouds and sea meet. She took no heed of, she did not even see, my gesture of farewell. I left her there inscrutable, a child with the face of a Sphinx. She had set me a riddle which I could not solve.

CHAPTER VII
COLONEL RAY'S RING

The ring lay on the table between us. Colonel Ray had not yet taken it up. In grim silence he listened to my faltering words. When I finished he smiled upon me as one might upon a child that needed humouring.

"So," he said, slipping the ring upon his finger, "you have saved me from the hangman. What remains? Your reward, eh?"

"It may seem to you," I answered hotly, "a fitting subject for jokes. I am sorry that my sense of humour is not in touch with yours. You are a great traveller, and you have shaken death by the hand before. For me it is a new thing. The man's face haunts me! I cannot sleep or rest for thinking of it—as I have seen it dead, and as I saw it alive pressed against my window that night. Who was he? What did he want with me?"

"How do you know," Ray asked, "that he wanted anything from you?"

"He looked in at my window."

"He might have seen me enter."

Then I told him what I had meant to keep secret.

"He asked for me in the village. He was directed to my cottage."

Ray had been filling his pipe. His fingers paused in their task. He looked at me steadily.

"How do you know that?" he asked.

"The person to whom he spoke in the village told me so."

"Then why did that person not appear at the inquest?"

"Because I asked her not to," I told him. "If she had given evidence the verdict must have been a different one."

"It seems to me," he said quietly, "that you have acted foolishly. If that young woman, whoever she may be, chooses to tell the truth later on you will be in an awkward position."

"If she had told the truth yesterday," I answered, "the position would have been quite awkward enough. Let that go! I want to know who that man was, what he wanted with me."

Colonel Ray shrugged his shoulders.

"My young friend," he said, "have you come from Braster to ask that question?"

"To give you the ring and to ask you that question."

"How do you know that the ring is mine?"

"I saw it on your finger when you were giving me wine."

"Then you believe," he said, "that I killed him?"

"It is no concern of mine," I cried hoarsely. "I do not want to know. I do not want to hear. But I tell you that the man's face haunts me. He asked for me in the village. I feel that he came to Rowchester to see me. And he is dead. Whatever he came to say or to tell me will be buried with him. Who was he? Tell me that?"

Ray smoked on for a few moments reflectively.

"Sit down, sit down!" he said gruffly, "and do abandon that tragical aspect. The creature was not worth all this agitation. He lived like a dog, and he died like one."

"It is true, then?" I murmured.

"If you insist upon knowing," Ray said coolly, "I killed him! There are insects upon which one's foot falls, reptiles which one removes from the earth without a vestige of a qualm, with a certain sense of relief. He was of this order."

"He was a human being," I answered.

"He was none the better for that," Ray declared. "I have known animals of finer disposition."

"You at least," I said fiercely, "were not his judge. You struck him in the dark, too. It was a cowardly action."

Ray turned his head. Then I saw that around his neck was a circular bandage.

"If it interests you to know it," he remarked drily, "I was not the assailant. But for the fact that I was warned it might have been my body which you came across on the sands. I started a second too soon for our friend—and our exchange of compliments sent him to eternity."

"It was in self-defence, then?"

"Scarcely that. He would have run away if he could. I decided otherwise."

"Tell me who he was," I insisted.

Ray shook his head.

"Better for you not to know," he remarked reflectively. "Much better."

My cheeks grew hot with anger.

"Colonel Ray," I said, "this may yet be a serious affair for you. Why you should assume that I am willing to be a silent accessory to your crime I cannot imagine. I insist upon knowing who this man was."

"You have come to London," Ray answered quietly, "to ask me this?"

"I have told you before why I am here," I answered. "I will not be put off any longer. Who was that man, and what did he want with me?"

For a period of time which I could not measure, but which seemed to me of great duration, there was silence between us. Then Ray leaned over towards me.

"I think," he said, "that it is my turn to talk. You have come to me like a hysterical schoolboy, you seem ignorant of the primeval elements of justice. After all it is not wonderful. As yet you have only looked in upon life. You look in, but you do not understand. You have called me a coward. It is only a year or so since His Majesty pinned a little cross upon my coat—for valour. I won that for saving a man's life. Mind you, he was a man. He was a man and a comrade. To save him I rode through a hell of bullets. It ought to have meant death. As a matter of fact it didn't. That was my luck. But you mustn't call me a coward, Ducaine. It is an insult to my decoration."

"Oh, I know that you are brave enough," I answered, "but this man was a poor weak creature, a baby in your hands."

"So are the snakes we stamp beneath our feet," he answered coolly. "Yet we kill them. In Egypt I have been in more than one hot corner where we fought hand to hand. I have killed men more than once. I have watched them galloping up with waving swords, and their fine faces ablaze with the joy of battle, and all the time one's revolver went spit, and the saddles were empty. Yet never once have I sent a brave man to his last account without regret, enemy and fanatic though he was. I am not a bloodthirsty man. When I kill, it is because necessity demands it. As for that creature whom you found in the marshes, well, if there were a dozen such in this room now, I would do my best to rid the earth of them. Take my advice. Dismiss the whole subject from your mind. Go back to Braster and wait. Something may happen within the next twenty-four hours which will be very much to your benefit. Go back to Braster and wait."

"You will tell me nothing, then?" I asked. "It is treating me like a child. I am not a sentimentalist. If the man deserved death the matter is between you and your conscience. But he came to Rowchester to see me. I want to know why."

"Go back to Rowchester and wait," Ray said. "I shall tell you nothing. Depend upon it that his business with you, if he had any, was evil business. He and his whole brood left their mark for evil wherever they crawled."

"His name?" I asked.

"Were there no papers upon him?" Ray demanded.

"None."

"So much the better," Ray declared grimly. "Now, my young friend, I have given you all the time I can spare. Beyond what I have said I shall say nothing. If you had known me better — you would not be here still."

So I left him. His words gave me no loophole of hope. His silence was the silence of a strong man, and I had no weapons with which to assail it. I had wasted the money which I could ill afford on this journey to London. Certainly Ray's advice was good. The sooner I was back in Braster the better.

From the station I had walked straight to Ray's house, and from Ray's house I returned, without any deviation, direct to the great terminus. For a man with less than fifty pounds in the world London is scarcely a hospitable city. I caught a slow train, and after four hours of jolting, cold, and the usual third-class miseries, alighted at Rowchester Junction. Already I had started on the three mile tramp home, my coat collar turned up as some slight protection against the drizzling rain, when a two-wheeled trap overtook me, and Mr. Moyat shouted out a gruff greeting. He raised the water-proof apron, and I clambered in by his side.

"Been to Sunbridge?" he inquired cheerfully.

"I have been to London," I answered.

"You haven't been long about it," he remarked. "I saw you on the eight-twenty, didn't I?"

I nodded.

"My business was soon over," I said.

"I've been to Sunbridge," he told me. "Went over with his Grace. My girl was talking about you the other night, Mr. Ducaine."

I started.

"Indeed?" I answered.

"Seemed to think," he continued, "that things had been growing a bit rough for you, losing those pupils after you'd been at the expense of taking the Grange, and all that, you know."

"It was rather bad luck," I admitted quietly.

"I've been wondering," he continued, with some diffidence, "whether you'd care for a bit of work in my office, just to carry you along till things looked up. Blanche, she was set upon it that I should ask you anyway. Of course, you being a college young gentleman might not care about it, but there's times when any sort of a job is better than none, eh?"

"It is very kind of you, Mr. Moyat," I answered, "and very kind of Miss Blanche to have thought of it. A week ago I shouldn't have hesitated. But within the last few days I have had a sort of offer—I don't know whether it will come to anything, but it may. Might I leave it open for the present?"

I think that Mr. Moyat was a little disappointed. He flicked the cob with the whip, and looked straight ahead into the driving mist.

"Just as you say," he declared. "I ain't particular in want of any one, but I'm getting to find my own bookkeeping a bit hard, especially now that my eyes ain't what they were. Of course it would only be a thirty bob a week job, but I suppose you'd live on that all right, unless you were thinking of getting married, eh?"

I laughed derisively.

"Married, Mr. Moyat!" I exclaimed. "Why, I'm next door to a pauper."

"There's such a thing," he remarked thoughtfully, "if one's a steady sort of chap, and means work, as picking up a girl with a bit of brass now and then."

"I can assure you, Mr. Moyat," I said as coolly as possible, "that anything of that sort is out of the question so far as I am concerned. I should never dream of even thinking of getting married till I had a home of my own and an income."

He seemed about to say something, but checked himself. We drove on in silence till we came to a dark pile of buildings standing a little way back from the road. He moved his head towards it.

"They tell me Braster Grange is took after all," he remarked. "Mr. Hulshaw told me so this morning."

I was very little interested, but was prepared to welcome any change in the conversation.

"Do you know who is coming there?" I asked.

"An American lady, I believe, name of Lessing. I don't know what strangers want coming to such a place, I'm sure."

I glanced involuntarily over my shoulder. Braster Grange was a long grim pile of buildings, which had been unoccupied for many years. Between it and the sea was nothing but empty marshland. It was one of the bleakest spots along the coast—to the casual observer nothing but an arid waste of sands in the summer, a wilderness of desolation in the winter. Only those who have dwelt in those parts are able to feel the fascination of that great empty land, a fascination potent enough, but of slow growth. Mr. Moyat's remark was justified.

We drove into his stable yard and clambered down.

"You'll come in and have a bit of supper," Mr. Moyat insisted.

I hesitated. I felt that it would be wiser to refuse, but I was cold and wet, and the thought of my fireless room depressed me. So I was ushered into the long low dining-room, with its old hunting prints and black oak furniture, and, best of all, with its huge log fire. Mrs. Moyat greeted me with her usual negative courtesy. I do not think that I was a favourite of hers, but whatever her welcome lacked in impressiveness Blanche's made up for. She kept looking at me as though anxious that I should remember our common secret. More than once I was almost sorry that I had not let her speak.

"You've had swell callers again," she remarked, as we sat side by side at supper-time. "A carriage from Rowchester was outside your door when I passed."

"Ah, he's a good sort is the Duke," Mr. Moyat declared appreciatively. "A clever chap, too. He's A1 in politics, and a first-class business man, chairman of the great Southern Railway Company, and on the board of several other City companies."

"I can't see what the gentry want to meddle with such things at all for," Mrs. Moyat said. "There's some as says as the Duke's lost more than he can afford by speculations."

"The Duke's a shrewd man," Mr. Moyat declared. "It's easy to talk."

"If he hasn't lost money," Mrs. Moyat demanded, "why is Rowchester Castle let to that American millionaire? Why doesn't he live there himself?"

"Prefers the East Coast," Mr. Moyat declared cheerfully. "More bracing, and suits his constitution better. I've heard him say so himself."

"That is all very well," Mrs. Moyat said, "but I can't see that Rowchester is a fit country house for a nobleman. What do you think, Mr. Ducaine?"

I was more interested in the discussion than anxious to be drawn into it, so I returned an evasive reply. Mrs. Moyat nodded sympathetically.

"Of course," she said, "you haven't seen the house except from the road, but I've been over it many a time when Mrs. Felton was housekeeper and the Duke didn't come down so often, and I say that it's a poor place for a Duke."

"Well, well, mother, we won't quarrel about it," Mr. Moyat declared, rising from the table. "I must just have a look at the mare. Do you look after Mr. Ducaine, Blanche."

To my annoyance the retreat of Mr. and Mrs. Moyat was evidently planned, and accelerated by a frown from their daughter. Blanche and I were left alone — whereupon I, too, rose to my feet."

"I must be going," I said, looking at the clock.

Blanche only laughed, and bade me sit down by her side.

"I'm so glad dad brought you in to-night," she said. "Did he say anything to you?"

"What about?"

"Never mind," she answered archly. "Did he say anything at all?"

"He remarked once or twice that it was a wet night," I said.

"Stupid!" she exclaimed. "You know what I mean."

"He did make me a very kind offer," I admitted.

She looked at me eagerly.

"Well?"

"I told him that I am expecting an offer of work of some sort from the Duke. Of course it may not come. In any case, it was very kind of Mr. Moyat."

She drew a little closer to me.

"It was my idea," she whispered. I put it into his head."

"Then it was very kind of you too," I answered. She was apparently disappointed. We sat for several moments in silence. Then she looked around with an air of mystery, and whispered still more softly into my ear —

"I haven't said a word about that — to anybody."

"Thank you very much," I answered. "I was quite sure that you wouldn't, as you had promised."

Again there was silence. She looked at me with some return of that half fearsome curiosity which had first come into her eyes when I made my request.

"Wasn't the inquest horrid?" she said. "Father says they were five hours deciding — and there's old Joe Hassell; even now he won't believe that — that — he came from the sea."

"It isn't a pleasant subject," I said quietly. "Let us talk of something else."

She was swinging a very much beaded slipper backwards and forwards, and gazing at it thoughtfully.

"I don't know," she said. "I can't help thinking of it sometimes. I suppose it is terribly wicked to keep anything back like that, isn't it?"

"If you feel that," I answered, "you had better go and tell your father everything."

She looked at me quickly.

"Now you're cross," she exclaimed. "I'm sure I don't know why."

"I am not cross," I said, "but I do not wish you to feel unhappy about it."

"I don't mind that," she answered, lifting her eyes to mine, "if it is better for you."

The door opened and Mr. Moyat appeared. Blanche was obviously annoyed,
I was correspondingly relieved. I rose at once, and took my leave.

"Blanche got you to change your mind?" he said, looking at me closely.

"Miss Moyat hasn't tried," I answered, shaking him by the hand. "We were talking about something else."

Blanche pushed past her father and came to let me out. We stood for a moment at the open door. She pointed down the street.

"It was just there he stopped me," she said in a low tone. "He was very pale, and he had such a slow, strange voice, just like a foreigner. It was in the shadow of the market-hall there. I wish I'd never seen him."

A note of real fear seemed to have crept into her voice. Her eyes were straining through the darkness. I forced a laugh as I lit my cigarette.

"You mustn't get fanciful," I declared. "Men die every day, you know, and I fancy that this one was on his last legs. Good-night."

Her lips parted as though in an answering greeting, but it was inaudible. As I looked round at the top of the street I saw her still standing there in the little flood of yellow light, gazing across towards the old market-hall.

CHAPTER VIII
A WONDERFUL OFFER

On my little table lay the letter I expected, large, square, and white. I tore it open with trembling fingers. The handwriting was firm and yet delicate. I knew at once whose it was.

"Rowchester, Tuesday.

"DEAR MR. DUCAINE,—My father wishes me to say that he and Lord Chelsford will call upon you to-morrow morning, between ten and eleven o'clock.—With best regards, I am,

"Yours sincerely,

"ANGELA HARBERLY."

The letter slipped from my hands on to the table. Lord Chelsford was a Cabinet Minister and a famous man. What could he have to do with any appointment which the Duke might offer me? I read the few words over and over again. The handwriting, the very faint perfume which seemed to steal out of the envelope, a moment's swift retrospective thought, and my fancy had conjured her into actual life. She was there in the room with me, slim and shadowy, with her quiet voice and movements, and with that haunting, doubtful look in her dark eyes. What had she meant by that curious warning? What was the knowledge or the fear which inspired it? If one could only understand!

I sat down in my chair and tried to read, but the effort was useless. Directly opposite to me was that black uncurtained window. Every time I looked up it seemed to become once more the frame for a white evil face. At last I could bear it no longer. I rose and left the house. I wandered capless across the marshes to where the wet seaweed lay strewn about, and the long waves came rolling shorewards; a wilderness now indeed of grey mists, of dark silent tongues of seawater cleaving the land. There was no wind-no other sound than the steadfast monotonous lapping of the waves upon the sands. Along that road he had come; the faintly burning light upon my table showed where he had pressed his face against the window. Then he had wandered on, past the storm-bent tree at the turn of the road pointing landwards. A few yards farther was the creek from which we had dragged him. The events of the night struggled to reconstruct themselves in my mind, and I fought against their slow coalescence. I did not wish to remember—to believe. In my heart I felt that for some hidden reason Ray was my friend. This visit of the Duke's, with whatever it might portend, was without doubt inspired by him. And, on the other hand, there was the warning of Lady Angela, so earnestly expressed, so solemn, almost sad. How could I see light through all these things? How could I hope to understand?

The Duke came punctually, spruce and debonnair, a small rose in his buttonhole, his wizened cheeks aglow with the smart of the stinging east wind. With him came Lord Chelsford, whose face and figure were familiar enough to me from the pages of the illustrated papers. Dark, spare, and tall, he spoke seldom, but I felt all the while the merciless investigation of his searching eyes. The Duke, on the other hand, seemed to have thrown aside some part of his customary reserve. He spoke at greater length and with more freedom than I had heard him.

"You see, Mr. Ducaine," he began, "I am not a man who makes idle promises. I am here to offer you employment, if you are open to accept a post of some importance, and also, to be frank with you, of some danger."

"If I am qualified for the post, your Grace," I answered, "I shall be only too willing to do my best. But you must excuse me if I express exactly what is in my mind. I am almost a stranger to you. I am a complete stranger to Lord Chelsford. How can you rely upon my trustworthiness? You must have so many young men to choose from who are personally known to you. Why do you come to me?"

The Duke smiled grimly.

"In the first place," he said, "we are only strangers from the personal point of view, which is possibly an advantage. I have in my pocket a close record of your days since you entered the university. I know those who have been your friends, your tastes, how you have spent your time. Don't be foolish, young sir," he added sharply, as he saw the colour rise in my cheeks: "you will have a trust reposed in you such as few men have ever borne before. This prying into your life is from no motives of private curiosity. Wait until you hear the importance of the things which I am going to say to you." I was impressed into silence. The Duke continued—"You have heard, my young friend," he said, "of the Committee of National Defence?" "I have read of it," I answered.

"Good! This committee has been formed and sanctioned by the War Office in consequence of the shocking revelations of inefficiency which came to light during the recent war. It occurred to the Prime Minister, as I dare say it did to most of the thinking men in the country, that if our unreadiness to take the offensive was so obvious, it was possible that our defensive precautions had also been neglected. A. board was therefore formed to act independently of all existing institutions, and composed chiefly of military and naval men. The Commander-in-Chief, Lord Chelsford, Colonel Ray, and myself are amongst the members. Our mandate is to keep our attention solely fixed upon the defences of the country, to elaborate different schemes for repelling different methods of attack, and in short to make ourselves responsible to the country for the safety of the Empire. Every harbour on the south and east coast is supposed to be known to us, every yard of railway feeding the seaports from London, all the secret fortifications and places, south of London, capable of being held by inferior forces. The mobilization of troops to any one point has been gone thoroughly into, and every possible movement and combination of the fleet. These are only a few of the things which have become our care, but they are sufficient for the purpose of illustration. The importance of this Board must be apparent to you; also the importance of absolute secrecy as regards its doings and movements."

I was fascinated by the greatness of the subject. However, I answered him as quickly as possible, and emphatically.

"The Board," the Duke continued, "has been meeting in London. For the last few months we have had business of the utmost importance on hand. But on January 10, that is just six weeks ago, we came to a full stop. The Commander-in-Chief had no alternative but temporarily to dissolve the assembly. We found ourselves in a terrible and disastrous position. Lord Ronald Matheson had been acting as secretary for us. We met always with locked doors, and the names of the twelve members of the Board are the most honoured in England. Yet twenty-four hours after our meetings a verbatim report of them, with full particulars of all our schemes, was in the hands of the French Secret Service."

"Good God!" I exclaimed, startled for the moment out of my respectful silence.

The Duke himself seemed affected by the revelation which he had made. He sat forward in his chair with puckered brows and bent head. His voice, which had been growing lower and lower, had sunk almost to a whisper. It seemed to me that he made a sign to Lord Chelsford to continue. Almost for the first time the man who had done little since his entrance save watch me, spoke.

"My own political career, Mr. Ducaine," he said, "has been a long one, but I have never before found myself confronted with such a situation. Even you can doubtless realize its effect. The whole good of our work is undone. If we cannot recommence, and with different results, I am afraid, as an Englishman, to say what may happen. War between England and France to-day would be like a great game of chess between two masters of equal strength — one having a secret knowledge of his opponent's each ensuing move. You can guess what the end of that would be. Our only hope is at once to reconstruct our plans. We are hard at it now by day and by night, but the time has arrived when we can go no further without a meeting, and the actual committal to paper and diagram of our new schemes. We have discussed the whole matter most carefully, and we have come to the following decision. We have reduced the number of the Board by half, those who have resigned, with certain exceptions, having done so by ballot. We have decided that instead of holding our meetings at the War Office they shall take place down here at the Duke's house, and so far as possible secretly. Then, as regards the secretaryship. No shadow of suspicion rests upon Lord Ronald any more than upon his predecessors, but, as you may have read in the newspapers, he has temporarily lost his reason owing to the shock, and has been obliged to go to a private home. We have decided to engage some one absolutely without political connexions, and whose detachment from political life must be complete. You have had a warm advocate in Colonel Mostyn Ray, and, subject to some stringent and absolute conditions, I may say that we have decided to offer you the post."

I looked from one to the other. I have no doubt that I looked as bewildered as I felt.

"I am a complete stranger to all of you," I murmured. "I am not deserving in any way of such a position."

Lord Chelsford smiled.

"You underrate yourself, young man," he said drily, "or your college professors have wandered from the truth. Still, your surprise is natural, I admit. I will explain a little further. Our choice is more limited than you might think. At least fifty names were proposed, all of them of young men of the highest character. Each one, however, had some possibly doubtful relative or association or custom in life. It is evident that there is treachery somewhere in the very highest quarters. These young men were sure to be brought into contact with it. Now it was Ray's idea to seek for some one wholly outside the diplomatic world, living in a spot remote from London, with as few friends as possible, who would have no sentimental objections to the surveillance of detectives. You appear to us to be suitable."

"It is a wonderful offer!" I exclaimed.

"In a sense it is," Lord Chelsford continued. "The remuneration, of course, will be high, but the post itself may not be a permanency, and you will live all the time at high pressure. The Duke will place a small house at your disposal, and it will be required that you form no new acquaintances without reference to him, nor must you leave this place on any account without permission. You will virtually be a prisoner, and if certain of my suspicions are correct you may even find the post one of great physical danger. On the other hand, you will have a thousand a year salary, and a sum of five thousand pounds in two years' time if all is well."

Excitement seemed to have steadied my nerves. I forgot all the minor tragedies which had been real enough things to face only a few hours ago. I spoke calmly and decisively.

"I accept, Lord Chelsford," I said. "I shall count my life a small thing indeed against my fidelity."

He drummed idly with his forefinger upon the table. His eyes were wandering around the room absently. His face was calm and expressionless.

"Very well, then," he said, "my business here is settled. I shall leave it with the Duke to acquaint you with the practical details of your work, and our arrangement."

He rose to his feet. The Duke glanced at his watch.

"You have only just time for the train," he remarked. "The car shall take you there. I prefer to walk back, and I have something further to say to Mr. Ducaine."

Lord Chelsford took leave of me briefly, and the Duke, after accompanying him outside, returned to his former seat. I ventured upon an incoherent attempt to express my gratitude, which he at once waved aside. He leaned over the table, and he fixed his eyes steadfastly upon me.

"I am able now," he said, "to ask you a question postponed from the other day. It is concerning the man who was found dead in the creek."

His merciless eyes noted my start.

"Ah!" he continued. "I can see that you know something. I have my suspicions about this man. You can now understand my interest when I hear of strangers in the neighbourhood. I do not believe that he was a derelict from the sea. Do you?"

"No," I answered.

He nodded.

"Am I right," he said, "in presuming that you know he was not?"

"I know that he was not," I admitted.

His fingers ceased their beating upon the table. His face became white and masklike.

"Go on," he said.

"I know that he came through Braster, and he asked for me. He looked in through the window of my cottage when Colonel Ray was with me. I saw him no more after that until I found him dead."

"Ray left you after you had seen this man's face at the window?"

"Yes."

"The wounds about the man's head and body. If he was not thrown up by the sea, can you explain them?"

"No," I answered with a shudder.

"At the inquest it was not mentioned, I think, that he had been seen in the village?"

"It was not," I admitted. "Most of the people were at Colonel Ray's lecture. He spoke to one girl, a Miss Moyat."

"She did not give evidence."

"I thought," I said in a low tone, "that she had better not."

"Did you hear anything after Ray left?" he asked suddenly.

I could have cried out, but my tongue seemed dry in my throat.

"There was a sound," I muttered, "I fancied that it was a cry. But I could not tell. The wind was blowing, and the sea and rain! No, I could not tell."

He rose up.

"You appear," he said drily, "to have discretion. Cultivate it! It is a great gift. I shall look for you at eleven o'clock in the morning. I am having a large house party this week, and amongst them will be our friends."

He left me without any further farewell, and turned slowly homewards. When he reached the bend in the road he paused, and remained there for several moments motionless. His eyes were fixed upon the small creek. He seemed to be measuring the distance between it and the road. He was still lingering there when I closed the door.

CHAPTER IX
TREACHERY

The sunlight was streaming through the window when at last my pen ceased to move. I rubbed my eyes and looked out in momentary amazement. Morning had already broken across the sea. My green-shaded lamp was burning with a sickly light. The moon had turned pale and colourless whilst I sat at my desk.

I stretched myself and, lighting a cigarette, commenced to collect my papers. Immediately a dark figure rose from a couch in the farther corner of the room and approached me.

"Can I get you anything, sir?"

I turned in my chair. The man-servant whom the Duke had put in charge of the "Brand," my present habitation, and who remained with me always in the room while I worked, stood at my elbow.

"I would like some coffee, Grooton," I said. "I am going to walk up to the house with these papers, and I shall want a bath and some breakfast directly I get back."

"Very good, sir. It shall be ready."

I folded up the sheets and maps, and placing them in an oilskin case, tied them round my body under my waistcoat. Then I withdrew all the cartridges save one from the revolver which had lain all night within easy reach of my right hand, and slipped it into my pocket.

"Coffee ready, Grooton?"

"In one moment, sir."

I watched him bending over the stove, pale, dark-visaged, with the subdued manners and voice which mark the aristocracy of servitude. My employer's confidence in him must be immense, for while he watched over me I was practically in his power.

"Have you been long with the Duke, Grooton?" I asked him.

"Twenty-one years, sir. I left his Grace to go to Lord Chelsford, who found me some work in London."

"Secret service work, wasn't it, Grooton?"

"Yes, sir."

"Interesting?"

"Some parts of it very interesting, sir."

I nodded and drank my coffee. Grooton was watching me with an air of respectful interest.

"You will pardon my remarking it, sir, but I hope you will try and get some sleep during the day. You are very pale this morning, sir."

I looked at the glass, and was startled at my own reflection. This was only my third day, and the responsibilities of my work were heavy upon me. My cheeks were sunken and there were black rings around my eyes.

"I will lie down when I come back, Grooton," I answered.

Outside, the fresh morning wind came like a sudden sweet tonic to my jaded nerves. I paused for a moment to face bareheaded the rush of it from the sea. As I stood there, drinking it in, I became suddenly aware of light approaching footsteps. Some one was coming towards the cottage from the Park.

I did not immediately turn my head, but every nerve in my body seemed to stiffen into quivering curiosity.

The pathway was a private one leading from the house only to the "Brand," and down the cliff to Braster. It was barely seven o'clock, and the footsteps were no labouring man's. I think that I knew very well who it was that came so softly down the cone-strewn path.

We faced one another with little of the mask of surprise. She came like a shadow, flitting between the slender tree trunks out into the sunshine, where for a moment she seemed wan and white. Her dark eyes flashed a greeting at me. I stood cap in hand before her. It was the first time we had met since I had taken up my abode at the "Brand."

"Good-morning, Mr. Ducaine," she said. "You need not look at me as though I were a ghost. I always walk before breakfast in the country."

"There is no better time," I answered.

"You look as though you had been up all night," she remarked.

"I had work to finish," I told her.

She nodded.

"So you would have none of my advice, Mr. Secretary," she said softly, coming a little nearer to me. "You are already installed."

"Already at work," I asserted.

She glanced towards the "Brand."

"I hope that you are comfortable," she said. "A couple of hours is short notice in which to make a place habitable."

"Grooton is a magician," I told her. "He has arranged everything."

"He is a wonderful servant," she said thoughtfully.

A white-winged bird floated over our heads and drifted away skywards.
She followed it with her eyes.

"You wonder at seeing me so early," she murmured. "Don't you think that it is worth while? Nothing ever seems so sweet as this first morning breeze."

I bowed gravely. She was standing bareheaded now at the edge of the cliff, watching the flight of the bird. It was delightful to see the faint pink come back to her cheeks with the sting of the salt wind. Nevertheless, I had an idea in my mind that it was not wholly for her health's sake that Lady Angela walked abroad so early.

"Tell me," she said presently, "have you had a visitor this morning?"

"What, at this hour?" I exclaimed.

"There are other early risers besides you and me," she said. "The spinney gate was open, so some one has passed through."

I shook my head.

"I have not seen or heard a soul," I told her. "I have just finished some work, and I am on my way up to the house with it."

"You really mean it?" she persisted.

"Of course I do," I answered her. "Grooton is the only person I have spoken to for at least nine hours. Why do you ask?"

She hesitated.

"My window looks this way," she said, "and I fancied that I saw some one cross the Park while I was dressing. The spinney gate was certainly open."

"Then I fancy that it has been open all night," I declared, "for to the best of my belief no one has passed through it save yourself. May I walk with you back to the house, Lady Angela? There is something which I should very much like to ask you."

She replaced her hat, which she had been carrying in her hand. I stood watching her deft white fingers flashing amongst the thick silky coils of her hair. The extreme slimness of her figure seemed accentuated by her backward poise. Yet perhaps I had never before properly appreciated its perfect gracefulness.

"I was going farther along the cliffs," she said, "but I will walk some of the way back with you. One minute."

She stood on the extreme edge, and, shading her eyes with her hand, she looked up and down the broad expanse of sand — a great untenanted wilderness. I wondered for whom or what she was looking, but I asked no question. In a few moments she rejoined me, and we turned inland.

"Well," she said, "what is it that you wish to say?"

"Lady Angela," I began, "a few weeks ago there was no one whose prospects were less hopeful than mine. Thanks to your father and Colonel Ray all that is changed. To-day I have a position I am proud of, and important work. Yet I cannot help always remembering this: I am holding a post which you warned me against accepting."

"Well?"

"I am very curious," I said. "I have never understood your warning. I believe that you were in earnest. Was it that you believed me incapable or untrustworthy, or —"

"You appear to me," she murmured, "to be rather a curious person."

I bent forward and looked into her face. There was in her wonderful eyes a glint of laughter which became her well. She walked with slow graceful ease, her hands behind her, her head almost on a level with my own. I found myself studying her with a new pleasure. Then our eyes met, and I looked away, momentarily confused. Was it my fancy, or was there a certain measure of rebuke in her cool surprise, a faint indication of her desire that I should remember that she was the Lady Angela Harberly, and I her father's secretary? I bit my lip. She should not catch me offending again, I determined.

"You must forgive me," I said stiffly, "but your warning seemed a little singular. If you do not choose to gratify my curiosity, it is of no consequence."

"Since you disregarded it," she remarked, lifting her dress from the dew-laden grass on to which we had emerged, "it does not matter, does it? Only you are very young, and you know little of the world. Lord Ronald was your predecessor, and he is in a lunatic asylum. No one knows what lies behind certain unfortunate things which have happened during the last months. There is a mystery which is as yet unsolved."

I smiled.

"In your heart you are thinking," I said, "that such an unsophisticated person as myself will be an easy prey to whatever snares may be laid for me. Is it not so?"

She looked at me with uplifted eyebrows.

"Others of more experience have been worsted," she remarked calmly.
"Why not you?"

"If that is a serious question," I said, "I will answer it. Perhaps my very inexperience will be my best friend."

"Yes?"

"Those before me," I continued, "have thought that they knew whom to trust. I, knowing no one, shall trust no one."

"Not even me?" she asked, half turning her head towards me.

"Not even you," I answered firmly.

A man's figure suddenly appeared on the left. I looked at him puzzled, wondering whence he had come.

"Here is your good friend, Colonel Mostyn Ray," she remarked, with a note of banter in her tone. "What about him?"

"Not even Colonel Mostyn Ray," I answered. "The notes which I take with me from each meeting are to be read over from my elaboration at the next. Nobody is permitted to hold a pen or to make a note whilst they are being read. Afterwards I have your father's promise that not even he will ask for even a cursory glance at them. I deliver them sealed to Lord Chelsford."

Ray came up to us. His dark eyebrows were drawn close together, and I noticed that his boots were clogged with sand. He had the appearance of a man who had been walking far and fast.

"You keep up your good habits, Lady Angela," he said, raising his cap.

"It is my only good one, so I am loth to let it go," she answered. "If you were as gallant as you appear to be energetic," she added, glancing at his boots, "you would have stopped when I called after you, and taken me for a walk."

His eyes shot dark lightnings at her.

"I did not hear you call," he said.

"You had the appearance of a man who intended to, hear nothing and see nothing," she remarked coolly. "Never mind! There will be no breakfast for an hour yet. You shall take me on to Braster Hill. Come!"

They left me at a turn in the path. I saw their heads close together in earnest conversation. I went on towards the house.

I entered by the back, and made my way across the great hall, which was still invaded by domestics with brushes and brooms. Taking a small key from my watch-chain, I unfastened the door of a room almost behind the staircase, and pushed it open. The curtains were drawn, and the room itself, therefore, almost in darkness. I carefully locked myself in, and turned up the electric light.

The apartment was a small one, and contained only a few pieces of heavy antique furniture. Behind the curtains were iron shutters. In one corner was a strong safe. I walked to it, and for the first time I permitted myself to think of the combination word. Slowly I fitted it together, and the great door swung open.

There were several padlocked dispatch-boxes, and, on a shelf above, a bundle of folded papers. I took this bundle carefully out and laid it on the table before me. I was on the point of undoing the red tape with which it was tied, when my fingers became suddenly rigid. I stared at the packet with wide-open eyes. I felt my breath come short and my brain reeling. The papers were there sure enough, but it was not at them that I was looking. It was the double knot in the pink tape which fascinated me.

CHAPTER X
AN EXPRESSION OF CONFIDENCE

I have no exact recollection of how long I spent in that little room. After a while I closed the door safe, and reset the combination lock with trembling fingers. Then I searched all round, but could find no traces of any recent intruder. I undid the heavy shutters, and let in a stream of sunshine. Outside, Ray and Lady Angela were strolling up and down the terrace. I watched the latter with fascinated eyes. It was from her that this strange warning had come to me, this warning which as yet was only imperfectly explained. What did she know? Whom did she suspect? Was it possible that she, a mere child, had even the glimmering of a suspicion as to the truth? My eyes followed her every movement. She walked with all the lightsome grace to which her young limbs and breeding entitled her, her head elegantly poised on her slender neck, her face mostly turned towards her companion, to whom she was talking earnestly. Even at this distance I seemed to catch the inspiring flash of her dark eyes, to follow the words which fell from her lips so gravely. And as I watched a new idea came to me. I turned slowly away and went in search of the Duke.

I found him sitting fully dressed in an anteroom leading from his bedroom, with a great pile of letters before him, and an empty postbag. He was leaning forward, his elbow upon the table, his head resting upon his right hand. Engrossed as I was with my own terrible discovery, I was yet powerfully impressed by his unfamiliar appearance. In the clear light which came flooding in through the north window he seemed to me older, and his face more deeply lined than any of my previous impressions of him had suggested. His eyes were fixed upon the mass of correspondence before him, most of which was as yet unopened, and his expression was one of absolute aversion. At my entrance he looked up inquiringly.

"What do you want, Ducaine?" he asked.

"I am sorry to have disturbed your Grace," I answered. "I have come to place my resignation in your hands."

His face was expressive enough in its frowning contempt, but he said nothing for a moment, during which his eyes met mine mercilessly.

"So you find the work too hard, eh?" he asked.

"The work is just what I should have chosen, your Grace," I answered. "I like hard work, and I expected it. The trouble is that I have succeeded no better than Lord Ronald."

My words were evidently a shock to him. He half opened his lips, but closed them again. I saw the hand which he raised to his forehead shake.

"What do you mean, Ducaine? Speak out, man."

"The safe in the study has been opened during the night," I said. "Our map of the secret fortifications on the Surrey downs and plans for a camp at Guilford have been examined."

"How do you know this?"

"I tied the red tape round them in a peculiar way. It has been undone and retied. The papers have been put back in a different order."

The Duke was without doubt agitated. He rose from his chair and paced the room restlessly.

"You are sure of what you say, Ducaine?" he demanded, turning, and facing me suddenly.

"Absolutely sure, your Grace," I answered.

He turned away from me.

"In my own house, under my own roof," I heard him mutter. "Good God!"

I had scarcely believed him capable of so much feeling. When he resumed his seat and former attitude I could see that his face was almost gray.

"This is terrible news," he said. "I am not at all sure, though, Mr. Ducaine, that any blame can attach itself to you."

"Your Grace," I answered, "there were three men only who knew the secret of that combination. One is yourself, another Colonel Ray, the third myself. I set the lock last night. I opened it this morning. I ask you, in the name of common sense, upon whom the blame is likely to fall? If I remain this will happen again. I cannot escape suspicion. It is not reasonable."

"The word was a common one," the Duke said half to himself. "Some one may have guessed it."

"Your Grace," I said, "is it likely that any one would admit the possibility of such a thing?"

"It may have been overheard."

"It has never been spoken," I reminded him. "It was written down, glanced at by all of us, and destroyed."

The Duke nodded.

"You are right," he admitted. "The inference is positive enough. The safe has been opened between the hours of ten at night and seven o'clock this morning by —"

"By either myself, Colonel Ray, or your Grace," I said.

"I am not sure that I am prepared to admit that," the Duke objected quietly.

"It is inevitable!" I declared.

"Only the very young use that word," the Duke said drily.

"I spoke only of what others must say," I answered.

"It is a cul de sac, I admit," the Duke said. "Nevertheless, Mr. Ducaine, I am not prepared without consideration to accept your resignation. I cannot see that our position would be improved in any way, and in my own mind I may add that I hold you absolved from suspicion."

I held myself a little more upright. The Duke spoke without enthusiasm, but with conviction.

"Your Grace is very kind," I answered gratefully, "but there are the others. They know nothing of me. It is inevitable that I should become an object of suspicion to them."

The Duke looked thoughtfully for several moments at the table before him. Then he looked up at me.

"Ducaine," he said, "I will tell you what I propose. You have done your duty in reporting this thing to me. Your duty ends there — mine begins. The responsibility, therefore, for our future course of action remains with me. You, I presume, are prepared to admit this."

"Certainly, your Grace," I answered.

"I see no useful purpose to be gained," the Duke continued, "in spreading this thing about. I believe that we shall do better by keeping our own counsel. You and I can work secretly in the matter. I may have some suggestions to make when I have considered it more fully; but for the present I propose that we treat the matter as a hallucination of yours. We shall hear in due course if this stolen information goes across the water. If it does — well, we shall know how to act."

"You mean this?" I asked breathlessly. "Forgive me, your Grace, but it means so much to me. You believe that we are justified?"

"Why not?" the Duke asked coldly. "It is I who am your employer. It is I who am responsible to the country for these things. You are responsible only to me. I choose that you remain. I choose that you speak of this matter only when I bid you speak."

To me it was relief immeasurable. The Duke's manner was precise, even cold. Yet I felt that he believed in me. I scarcely doubted but that he had suspicions of his own. I, at any rate, was not involved in them. I could have wrung him by the hand but for the inappropriateness of such a proceeding. So far as he was concerned I could see that the matter was already done with. His attention was beginning to wander to the mass of letters before him.

"Would you allow me to help your Grace with your correspondence?" I suggested. "I have no work at present."

The Duke shook his head impatiently.

"I thank you," he said. "My man of business will be here this morning, and he will attend to them. I will not detain you, Mr. Ducaine."

I turned to leave the room, but found myself face to face with a young man in the act of entering it.

"Blenavon!" the Duke exclaimed.

"How are you, sir?" the newcomer answered. "Sorry I didn't arrive in time to see you last night. We motored from King's Lynn, and the whole of this respectable household was in bed."

I knew at once who he was. The Duke looked towards me.

"Ducaine," he said, "this is my son, Lord Blenavon."

Lord Blenavon's smile was evidently meant to be friendly, but his expression belied it. He was slightly taller than his father, and his cast of features was altogether different. His cheeks were pale, almost sunken, his eyes were too close together, and they had the dimness of the roué or the habitual dyspeptic. His lips were too full, his chin too receding, and he was almost bald.

"How are you, Mr. Ducaine?" he said. "Awful hour to be out of bed, isn't it? and all for the slaying of a few fat and innocent birds. Let me see, wasn't I at Magdalen with you?"

"I came up in your last year," I reminded him.

"Ah, yes, I remember," he drawled. "Terrible close worker you were, too. Are you breakfasting down stairs, sir?"

"I think that I had better," the Duke said. "I suppose you brought some men with you?"

"Half a dozen," Lord Blenavon answered, "including his Royal Highness."

The Duke thrust all his letters into his drawer, and locked them up with a little exclamation of relief.

"I will come down with you," he said. "Mr. Ducaine, you will join us."

I would have excused myself, for indeed I was weary, and the thought of a bath and rest at home was more attractive. But the Duke had a way of expressing his wishes in a manner which it was scarcely possible to mistake, and I gathered that he desired me to accept his invitation. We all descended the stairs together.

CHAPTER XI
HIS ROYAL HIGHNESS

The long dining-room was almost filled with a troop of guests who had arrived on the previous day. Most of the men were gathered round the huge sideboard, on which was a formidable array of silver-covered hot-water dishes. Places were laid along the flower-decked table for thirty or forty. I stood apart for a few moments whilst the Duke was greeting some of his guests. Ray, who was sitting alone, motioned me to a place by him.

"Come and sit here, Ducaine," he said; "that is," he added, with a sudden sarcastic gleam in his dark eyes, "unless you still have what the novelists call an unconquerable antipathy to me. I don't want to rob you of your appetite."

"I did not expect to see you down here again so soon, Colonel Ray," I answered gravely. "I congratulate you upon your nerves."

Ray laughed softly to himself.

"You would have me go shuddering past the fatal spot, I suppose, with shaking knees and averted head, eh? On the contrary, I have been down on the sands for more than an hour this morning, and have returned with an excellent appetite."

I looked at him curiously.

"I saw you returning," I said. "Your boots looked as though you had been wading in the wet sand. You were not there without a purpose."

"I was not," he admitted. "I seldom do anything without a purpose."

For a moment he abandoned the subject. He proceeded calmly with his breakfast, and addressed a few remarks to a man across the table, a man with short cropped hair and beard, and a shooting dress of sombre black.

"You are quite right," he said, turning towards me suddenly. "I had a purpose in going there. I thought that the gentleman whose untimely fate has enlisted your sympathies might have dropped something which would have been useful to me."

For the moment I forgot this man's kindness to me. I looked at him with a shudder.

"If you are in earnest," I said, "I trust that you were unsuccessful."

I fancied that there was that in his glance which suggested the St. Bernard looking down on the terrier, and I chafed at it.

"It would have been better for you," he said, grimly, "had my search met with better result."

"For me?" I repeated.

"For you! Yes! The man came to see you. If he had been alive you might have been in his toils by now. He was a very cunning person, and those who sent him were devils."

"How do you know these things?" I asked, amazed.

"From the letters which I ripped from his coat," he answered.

"He came to Braster to see me, then?" I exclaimed.

"Precisely."

"And the letters which you took from him — were they addressed to me?"

"They were."

I was getting angry, but Ray remained imperturbable.

"I think," I said, "you will admit that I have a right to them."

"Not a shadow of a doubt of it," he answered. "In fact, it was so obvious that I destroyed them."

"Destroyed my letters!"

"Precisely! I chose that course rather than allow them to fall into your hands."

"You admit, then," I said, "that I had a right to them."

"Indubitably. But they do not exist."

"You read them, without doubt. You can acquaint me with their contents."

"Some day," he said, "I probably shall. But not yet. Believe me or not, as you choose, but there are certain positions in which ignorance is the only possible safe state. You are in such a position at the present moment."

"Are you," I asked, "my moral guardian?"

"I have at least," he said, "incurred certain responsibilities on your behalf. You could no longer hold your present post and be in communication with the sender of those letters."

My anger died away despite myself. The man's strength and honesty of purpose were things which I could not bring myself to doubt. I continued my breakfast in silence.

"By-the-bye," he remarked presently, "you, too, my young friend, were out early this morning."

"I was writing all night," I answered. "I had documents to put in the safe."

He shot a quick searching glance at me.

"You have been to the safe this morning, then?"

I answered him with a composure at which I inwardly marvelled.

"Certainly! It was the object of my coming here."

"You entered the room with the Duke. Was he in the study at that hour?"

"No, I went upstairs to him. I had a question to ask."

"And you have met Lord Blenavon? What do you think of him?"

"We were at Magdalen together for a term," I answered. "He was good enough to remember me."

Ray smiled, but he did not speak another word to me all the breakfast-time. Once I made a remark to him, and his reply was curt, almost rude. I left the room a few minutes afterwards, and came face to face in the hall with Lady Angela.

"I am glad, Mr. Ducaine," she remarked, "that your early morning labours have given you an appetite. You have been in to breakfast, have you not?"

"Your father was good enough to insist upon it," I answered.

"You have seen him already this morning, then?"

"For a few minutes only," I explained. "I went up to his room."

"I trust so far that everything is going on satisfactorily?" she inquired, raising her eyes to mine.

I did not answer her at once. I was engaged in marvelling at the wonderful pallor of her cheeks.

"So far as I am concerned, I think so," I said. "Forgive me, Lady Angela," I added, "but I think that you must have walked too far this morning. You are very pale."

"I am tired," she admitted.

There was a lounge close at hand. She moved slowly towards it, and sat down. There was no spoken invitation, but I understood that I was permitted to remain with her.

"Do you know," she said, looking round to make sure that we were alone, "I dread these meetings of the Council. I have always the feeling that something terrible will happen. I knew Lord Ronald very well, and his mother was one of my dearest friends. I am sure that he was perfectly innocent. And to-day he is in a madhouse. They say that he will never recover."

I did not wish to speak about these things, even with Lady Angela. I tried to lead the conversation into other channels, but she absolutely ignored my attempt.

"There is something about it all so grimly mysterious," she said. "It seems almost as though there must be a traitor, if not in the Council itself, in some special and privileged position."

She looked up at me as though asking for confirmation of her views. I shook my head.

"Lady Angela," I said, "would you mind if I abstained from expressing any opinion at all? It is a subject which I feel it is scarcely right for me to discuss."

She looked at me with wide-open eyes, a dash of insolence mingled with her surprise. I do not know what she was about to say, for at that moment the young man with the sombre shooting suit and closely cropped hair paused for a moment on his way out of the breakfast-room. He glanced at me, and I received a brief impression of an unwholesome-looking person with protuberant eyeballs, thin lashes, and supercilious mouth.

"I trust that the day's entertainment will include something more than a glimpse of Lady Angela," he said, with a low bow.

She raised her eyes. It seemed to me, who was watching her closely, that she shrank a little back in her seat. I was sure that she shared my instinctive dislike of the man.

"I think not," she said. "Perhaps you are expecting me to come down with the lunch and compliment you all upon your prowess."

"It would be delightful!" he murmured.

She shook her head.

"There are too many of you, and I am too few," she said lightly. "Besides, shooting is one of the few sports with which I have no sympathy at all. I shall try and get somewhere away from the sound of your guns."

"I myself," he said, "am not what you call a devotee of the sport. I wonder if part of the day one might play truant. Would Lady Angela take pity upon an unentertained guest?"

"I should find it a shocking nuisance," she said, coolly. "Besides, it would not be allowed. You will find that when my father has once marshalled you, escape is a thing not to be dreamed of. Every one says that he is a perfect martinet where a day's shooting is concerned."

He smiled enigmatically. "We shall see," he remarked, as he turned away. Lady Angela watched him disappear. "Do you know who that is?" she asked me. I shook my head. "Some one French, very French," I remarked. "He should be," she remarked. "That is Prince Henri de Malors. He represents the hopes of the Royalists in France."

"It is very interesting," I murmured. "May I ask is he an old family friend?"

"Our families have been connected by marriage," she answered. "He and Blenavon saw a great deal of one another in Paris, very much to the disadvantage of my brother, I should think. I believe that there was some trouble at the Foreign Office about it."

"It is very interesting," I repeated.

"Blenavon was very foolish," she declared. "It was obviously a most indiscreet friendship for him, and Paris was his first appointment. But I must go and speak to some of these people."

She rose and left me a little abruptly. I escaped by one of the side entrances, and hurried back to my cottage.

CHAPTER XII
AN ACCIDENT

The Prince accepted my most comfortable easy chair with an air of graceful condescension. Lady Angela had already seated herself. It was late in the afternoon, and Grooton was busy in the room behind, preparing my tea.

"The Prince did not care to shoot to-day," Lady Angela explained, "and I have been showing him the neighbourhood. Incidentally, I am dying for some tea, and the Prince has smoked all his cigarettes."

The Prince raised his hand in polite expostulation, but he accepted a cigarette with a little sigh of relief.

"You have found a very lonely spot for your dwelling-house, Mr. Ducaine," he said. "You English are so fond of solitude."

"It suits me very well," I answered, "for just now I have a great deal of work to do. I am safely away from all distractions here."

Lady Angela smiled at me.

"Not quite so safe perhaps, Mr. Ducaine, as you fondly imagined," she remarked. "I am afraid that we disturbed you. You look awfully busy."

She glanced towards my writing-table. It was covered with papers, and a map of the southern counties leaned up against the wall. The Prince also was glancing curiously in the same direction.

"I have finished my work for the day," I said, rising. "If you will permit me, I will put it away."

Grooton brought in tea. The Prince was politely curious as to the subject matter of those closely written sheets of paper.

"You are perhaps interested in literature, Mr. Ducaine," he remarked.

"Immensely," I answered, waving my hand towards my bookshelves.

"But you yourself—you no doubt write?"

"Oh, one tries," I answered, pouring out the tea.

"It may be permitted then to wish you success," he remarked dryly.

"You are very good," I answered.

Lady Angela calmly interposed. The Prince ate buttered toast and drank tea with a bland affectation of enjoyment. They rose almost immediately afterwards.

"You are coming up to the house this evening, Mr. Ducaine?" Lady Angela asked.

"I am due there now," I answered. "If you will allow me, I will walk back with you."

The Prince touched my arm as Lady Angela passed out before us.

"I am anxious, Mr. Ducaine," he said, looking me in the face, "for a few minutes' private conversation with you. I shall perhaps be fortunate enough to find you at home to-morrow."

He did not wait for my answer, for Lady Angela looked back, and he hastened to her side. He seemed in no hurry, however, to leave the place. The evening was cloudy and unusually dark. A north wind was tearing through the grove of stunted firs, and the roar of the incoming sea filled the air with muffled thunder. The Prince looked about him with a little grimace.

"It is indeed a lonely spot," he remarked. "One can imagine anything happening here. Did I not hear of a tragedy only the other day—a man found dead?"

"If you have a taste for horrors, Prince," I remarked, "you can see the spot from the edge of the cliff here."

The Prince moved eagerly forward.

"I disclaim all such weakness," he said, "but the little account which I read, or did some one tell me of it?—ah, I forget; but it interested me."

I pointed downwards to where the creek-riven marshes merged into the sands.

"It was there—a little to the left of the white palings," I said. "The man was supposed to have been cast up from the sea."

He measured the distance with his eye. I anticipated his remark.

"The tide is only halfway up now," I said, "and on that particular night there was a terrible gale."

"Nevertheless," he murmured, half to himself, "it is a long way. Was the man what you call identified, Mr. Ducaine?"

"No!"

"There were no letters or papers found upon him?"

"None."

The Prince looked at me sharply.

"That," he said softly, "was strange. Does it not suggest to you that he may have been robbed?"

"I had not thought of it," I answered. "The verdict, I believe, was simply Found drowned."

"Found drowned," the Prince repeated. "Ah! Found drowned. By-the-bye," he added suddenly, "who did find him?"

"I did," I said coolly.

"You?" The Prince peered at me closely through the dim light. "That," he said reflectively, "is interesting."

"You find it so interesting," I remarked, "that perhaps you could help to solve the question of the man's identity."

He seemed startled.

"I?" he exclaimed. "But, no. Why should you think that?"

I turned to join Lady Angela. He did not immediately follow.

"Why did you bring him?" I asked her softly. "You had some reason."

"He was making inquiries about you," she answered, "secretly and openly. I thought you ought to know, and I could think of no other way of putting you on your guard."

"The Prince of Malors!" I murmured. "He surely would not stoop to play the spy."

She was silent, and moved a step or two farther away from the spot where he still stood as though absorbed. His angular figure was clearly defined through the twilight against the empty background of space. He was on the very edge of the cliff, almost looking over.

"I know very little about him myself," she said hurriedly, "but I have heard the others talk, Lord Chelsford especially. He is a man, they say, with a twofold reputation. He has played a great part in the world of pleasure, almost a theatrical part; but, you know, the French people like that."

"It is true," I murmured. "They love their heroes decked in tinsel." She nodded.

"They say that it is part of a pose, and that he has serious political ambitions. He contemplates always some great scheme which shall make him the idol, if only for a day, of the French mob. A day would be sufficient, for he would strike while—Prince, be careful," she called out. "Ah!"

We heard a shrill cry, and we saw the Prince sway on the verge of the cliff. He threw up his arms and clutched wildly at the air, but he was too late to save himself. We saw the ground crumble beneath his feet, and with a second cry of despair he disappeared.

Grooton, Lady Angela, and I reached the edge of the cliff at about the same moment. We peered over in breathless anxiety. Lady Angela clutched my arm, and for a moment I did not in the least care what had happened to the Prince.

"Don't be frightened," I whispered. "The descent is not by any means sheer. He can't possibly have got to the bottom. I will clamber down and look for him,"

She shuddered.

"Oh, you mustn't," she exclaimed. "It is not safe. How terrible it looks down there!"

I raised my voice and shouted. Almost immediately there came an answer.

"I am here, my friends, in the middle of a bush. I dare not move. It is so dark I cannot see where to put my foot. Can you lower me a lantern, and I will see if I can climb up?"

Grooton hastened back to the cottage.

"I think you will be all right," I cried out. "It is not half as steep as it looks."

"I believe," he answered, "that I can see a path up. But I will wait until the lantern comes."

The lantern arrived almost immediately. We lowered it to him by a rope, and he examined the face of the cliff.

"I think that I can get up," he cried out, "but I should like to help myself with the rope. Can you both hold it tightly?"

"All right," I answered. "We've got it."

He clambered up with surprising agility. But as he reached the edge of the cliff he groaned heavily.

"Are you hurt?" Lady Angela asked.

"It is my foot," he muttered, "my left foot. I twisted it in falling."

Grooton and I helped him to the cottage. He hobbled painfully along with tightly clenched lips.

"I shall have to ask for a pony cart to get up to the house, I am afraid," he said. "I am very sorry to give you so much trouble, Mr. Ducaine."

"The trouble is nothing,". I answered, "but I am wondering how on earth you managed to fall over the cliff."

"I myself, I scarcely know," he answered, as he sipped the brandy which Grooton had produced. "I am subject to fits of giddiness, and one came over me as I stood there looking down. I felt the ground sway, and remember no more. I am very sorry to give you tall this trouble, but indeed I fear that I cannot walk."

"We will send you down a cart," I declared. "You will have rather a rough drive across the grass, but there is no other way."

"You are very kind," he declared. "I am in despair at my clumsiness."

I gave him my box of cigarettes. Lady Angela hesitated.

"I think," she said, "that I ought to stay with you, Prince, while Mr. Ducaine goes up for the cart."

"Indeed, Lady Angela, you are very kind," he answered, "but I could not permit it. I regret to say that I am in some pain, and I have a weakness for being alone when I suffer. If I desire anything Mr. Ducaine's servant will be at hand."

So we left him there. At any other time the prospect of that walk with Lady Angela would have filled me with joy. But from the first moment of leaving the cottage I was uneasy.

"What do you think of that man?" I asked her abruptly. "I mean personally?"

"I hate him," she answered coolly. "He is one of those creatures whose eyes and mouth, and something underneath his most respectful words, seem always to suggest offensive things. I find it very hard indeed to be civil to him."

"Do you happen to know what Colonel Ray thinks of him?" I asked her.

"I have no special knowledge of Colonel Ray's likes or dislikes," she answered.

"Forgive me," I said. "I thought that you and he were very intimate, and that you might know. I wonder whether he takes the Prince seriously."

"Colonel Ray is one of my best friends," she said, "but I am not in his confidence."

A slight reserve had crept into her tone. I stole a glance at her face; paler and more delicate than ever it seemed in the gathering darkness. Her lips were firmly set, but her eyes were kind. A sudden desire for her sympathy weakened me.

"Lady Angela," I said, "I must talk to some one. I do not know whom to trust. I do not know who is honest. You are the only person whom I dare speak to at all."

She looked round cautiously. We were out of the plantation now, in the open park, where eavesdropping was impossible.

"You have a difficult post, Mr. Ducaine," she said, "and you will remember — "

"Oh, I remember," I interrupted. "You warned me not to take' it. But think in what a position I was. I had no career, I was penniless. How could I throw away such a chance?"

"Something has happened — this morning, has it not?" she asked. I nodded.

"Yes."

She waited for me to go on. She was deeply interested. I could hear her breath coming fast, though we were walking at a snail's pace. I longed to confide in her absolutely, but I dared not.

"Do not ask me to tell you what it was," I said. "The knowledge would only perplex and be a burden to you. It is all the time like poison in my brain."

We were walking very close together. I felt her fingers suddenly upon my arm and her soft breath upon my cheek.

"But if you do not tell me everything—how can you expect my sympathy, perhaps my help?"

"I may not ask you for either," I answered sadly. "The knowledge of some things must remain between your father and myself."

"Between my father—and yourself!" she repeated.

I was silent, and then we both started apart. Behind us we could hear the sound of footsteps rapidly approaching, soft quick footsteps, muffled and almost noiseless upon the spongy turf. We stood still.

CHAPTER XIII
A BRIBE

I wheeled round and peered into the darkness. Lady Angela's fingers clutched my arm. I could feel that she was trembling violently. It was Grooton whose figure loomed up almost immediately before us—Grooton, bareheaded and breathless. "What is it?" I exclaimed quickly. "I think, sir, that you had better return," he panted.

He pointed over his shoulder towards the "Brand," and I understood. In a moment I was on my way thither, running as I had not done since my college days. I stumbled over antheaps, and more than once I set my foot in a rabbit hole, but somehow I kept my balance. As I neared the cottage I slackened my speed and proceeded more stealthily. I drew close to the window and peered in. Grooton had been right indeed to fetch me. The Prince was standing before my desk, with a bundle of papers in his hand. I threw open the door and entered the room. Swift though my movement had been, a second's difficulty with the catch had given the Prince his opportunity. He was back in his easy chair when I entered, reclining there with half-closed eyes. He looked up at me with well simulated surprise.

"You are soon back, Mr. Ducaine," he remarked calmly. "Did you forget something?"

"I forgot," I answered, struggling to recover my breath, "to lock up my desk."

"An admirable precaution," he admitted, watching as I gathered my papers together, "especially if one has valuables. It is an exposed spot this, and very lonely."

"I am curious," I said, leaning against the table and facing him, "I am curious to know which of my poor possessions can possibly be of interest or value to the Prince of Malors."

The calm hauteur of his answering stare was excellently done. I had a glimpse now of the aristocrat.

"You speak in enigmas, young man," he said. "Kindly be more explicit."

"My language can scarcely be more enigmatic than your actions," I answered. "I was fool enough to trust you and I left you here alone. But you were not unobserved, Prince. My servant, I am thankful to say, is faithful. It was he who summoned me back."

"Indeed!" he murmured.

"I might add," I continued, "that I took the liberty of looking in through the side window there before entering."

"If it amused you to do so, or to set your servant to spy upon me," he said, "I see no reason to object. But your meaning is still unexplained."

"The onus of explanation," I declared, "appears to me to rest with you, Prince. I offered the hospitality of my room, presumably to a gentleman—not to a person who would seize that opportunity to examine my private papers."

"You speak with assurance, Mr. Ducaine."

"The assurance of knowledge," I answered. "I saw you at my desk from outside."

"You should consult an oculist," he declared. "I have not left this chair. My foot is still too painful."

"You lie well, Prince," I answered, "but not well enough."

He looked at me thoughtfully.

"I am endeavouring," he said, "to accommodate myself to the customs of this wonderful country of yours. In France one sends one's seconds. What do you do here to a man who calls you a liar?"

"We treat him," I answered hotly, "as the man deserves to be treated who abuses the hospitality of a stranger, and places himself in the position of a common thief."

The Prince shrugged his shoulders lightly, and helped himself to one of my cigarettes.

"You are very young, Mr. Ducaine," he said, looking at me thoughtfully. "You have no doubt your career to make in the world.

So, in a greater sense of the word, have I. I propose, if you will allow me, to be quite frank with you."

"I have no wish for your confidences, Prince," I answered. "They cannot possibly concern or interest me."

"Do not be too sure of that," he said. "Like all young men of your age, you jump too readily at conclusions. It is very possible that you and I may be of service to one another, and I may add that those who have been of service to the Prince of Malors have seldom had cause to regret it."

"This conversation," I interposed, "seems to me to be beside the point. I have no desire to be of service to you. My inclinations are rather the other way."

"The matter may become more clear to you if you will only curb your impatience, my young friend," the Prince said. "It is only my ambition to serve my country, to command the gratitude of a nation which to-day regards both me and mine with mingled doubt and suspicion. I have ambitions, and I should be an easy and generous master to serve."

"I am honoured with your confidence, Prince, but I still fail to see how these matters concern me," I said, setting my teeth hard.

"With your permission I will make it quite clear," he continued. "For years your War Office has suffered from constant dread of an invasion by France. The rumour of our great projected manoeuvres in the autumn have inspired your statesmen with an almost paralysing fear. They see in these merely an excuse for marshalling and equipping an irresistible army within striking distance of your Empire. Personally I believe that they are entirely mistaken in their estimate of my country's intentions. That, however, is beside the mark. You follow me?"

"Perfectly," I assured him. "This is most interesting, although as yet it seems to me equally irrelevant."

"Your War Office," the Prince continued, "has established a Secret Council of Defence, whose only task it is to plan the successful resistance to that invasion, if ever it should take place. You, Mr. Ducaine, are, I believe, practically the secretary of that Council. You have to elaborate the digests of the meetings, to file schemes for the establishment of fortifications and camps; in a word, the result of these meetings passes through your hands. I will not beat about the bush, Mr. Ducaine. You can see that you have something in your keeping which, if passed on to me, would accomplish my whole aim. The army would be forced to acknowledge my claim upon them; the nation would hear of it."

"Well," I asked, "supposing all you say is true? What then?"

"You are a little obtuse, Mr. Ducaine," the Prince said softly. "If twenty thousand pounds would quicken your understanding—"

I picked up a small inkpot from the side of the table and hurled it at him. He sprang aside, but it caught the corner of his forehead, and he gave a shrill cry of pain. He struck a fierce blow at me, which I parried, and a moment later we were locked in one another's arms. I think that we must have been of equal strength, for we swayed up and down the room, neither gaining the advantage, till I felt my breath come short and my head dizzy. Nevertheless, I was slowly gaining the mastery. My grasp upon his throat was tightening. I had hold of his collar and tie, and I could have strangled him with a turn of my wrist. Just then the door opened. There was a quick exclamation of horrified surprise in a familiar tone. I threw him from me to the ground, and turned my head. It was Lady Angela who stood upon the threshold.

CHAPTER XIV
A RELUCTANT APOLOGY

Lady Angela looked at us both in cold surprise.

"Mr. Ducaine! Prince!" she exclaimed. "What is the meaning of this extraordinary exhibition?"

The Prince, whose sangfroid was marvellous, rose to his feet, and began to wipe his forehead with a spotless cambric handkerchief.

"My dear Lady Angela," he said, "I am most distressed that you should have been a witness of this—extraordinary incident. I have been trying to adapt myself to the methods of your country, but, alas! I cannot say that I am enamoured of them. Here, it seems, that gentlemen who differ must behave like dustmen. Will you pardon me if I turn my back to you for a moment? I see a small mirror, and I am convinced that my tie and collar need readjustment."

"But why quarrel at all?" she exclaimed. "Mr. Ducaine," she added, turning coolly to me, "I trust you have remembered that the Prince is my father's guest."

I was speechless, but the Prince himself intervened.

"The blame, if any," he declared, "was mine. Mr. Ducaine appeared to misunderstand me from the first. I believe that his little ebullition arose altogether from too great zeal on behalf of his employers. I congratulate him upon it, while I am bound to deprecate his extreme measures."

"And you, Mr. Ducaine," she asked, turning towards me, "what have you to say?"

"Nothing," I declared, stung by her tone and manner as much as by his coolness, "except that I found the Prince of Malors meddling with my private papers, and subsequently I interrupted him in the offer of a bribe."

The Prince smoothed his necktie, which he had really tied very well, complacently.

"The personal belongings of Mr. Ducaine," he said calmly, "are without interest to me. I fancy that the Prince of Malors can ignore any suggestions to the contrary. As for the bribe, Mr. Ducaine talks folly. I am not aware that he has anything to sell, and I decline to believe him a blackmailer. I prefer to look upon him as a singularly hot-headed and not over-intelligent person, who takes very long jumps at conclusions. Lady Angela, I find my foot much better. May I have the pleasure of escorting you to the house?"

I held my tongue, knowing very well that the Prince played his part solely that I might be entrapped into speech. But Lady Angela seemed puzzled at my silence. She looked at me for a moment inquiringly out of her soft dark eyes. I made no sign. She turned away to the Prince.

"If you are sure that you can walk without pain," she said. "We will not trouble you, Mr. Ducaine," she added, as I moved to open the door.

So they left me alone, and I was not sure whether the honours remained with him or with me. He had never for a moment lost his dignity, nor had he even looked ridiculous when calmly rearranging his tie and collar. I laughed to myself bitterly as I prepared to follow them. I was determined to lay the whole matter before the Duke at once.

As I reached the terrace I saw a man walking up and down, smoking a pipe. He stood at the top of the steps and waited for me. It was Colonel Ray. He took me by the arm.

"I have been waiting for you, Ducaine," he said. "I was afraid that I might miss you, or I should have come down."

"I am on my way to the Duke," I said, "and my business is urgent."

"So is mine," he said grimly. "I want to know exactly what has passed between you and the Prince of Malors."

"I am not at all sure, Colonel Ray," I answered, "that I am at liberty to tell you. At any rate, I think that I ought to see the Duke first."

His face darkened, his eyes seemed to flash threatening fires upon me. He was smoking so furiously that little hot shreds of tobacco fell from his pipe.

"Boy," he exclaimed, "there are limits even to my forbearance. You are where you are at my suggestion, and I could as easily send you adrift. I do not say this as a threat, but I desire to be treated with common consideration. I appeal to your reason. Is it well to treat me like an enemy?"

"Whether you are indeed my friend or my enemy I am not even now sure," I answered. "I am learning to be suspicious of every person and thing which breathes. But as for this matter between the Prince and myself, it can make little difference who knows the truth. He shammed a fall over the cliff and a sprained ankle. Lady Angela and I started for the house to send a cart for him, but, before we were halfway across the Park, Grooton fetched me back. I found the Prince examining the papers on which I had been working, and when I charged him with it he offered me a bribe."

"And you?"

"I struck him!"

Ray groaned.

"You struck him! And you had him in your power—to play with as you would. And you struck him! Oh, Ducaine, you are very, very young. I am your friend, boy, or rather I would be if you would let me. But I am afraid that you are a blunderer."

I faced him with white face.

"I seem to have found my way into a strange place," I answered. "I have neither wit nor cunning enough to know true men from false. I would trust you, but you are a murderer. I would have trusted the Prince of Malors, but he has proved himself a common adventurer. So I have made up my mind that all shall be alike. I will be neither friend nor foe to any mortal, but true to my country. I go my way and do my duty, Colonel Ray."

He blew out dense volumes of smoke, puffing furiously at his pipe for several minutes. There seemed to be many things which he had it in his mind to say to me. But, as though suddenly altering his purpose, he stood on one side.

"You shall go your own way," he said grimly. "The Lord only knows where it will take you."

It took me in the first place to the Duke, to whom I recounted briefly what had happened. I could see that my story at once made a deep impression upon him. When I had finished he sat for several minutes deep in thought. For the first time since I had known him he seemed nervous and ill at ease. He was unusually pale, and there were deep lines engraven about his mouth. One hand was resting upon the table, and I fancied that his fingers were shaking.

"The Prince of Malors," he said at last, and his voice lacked altogether its usual ring of cool assurance, "is of Royal blood. He is not even in touch with the political powers of France to-day. He may have been guilty of a moment's idle curiosity — "

"Your Grace must forgive me," I interrupted, "but you are overlooking facts. The fall over the cliff was premeditated, the sprained foot was a sham, the whole affair was clearly planned in order that he might be left alone in my room. Besides, there is the bribe."

The Duke folded his hands nervously together. He looked away from me into the fire.

"It is a very difficult position," he declared, "very difficult indeed. The Prince has been more than a friend to Blenavon. He has been his benefactor. Of course he will deny this thing with contempt. Let me think it out, Ducaine."

"By all means, your Grace," I answered, a little nettled at his undecided air. "So far as I am concerned, my duty in the matter ends here. I have, told you the exact truth concerning it, and it seems to me by no means improbable that the Prince has been in some way responsible for those former leakages."

The Duke shook his head slowly.

"It is impossible," he said.

"Your Grace is the best judge," I answered.

"The Prince was not in the house last night when the safe was opened, he objected.

"He probably has accomplices," I answered. "Besides, how do we know that he was not here?"

"Even if he were," the Duke said, raising his head, "how could he have known the cipher?"

I made no answer at all. It seemed useless to argue with a man who had evidently made up his mind not to be convinced.

"Have you mentioned this matter to any one?" the Duke asked.

"To Colonel Ray only, your Grace," I answered.

"Ray!" The Duke was silent for a moment. He was looking steadily into the fire. "You told Ray what you have told me?"

"In substance, yes, your Grace. In detail, perhaps not so fully."

"And he?"

"He did not doubt my story, your Grace," I said quietly.

The Duke frowned across at me.

"Neither do I, Ducaine," he declared. "It is not a question of veracity at all. It is a question of construction. You are young, and these things are all new to you. The Prince might have been trying you, or something which you did not hear or have forgotten might throw a different light upon his actions and suggestion. I beg that you will leave the matter entirely in my hands."

I abandoned the subject then and there. But as I left the room I came face to face with Blenavon, who was loitering outside. He at once detained me. His manner since the morning had altered. He addressed me now with hesitation, almost with respect.

"Can you spare me a few minutes, Mr. Ducaine?" he asked. "I will not detain you long."

"I am at your service, Lord Blenavon," I answered. "We will go into the hall and have a smoke," he suggested, leading the way. "To me it seems the only place in the house free from draughts."

I followed him to where, in a dark corner of the great dome-shaped hall, a wide cushioned lounge was set against the wall. He seated himself and motioned me to follow his example. For several moments he remained silent, twisting a cigarette with thin nervous fingers stained yellow with nicotine. Every now and then he glanced furtively around. I waited for him to speak. He was Lady Angela's brother, but I disliked and distrusted him.

He finally got his cigarette alight, and turned to me.

"Mr. Ducaine," he said, "I want you to apologize to my friend, the Prince of Malors, for your behaviour this afternoon."

"Apologize to the Prince!" I exclaimed. "Why should I?"

"Because this is the only condition on which he will consent to remain here."

"I should have thought," I said, "that his immediate departure was inevitable. I detected him in behaviour—"

"That is just where you are wrong," Blenavon interrupted eagerly. "You were mistaken, entirely mistaken."

I laughed, a little impolitely, I am afraid, considering that this was the son of my employer.

"You know the circumstances?" I asked. He nodded.

"The Prince has explained them to me. It was altogether a misunderstanding. He felt his foot a little easier, and he was simply looking for a newspaper or something to read until you returned. Inadvertently he turned over some of your manuscript, and at that moment you entered."

"Most inopportunely, I am afraid," I answered, with an unwilling smile.
"I am sorry, Lord Blenavon, that I cannot accept this explanation of the
Prince's behaviour. I am compelled to take the evidence of my eyes and
ears as final."

Blenavon sucked at his cigarette fiercely for a minute, threw it away, and commenced to roll another.

"It's all rot!" he exclaimed. "Malors wouldn't do a mean action, and, besides, what on earth has he to gain? He is a fanatical Royalist. He is not even on speaking terms with the Government of France to-day."

"I perceive," I remarked, looking at him closely, "that you are familiar with the nature of my secretarial work."

He returned my glance, and it seemed to me that there was some hidden meaning in his eyes which I failed to catch.

"I am in my father's confidence," he said slowly.

There was a moment's silence. I was listening to a distant voice in the lower part of the hall.

"Am I to take it, Mr. Ducaine, then," he said at last, "that you decline to apologize to the Prince?"

"I have nothing to apologize for," I answered calmly. "The Prince was attempting to obtain information in an illicit manner by the perusal of papers which were in my charge."

Blenavon rose slowly to his feet. His eyes were fixed upon the opposite corner of the hall. Lady Angela, who had just descended the stairs, was standing there, pale and unsubstantial as a shadow, and it seemed to me that her eyes, as she looked across at me, were full of trouble. She came slowly towards us. Blenavon laid his hand upon her arm.

"Angela," he said, "Mr. Ducaine will not accept my word. I can make no impression upon him. Perhaps he will the more readily believe yours."

"Lady Angela will not ask me to disbelieve the evidence of my own senses," I said confidently.

She stood between us. I was aware from the first of something unfamiliar in her manner, something of which a glimmering had appeared on our way home through the wood.

"It is about Malors, Angela," he continued. "You were there. You know all that happened. Malors is very reasonable about it. He admits that his actions may have seemed suspicious. He will accept an apology from Mr. Ducaine, and remain."

She turned to me.

"And you?" she asked.

"The idea of an apology," I answered, "appears to me ridiculous. My own poor little possessions were wholly at his disposal. I caught him, however, in the act of meddling with papers which are mine only on trust."

Lady Angela played for a moment with the dainty trifles which hung from her bracelet. When she spoke she did not look at me.

"The Prince's explanation," she said, "is plausible, and he is our guest. I think perhaps it would be wisest to give him the benefit of the doubt."

"Doubt!" I exclaimed, bewildered. "There is no room for doubt in the matter."

Then she raised her eyes to mine, and I saw there new things. I saw trouble and appeal, and behind both the shadow of mystery.

"Have you spoken to my father?" she asked.

"Yes," I answered.

"Did he accept — your view?"

"He did not," I answered bitterly. "I could not convince him of what I saw with my own eyes."

"You have done your duty, then," she said softly. "Why not let the rest go? As you told us just now, this is not a personal matter, and there are reasons why he did not wish the Prince to leave suddenly."

I was staggered. I held my peace, and the two stood watching me. Then I heard footsteps approaching us, and a familiar voice.

"What trio of conspirators is this talking so earnstly in the shadows? Ah!"

The Prince had seen me, and he stood still. I faced him at once.

"Prince," I said, "it has been suggested to me that my eyesight is probably defective. It is possible in that case that I have not seen you before to-day, that the things with which I charge you are false, that in all probability you were in some other place altogether. If this is so, I apologize for my remarks and behaviour towards you."

He bowed with a faint mirthless smile.

"It is finished, my young friend," he declared. "I wipe it from my memory." It seemed to me that I could hear Blenavon's sigh of relief, that the shadow had fallen from Lady Angela's face. There was a little murmur of satisfaction from both of them. But I turned abruptly, and with scarcely even an attempt at a conventional farewell I left the house, and walked homewards across the Park.

CHAPTER XV
TWO FAIR CALLERS

After three days the house party at Rowchester was somewhat unexpectedly broken up. Lord Chelsford departed early one morning by special train, and the Duke himself and the remainder of his guests left for London later on in the day. I remained behind with three weeks' work, and a fear which never left me by day or by night. Yet the relief of solitude after the mysteries of the last few days was in itself a thing to be thankful for.

For nine days I spoke with no one save Grooton. For an hour every afternoon, and for rather longer at night, I walked on the cliffs or the sands. Here on these lonely stretches of empty land I met no one, saw no living thing save the seagulls. It was almost like a corner of some forgotten land. These walks, and an occasional few hours' reading, were my sole recreation.

It was late in the afternoon when I saw a shadow pass my window, and immediately afterwards there was a timid knock at the door. Grooton had gone on his daily pilgrimage with letters to the village, so I was obliged to open it myself. To my surprise it was Blanche Moyat who stood upon the threshold. She laughed a little nervously.

"I'm no ghost, Mr. Ducaine," she said, "and I shan't bite!"

"Forgive me," I answered. "I was hard at work and your knock startled me. Please come in."

I ushered her into my sitting-room. She was wearing what I recognized as her best clothes, and not being entirely at her ease she talked loudly and rapidly.

"Such a stranger as you are, Mr. Ducaine," she exclaimed. "Fancy, it's getting on for a month since we any of us saw a sign of you, and

I'm sure never a week used to pass but father'd be looking for you to drop in. We heard that you were living here all by yourself, and this morning mother said, perhaps he's ill. We tried to get father to come up and see, but he's off to Downham market to-day, and goodness knows when he'd find time if we left it to him. So I thought I'd come and find out for myself."

"I am quite well, thanks, Miss Moyat," I answered, "but very busy. The Duke has been giving me some work to do, and he has lent me this cottage, so that I shall be close at hand. I should have looked you up the first time I came to Braster, but as a matter of fact I have not been there since the night of my lecture."

She was nervously playing with the fastening of her umbrella, and it seemed to me that her silence was purposeful. I ventured some remark about the weather, which she interrupted ruthlessly.

"It's a mile and a half to our house from here," she said, "not a step farther. I don't see why you shouldn't have made a purpose journey."

I ignored the reproach in her eyes, as I had every right to do. But I began to understand the reason of her nervousness and her best clothes, and I prayed for Grooton's return.

"If I had had an evening to myself," I said, "I should certainly have paid your father a visit. But as it happens, the Duke has required me at the house every night while he was here, and he has left me enough work to do to keep me busy night and day till he comes back."

She looked down upon the floor.

"I had to come and see you," she said in a low tone. "Sometimes I can't sleep for thinking of it. I feel that I haven't done right."

I knew, of course, what she meant.

"I thought we had talked all that out long ago," I answered, a little wearily. "You would have been very foolish if you had acted differently. I don't see how else you could have acted."

"Oh, I don't know," she said. "We were always brought up very particular — especially about telling the truth."

"Well, you haven't said anything that wasn't the truth," I reminded her.

"Oh, I don't know. I haven't said what I ought to say," she declared. "It seems all right when you are with me, and talk about it," she continued slowly, raising her eyes to mine. "It's when I don't see you for weeks and weeks that it seems to get on my mind, and I get afraid. I don't understand it, I don't understand it even now."

"Don't understand what?" I repeated.

She looked around. Her air of troubled mystery was only half assumed.

"How that man died!" she whispered.

"I can assure you that I did not kill him, if that is what you mean," I told her coolly. "The matter is over and done with. I think that you are very foolish to give it another thought."

She shuddered.

"Men can forget those things easier," she said. "Perhaps he had a wife and children. Perhaps they are wondering all this time what has become of him."

"People die away from their homes and families every day, every hour," I answered. "It is only morbid to brood over one particular example."

"Father would never forgive me if he knew," she murmured, irrelevantly.
"He hates us to do anything underhand."

I heard Grooton return with a sigh of relief.

"You will have some tea," I suggested.

She shook her head and stood up. I did not press her.

"No, I won't," she said. "I am sorry I came. I don't understand you, Mr. Ducaine. You seem to have changed altogether just these last few weeks. I can see that you are dying to get rid of me now, but you were glad enough to see me, or at any rate you pretended to be, once."

My breath was a little taken away. I looked at her in surprise. Her cheeks were flushed, her voice had shaken with something more like anger than any form of pathos. I was at a loss how to answer her, and while I hesitated the interruption which I had been praying for came, though from a strange quarter. My door was pushed a few inches open, and I heard Lady Angela's clear young voice.

"Are you there, Mr. Ducaine? May I come in?"

Before I could answer she stood upon the threshold, I saw the delightful little smile fade from her lips as she looked in. She hesitated, and seemed for a moment about to retreat.

"Please come in, Lady Angela," I begged, eagerly.

She came slowly forward.

"I must apologize for my abominable country manners," she said, resting the tips of her fingers for a moment in mine. "I saw your door was not latched, and it never occurred to me to knock."

"It was not necessary," I assured her. "A front door which does not boast a knocker or a bell must expect to be taken liberties with. But it is a great surprise to see you here. I had no idea that any one was at Rowchester, or expected there, except Lord Blenavon. Has the Duke returned?"

She shook her head.

"I came down alone," she answered. "I found London dull. Let me see, I am sure that I know your face, do I not?" she added, turning to Blanche Moyat with a smile. "You live in Braster, surely?"

"I am Miss Moyat," Blanche answered quietly.

"Of course. Dear me! I ought to have recognized you. We have been neighbours for a good many years."

"I will wish you good-afternoon, Mr. Ducaine," Blanche said, turning to me. "Good-afternoon — your Ladyship," she added a little awkwardly.

I opened the door for her.

"I will come down and see your father the first evening I have to spare," I said. "I hope you will tell him from me that I should have been before, but for the luxury of having some work to do."

"I will tell him," she said almost inaudibly.

"And thank you very much for coming to inquire after me," I added. "Good-afternoon."

"Good-afternoon, Mr. Ducaine."

I closed the door. Lady Angela was lounging in my easy chair with a slight smile upon her lips.

"Two lady callers in one afternoon, Mr. Ducaine," she remarked quietly.

"You will lose your head, I am afraid."

"I can assure you, Lady Angela," I answered, "that there is not the slightest fear of such a catastrophe."

She sat looking meditatively into the fire, swinging her dogskin gloves in her hands. She wore a plain pearl grey walking dress and deerstalker hat with a single quill in it. The severe but immaculate simplicity of her toilette might have been designed to accentuate the barbarities of Blanche Moyat's cheap finery.

"I understood that you would be in town for at least three weeks," I remarked. "I trust that his Grace is well."

"I trust that he is," she answered. "I see nothing of him in London. He has company meetings and political work every moment of his time. I do not believe that there is any one who works harder."

"He has, at least," I remarked, "the compensation of success."

"You are wondering, I suppose," she said, looking up at me quickly, "what has brought me back again so soon."

"I certainly did not expect you," I admitted.

She rose abruptly.

"Come outside," she said, "and I will show you. Bring your hat."

We passed into the March twilight. She led the way down the cliff and towards the great silent stretch of salt marshes. An evening wind, sharp with brine, was blowing in from the ocean, stirring the surface of the long creeks into silent ripples, and bending landwards the thin streaks of white smoke rising amongst the red-tiled roofs of the village. I felt the delicate sting of it upon my cheeks. Lady Angela half closed her eyes as she turned her face seawards.

"I came for this," she murmured. "There is nothing like it anywhere else."

We stood there in silence for several long minutes. Then she turned to me with a little sigh.

"I am content," she said. "Will you come up and dine with us to-night? Blenavon will be there, you know." I hesitated.

"I am afraid it is rather a bother to you to leave your work," she continued, "but I am not offering you idle hospitality. I really want you to come."

"In that case," I answered, "of course I shall be delighted."

She pointed to Braster Grange away on the other side of the village. I noticed for the first time that it was all lit up.

"Have you heard anything of our new neighbours?" she asked.

"Only their names," I answered. "I did not even know that they had arrived."

"There is only a woman, I believe," she said. "I have met her abroad, and I dislike her — greatly. I hear that my brother spends most of his time with her, and that he has dined there the last three nights. It is not safe or wise of him, for many reasons. I want to stop it. That is why I have asked you to come to us."

"It is quite sufficient," I told her. "If you want me for any reason I will come. I am two days ahead of my work."

We threaded our way amongst the creeks. All the time the salt wind blew upon us, and the smell of fresh seaweed seemed to fill the air with ozone. Just as we came in sight of the road we heard the thunder of hoofs behind. We turned around. It was Blenavon, riding side by side with a lady who was a stranger to me. Her figure was slim but elegant. I caught a glimpse of her face as they flashed by, and it puzzled me. Her hair was almost straw coloured, her complexion was negative, her features were certainly not good. Yet there was something about her attractive, something which set me guessing at once as to the colour of her eyes, the quality of her voice, if she should speak. Blenavon reined in his horse.

"So you have turned up, Angela," he remarked, looking at her a little nervously. "You remember Mrs. Smith-Lessing, don't you — down at Bordighera, you know?"

Angela shook her head, but she never glanced towards the woman who sat there with expectant smile.

"I am afraid that I do not," she said. "I remember a good many things about Bordighera, but — not Mrs. Smith-Lessing. I shall see you at dinner-time, Blenavon. I have some messages for you."

I saw the whip come down upon the woman's horse, but I did not dare to look into her face. Blenavon, with a smothered oath and a black look at his sister, galloped after her. I rejoined Lady Angela, who was already in the road.

"Dear me," she said, "what a magnificent nerve that woman must have! To dare to imagine that I should receive her! Why, she is known in every capital in Europe—a police spy, a creature whose brains and body and soul are to be bought by any one's gold."

"What on earth can such a woman want here?" I remarked.

"In hiding, very likely," Lady Angela remarked. "Or perhaps she may be an additional complication for you."

I laughed a little scornfully.

"You, too, are getting suspicious," I declared. "The Prince and Mrs. Smith-Lessing are a strong combination."

"Be careful then that they are not too strong for you," she answered, smiling. "I have heard a famous boast of Mrs. Smith-Lessing's, that never a man nor a lock has yet resisted her."

I thought of her face as I had seen it in the half light—a faint impression of delicate colourlessness, and for the life of me I could not help a little shiver. Lady Angela looked at me in surprise.

"Are you cold?" she asked. "Let us walk more quickly."

"It is always cold at this time in the evening," I remarked. "It is the mist coming up from the marshes. One feels it at unexpected moments."

"I am not going to take you any farther," she declared, "especially as you are coming up to-night. Eight o'clock, remember. Go and salve your conscience with some work."

I protested, but she was firm. So I stood by the gate and watched her slim young figure disappear in the gathering shadows.

CHAPTER XVI
LADY ANGELA'S ENGAGEMENT

I dined that night at Rowchester. Lord Blenavon was sulky, and Lady Angela was only fitfully gay. It was not altogether a cheerful party. Lady Angela left us the moment Blenavon produced his cigarette-case.

"Do not stay too long, Mr. Ducaine," she said, as I held the door open for her. "I want a lesson at billiards."

I bowed and returned to my seat. Blenavon was leaning back in his chair, smoking thoughtfully.

"My sister," he remarked, looking up at the ceiling and speaking as though to himself, "would make an admirable heroine for the psychological novelist. She is a bundle of fancies; one can never rely upon what she is going to do. What other girl in the world would get engaged on the Thursday, and come down here on the Friday to think it over—leaving, of course, her fiance in town? Doesn't that strike you as singular?"

"Is it," I asked calmly, "a genuine case?"

Lord Blenavon nodded.

"I do not think that it is a secret," he said, helping himself to wine and passing the decanter. "She has made up her mind at last to marry Mostyn Ray. The affair has been hanging about for more than a year. In fact, I think that there was something said about it before Ray went abroad. Personally, I think that he is too old. I don't mind saying so to you, because that has been my opinion all along. However, I suppose it is all settled now."

I kept my eyes fixed upon the wineglass in front of me, but the things which I saw, no four walls had ever enclosed. One moment the rush of the sea was in my ears, another I was lying upon the little horsehair couch in my sitting-room. I felt her soft white fingers upon my pulse and forehead. Again I saw her leaning down from the saddle of her great brown horse, and heard her voice, slow, emotionless, yet always with its strange power to play upon my heartstrings. And yet, while the grey seas of despair were closing over my head, I sat there with a stereotyped smile upon my lips, fingering carelessly the stem of my wineglass, unwilling guest of an unwilling host. I do not know how long we sat there in silence, but it seemed to me an eternity, for all the time I knew that Blenavon was watching me. I felt like a victim upon the rack, whilst he, the executioner, held the cords. I do not think, however, that he learnt anything from my face.

With a little shrug of the shoulders he abandoned the subject.

"By-the-bye, Ducaine," he said, "I hope you won't mind my asking you a rather personal question."

"If it is only personal," I answered quietly, "not at all. As you know, I may not discuss any subject connected with my work."

"Quite so! I only want to know whether your secretarial duties begin and end with your work on the Council of Defence, or are you at all in my father's confidence as regards his private affairs?"

"I am temporary secretary to the Council of Defence only, Lord Blenavon," I answered. "I know nothing whatever of your father's private affairs. He has his own man of business."

I am not sure whether he believed me. He cracked some walnuts and commenced peeling them.

"My father will never listen to me," he said, "but I feel sure that he makes a mistake in becoming a director of all these companies. Politics should be quite sufficient to engross his time, and the money cannot be so much of an object to him. I don't suppose his holdings are large, but I am quite sure that one or two of those Australian gold mines are dicky, and you know he was an enormous holder of Chartereds, and wouldn't sell, worse luck! Of course I'm not afraid of his losing in the long run, but it isn't exactly a dignified thing to be associated with these concerns that aren't exactly A1. His name might lead people into speculations who couldn't altogether afford it."

"I know nothing whatever of these matters," I answered, "but from what I have seen of your father I should imagine that he is remarkably able to guard his own interests."

Blenavon nodded.

"I suppose that is true," he admitted. "But when he is already a rich man, with very simple tastes, I am rather surprised that he should care to meddle with such things."

"Playing at commerce," I remarked, "has become rather a hobby with men of leisure lately."

"And women, too," Blenavon assented. "Rather an ugly hobby, I call it."

A servant entered and addressed Blenavon. "The carriage is at the door, your Lordship," he announced.

Blenavon glanced at his watch and rose.

"I shall have to ask you to excuse me, Ducaine," he said. "I was to have dined out to-night, and I must go and make my peace. Another glass of wine?"

I rose at once.

"Nothing more, thank you," I said. "I will just say good-night to your sister."

"She's probably in the drawing-room," he remarked. "If not, I will make your excuses when I see her."

Blenavon hurried out. A few moments later I heard the wheels of his carriage pass the long front of the house and turn down the avenue. I lingered for a moment where I was. The small oak table at which we had dined seemed like an oasis of colour in the midst of an atmosphere of gloom. The room was large and lofty, and the lighting was altogether inadequate. From the walls there frowned through the shadows the warlike faces of generations of Rowchesters. At the farther end of the apartment four armed giants stood grim and ghostlike in the twilight, which seemed to supply their empty frames with the presentment of actual warriors. I looked down upon the table, all agleam with flowers, and fruit, and silver, over which shone the red glow of the shaded lamps. Exactly opposite to me, in that chair now pushed carelessly back, she had sat, so close that my hand could have touched hers at any moment, so close that I had been able to wonder more than ever before at the marvellous whiteness of her skin, the perfection of her small, finely-shaped features, the strange sphinxlike expression of her face, always suggestive of some great self-restraint, mysterious, and subtly stimulating. And as I stood there she seemed again to be occupying the chair, at first a faint shadowy presence, but gaining with every second shape and outline, until I could scarcely persuade myself that it was not she who sat there, she whose eyes more than once during dinner-time had looked into mine with that curious and instinctive demand for sympathy, even as regards the things of the moment, the passing jest, the most transitory of emotions. A few minutes ago I had felt that I knew her better than ever before in my life, and now the chair was empty. My heart was beating at the imaginary presence of the vainest of shadows. She was going to marry Colonel Mostyn Ray.

And then I stood as though suddenly turned to stone. Before me were the great front windows of the castle. Beyond, eastwards, stretched the salt marshes, the salt marshes riven with creeks. Once more my unwilling hands touched that huddled-up heap of extinct humanity. I saw the dead white face, which the sun could never warm again, and I felt the hands, cold, clammy, horrible. Ray was a soldier, and life and death had become phrases to him; but I—it was the first dead man I had ever seen, and the horror of it was cold in my blood. Ray had murdered him, fought with him, perhaps, but killed him. What would she say if she knew? Would his hands be clean to her, or would the horror rise up like a red wall between them?

"Will you take coffee, sir?"

I set my teeth and turned slowly round. I even took the cup from the tray without spilling it.

"What liqueur may I bring you, sir?" the man asked.

"Brandy," I answered.

In a few minutes I was laughing at myself, not quite naturally, perhaps, but only I could know that. I was getting to be a morbid, nervous person. It was the solitude! I must get away from it all before long. Fate had been playing strange tricks with me. Life, which a few months ago had been a cold and barren thing, was suddenly pressed to my lips, a fantastic, intoxicating mixture. I had drawn enough poison into my veins. I would have no more. I swore it.

* * * * *

I tried to leave the castle unnoticed, but the place was alive with servants. One of them hurried up to me as I tried to reach my hat and coat.

"Her ladyship desired me to say that she was in the billiard-room, sir," he announced.

"Will you tell Lady Angela—" and then I stopped. The door of the billiard-room was open, and Lady Angela stood there, the outline of her figure sharply defined against a flood of light. She had a cue in her hand, and she looked across at me.

"You are a long time, Mr. Ducaine. I am waiting for you to give me a lesson at billiards."

I crossed the hall to her side.

"I thought that as Lord Blenavon had gone out—"

She shrugged her shoulders.

"That you would evade your duty, which is clearly to stay and entertain your hostess."

She closed the door and glanced at me curiously.

"What has happened to you?" she asked. "You look as though you had been with ghosts."

"Is it so impossible?" I asked, moving a little nearer to the huge log fire. "What company is more terrifying than the company of our dead thoughts and dead hopes and dead memories?"

"Really, I am afraid that Blenavon must have been a very depressing companion!" she said, leaning her elbow upon the broad mantelpiece.

It was absurd! I tried to shake myself free from the miseries of the last hour.

"I am afraid it must have been the other way," I said, "for your brother has gone out."

"Yes," she said quietly, "he has gone to that woman at Braster Grange. I wish I knew what brought her into this part of the country."

I looked round at the billiard-table.

"Did you mean that you would like a game?" I asked. "I am rather out of practice, but I used to fancy myself a little."

"I have no doubt," she answered, sinking into a low chair, "that you are an excellent player, but I am willing to take it for granted. I do not wish to play billiards. Draw that chair up to the fire and talk to me."

It was of all things what I wished to avoid that night. But there was no escape. I obeyed her.

"What your brother has told me is, I presume, no secret," I said. "I am to wish you happiness, am I not?"

She looked up at me in quick surprise.

"Did Blenavon tell you—"

"That you had promised to marry Colonel Mostyn Ray. Yes."

"That is very strange," she said thoughtfully. "Blenavon is not as a rule needlessly communicative, and at present it is almost a secret."

"Nevertheless," I said, turning slowly towards her, "I presume that it is true."

"It is perfectly true," she answered.

There was silence between us for several minutes. One of the footmen came softly in to see whether we required a marker, and finding us talking, withdrew. I was determined that the onus of further speech should remain with her.

"You are surprised?" she asked at last.

"Very."

"And why?"

"I scarcely know," I answered, "except that I have never associated the thought of marriage with Colonel Ray, and he is very much older than you."

"Yes, he is a great deal older," she answered. "I think that his history has been rather a sad one. He was in love for many years with a woman who married—some one else. I have always felt sorry for him ever since I was a little girl."

"Do you know who that woman was?"

"I have never heard her name," she answered.

I found courage to lift my eyes and look at her.

"May I ask when you are going to be married?"

Her eyes fell. The question did not seem to please her.

"I do not know," she said. "We have not spoken of that yet. Everything is very vague."

"Colonel Ray is coming down here, of course?" I remarked.

"Not to my knowledge," she declared. "Not at any rate until the next meeting of the Council. I shall be back in town before then."

"I begin to believe," I said, with a grim smile, "that your brother was right."

"My brother right?"

"He finds you enigmatic! You become engaged to a man one day, and you leave him the next — without apparent reason."

She was obviously disturbed. A slight wave of trouble passed over her face. Her eyes failed to meet mine.

"That I cannot altogether explain to you," she said. "There are reasons why I should come, but apart from them this place is very dear to me. I think that whenever anything has happened to me I have wanted to be here. You are a man, and you will not altogether understand this."

"Why not?" I protested. "We, too, have our sentiment, the sentiment of places as well as of people. If I could choose where to die I think that it would be here, with my windows wide open and the roar of the incoming tide in my ears."

"For a young man," she remarked, looking across at me, "I should consider you rather a morbid person."

"There are times," I answered, "when I feel inclined to agree with you. To-night is one of them."

"That," she said coolly, "is unfortunate. You have been over-working."

"I am worried by a problem," I told her. "Tell me, are you a great believer in the sanctity of human life?"

"What a question!" she murmured. "My own life, at any rate, seems to me to be a terribly important thing."

"Suppose you had a friend," I said, "who was one night attacked in a quiet spot by a man who sought his life, say, for the purpose of robbery. Your friend was the stronger and easily defended himself. Then he saw that his antagonist was a man of ill repute, an evildoer, a man whose presence upon the earth did good to no one. So he took him by the throat and deliberately crushed the life out of him. Was your friend a murderer?"

She smiled at me—that quiet, introspective smile which I knew so well.

"Does the end justify the means? No, of course not. I should have been very sorry for my friend; but if indeed there is a Creator, it is He alone who has power to take back what He has given."

"Your friend, then—"

"Don't call him that!"

I rose up and moved towards the door. I think that she saw something in my face which checked any attempt she might have made to detain me.

"You must forgive me," I said. "I cannot stay."

She said nothing. I looked back at her from the door. Her eyes were fixed upon me, a little distended, full of mute questioning. I only shook my head. So I left her and passed out into the night.

CHAPTER XVII
MORE TREACHERY

There followed for me a period of unremitting hard work, days during which I never left my desk save at such hours when I knew that the chances of meeting any one scarcely existed. Several times I saw Lady Angela from my window on the sands below, threading her way across the marshes to the sea. Once she passed my window very slowly, and with a quick backward glance as she turned to descend the cliff. But I sat still with clenched teeth. I had nailed down my resolutions, I had determined to hold fast to such threads of my common sense as remained. Only in the night-time, when sleep mocked me and all hope of escape was futile, was I forced to grapple with this new-born monster of folly. It drove me up across the Park to where the house, black and lightless, rose a dark incongruous mass above the trees, down to the sea, where the wind came booming across the bare country northwards, and the spray leaped white and phosphorescent into the night like flakes of wind-hurled snow. I stood as close to the sea as I dared, and I prayed. Once I saw morning lighten the mass of clouds eastwards, and the grey dawn break over the empty waters. I heard the winds die away, and I watched the sea grow calm. Far across on the horizon there was faint glimmer of cold sunlight. Then I went back to my broken rest. It was my solitude in those days which drove me to seek peace or some measure of it from these things.

At last a break came, a summons to London to a meeting of the Council. I was just able to catch my train and reach the War Office at the appointed time. There were two hours of important work, and I noticed a general air of gravity on the faces of every one present. After it was over Ray came to my side.

"Ducaine," he said, "Lord Chelsford wishes to speak' to you for a few moments. Come this way."

He led me into a small, barely-furnished room, with high windows and only one door. It was empty when we entered it. Ray looked at me as he closed the door, and I fancied that for him his expression was not unfriendly.

"Ducaine," he said, "there has been some more of this damned leakage. Chelsford will ask you questions. Answer him simply, but tell him everything — everything, you understand."

"I should not dream of any concealment," I answered.

"Of course not! But it is possible — Ah!"

He broke off and remained listening. There was the sound of a quick footstep in the hall.

"Now you will understand what I mean," he whispered. "Remember!"

It was not Chelsford, but the Duke, who entered and greeted me cordially. With a farewell nod to me Ray disappeared. The Duke looked round and watched him close the door. Then he turned to me.

"Ducaine," he said, "a copy of our proposed camp at Winchester, and the fortifications on Bedler's Hill, has reached Paris."

"Your Grace," I answered, "it was I who pointed out to you that our papers dealing with those matters had been tampered with. I am waiting now to be cross-questioned by Lord Chelsford. I have done all that is humanly possible. It goes without saying that my resignation is yours whenever you choose to ask for it."

The Duke sat down and looked at me thoughtfully.

"Ducaine," he said, "I believe in you."

I drew a little breath of relief. The Duke was a hard man and a man of few words. I felt that in making that speech he had departed a great deal from his usual course of action, and I knew that he meant it.

"I am very much obliged to your Grace," I answered.

"I think," he continued, "that Lord Chelsford and in fact all the others are inclined to accept you on my estimate. We all of us feel that we are the victims of some unique and very marvellous piece of roguery on the part of some one or other. I believe myself that we are on the eve of a discovery."

"Thank Heaven!" I murmured.

"We shall only succeed in unravelling this mystery," the Duke continued deliberately, "by very cautious and delicate manoeuvring. I have an idea which I propose to carry out. But its success depends largely upon you."

"Upon me?" I repeated, amazed.

"Exactly! Upon your common sense and judgment." The Duke paused to listen for a moment. Then he continued, speaking very slowly, and leaning over towards me—

"Lord Chelsford proposes for his own satisfaction to cross-examine you. It occurs to me that you will probably tell him of your fancied disturbance of those papers in the safe, and of your little adventure with the Prince of Malors." I looked at him in surprise. "Have they not all been told of this?" I asked. "No."

There was a moment's dead silence. I was a little staggered. The Duke remained imperturbable.

"They have not been told," he repeated. "No one has been told. The matter was one for my discretion, and I exercised it."

There seemed to be no remark which I could make, so I kept silence.

"We have discussed this matter before," the Duke said, "and my firm conviction is that you were mistaken. That safe could only have been opened by yourself, Ray, or myself. I think I am justified in saying that neither of us did open it."

"Nevertheless that safe was opened," I objected. "Those were the very papers, copies of which have found their way to Paris."

"Exactly," the Duke answered. "Only you must remember that every member of the Board was sufficiently acquainted with their contents to have sent those particulars to Paris, without opening the safe for a further investigation of them. Any statement of your suspicion would only result in attention being diverted from the proper quarters to members of my household. I believe that even if you are right, even if those papers were disturbed, it was done simply to throw dust in your eyes. Do you follow me?"

"Yes, your Grace," I answered.

"Lord Chelsford, if you were able to convince him, would most certainly be misled in this direction. That is why I have kept your report to myself. That is why my advice to you now is to say nothing about your imagined displacement of those papers. That is my advice. You understand?"

"Yes, your Grace," I repeated.

"With regard to the Prince of Malors," the Duke continued, "my firm conviction is that you were mistaken. Malors is not a politician. He has nothing whatever to gain or lose in this matter. He is a member of one of the most ancient houses of Europe, a house which for generations has been closely connected with my own. I absolutely decline to believe that whilst under my roof a Malors could lower himself to the level of a common spy. Such an accusation brought against him would be regarded as a blot upon my hospitality. Further, it would mean the breaking off of my ancient ties of friendship. I am very anxious, therefore, that you should bring yourself to accept my view as to this episode also."

"Your Grace," I answered, "you ask me very hard things."

He looked at me with his clear cold eyes.

"Surely not too hard, Mr. Ducaine," he said. "I ask you to accept my judgment. Consider for a moment. You are a young man, little more than a boy. I for forty years have been a servant of my country, both in the field and as a lawmaker. I am a Cabinet Minister. I have a life-long experience of men and their ways. My judgment in this matter is that you were mistaken, and much mischief is likely to ensue if the Prince of Malors should find himself an object of suspicion amongst us."

"Your Grace," I said, "forgive me, but why do you not say these things to the Board, or to Lord Chelsford and Colonel Ray after they have heard my story?"

"Because," the Duke answered, "I have no confidence in the judgment of either of them. Both in their way are excellent men, but they are of this new generation, who do not probe beneath the surface, who form their opinions only from the obvious. It is possible that after hearing your story they might consider the problem solved.

I am, at any rate, convinced that they would commence a search for its solution in altogether wrong quarters."

"Your Grace," I said firmly, "I am very sorry indeed that I cannot take your advice. I think it most important that Lord Chelsford should know that those papers were tampered with. And as regards the Prince of Malors, whatever his motive may have been, I discovered him in the act of perusing the documents relating to the subway of Portsmouth. I cannot possibly withhold my knowledge of these things from Lord Chelsford. In fact, I think it is most important that he should know of them."

The Duke rose slowly to his feet. He showed no sign of anger.

"If you prefer your own judgment to mine, Mr. Ducaine," he said, "I have no more to say. I have taken you into my confidence, and I have endeavoured to show you your most politic course of behaviour. If your views are so far opposed, you must not consider it an injustice if I decide that a person of more judgment is required successfully to conduct the duties of secretary to the Council."

"I can only thank your Grace for your past kindness," I answered with sinking heart.

He looked across at me with still cold eyes.

"Do not misunderstand me," he said. "I do not dismiss you. I shall leave that to the Board. If my colleagues are favourably disposed towards you I shall not interfere. Only so far as I am concerned you must take your chance."

"I quite understand your Grace," I declared. "I think that you are treating me very fairly."

The Duke leaned back in his chair.

"Here they come!" he remarked.

CHAPTER XVIII
IN WHICH I SPEAK OUT

The door was thrown open. Lord Chelsford and Colonel Ray entered together. The Commander-in-Chief accompanied them, and there was also present a person who sat a little apart from the others, and who, I learned afterwards, was a high official in the secret service. More than ever, perhaps, I realized at that moment in the presence of these men the strangeness of the events which for a short space of time, at any rate, had brought me into association with persons and happenings of such importance.

Lord Chelsford seated himself at the open desk opposite to the Duke. As was his custom, he wasted no time in preliminaries.

"We wish for a few minutes' conversation with you, Mr. Ducaine," he said, "on the subject of this recent leakage of news concerning our proceedings on the Council of Defence. I need not tell you that the subject is a very serious one."

"I quite appreciate its importance, sir," I answered.

"The particular documents of which we have news from Paris," Lord Chelsford continued, "are those having reference to the proposed camp at Winchester and the subway at Portsmouth. I understand, Mr. Ducaine, that these were drafted by you, and placed in a safe in the library of Rowchester on the evening of the eighteenth of this month."

"That is so, sir," I answered. "And early the next morning I reported to the Duke that the papers had been tampered with."

There was a dead silence for several moments. Lord Chelsford glanced at the Duke, who sat there imperturbable, with a chill, mirthless smile at the corner of his lips. Then he looked again at me, as though he had not heard aright.

"Will you kindly repeat that, Mr. Ducaine?" he said.

"Certainly, sir," I answered. "I had occasion to go to the safe again early on the morning of the nineteenth, and I saw at once that the documents in question had been tampered with. I reported the matter at once to his Grace."

The eyes of every one were bent upon the Duke. He nodded his head slowly.

"Mr. Ducaine," he said, "certainly came to me and made the statement which he has just repeated. I considered the matter, and I came to the conclusion that he was mistaken. I was sure of it then. I am equally sure of it now."

"Tell us, Mr. Ducaine," Lord Chelsford said, "what your reasons were for making such a statement."

I took a piece of red tape and a newspaper from the table before which I stood. I folded up the newspaper and tied the tape around it.

"When I put those documents away," I said, "I tied them up with a knot like this, of my own invention, which I have never seen used by anybody else. In the morning I found that my knot had been untied, and that the tape around the papers had been re-tied in an ordinary bow."

"Will you permit me for a moment," the Duke interposed. "The safe, I believe, Mr. Ducaine, was secured with a code lock, the word of which was known to-whom?"

"Yourself, sir, Colonel Ray, and myself."

The Duke nodded.

"If I remember rightly," he said, "the code word was never mentioned, but was written on a piece of paper, glanced at by each of us in turn, and immediately destroyed."

"That is quite true, sir."

"Now, do you believe, Mr. Ducaine," the Duke continued, "that it was possible for any one else except us the to have attained to the knowledge of that word."

"I do not sir," I admitted.

"Do you believe that it was possible for any one to have opened the safe without the knowledge of that word?"

"Without breaking it open, no, sir."

"There were no signs of the lock having been tampered with when you went to it in the morning?" "None, sir."

"It was set at the correct word, the word known only to Colonel Ray, myself, and yourself?" "Yes, sir."

The Duke leaned back in his chair and addressed Lord Chelsford.

"For the reasons which you have heard from Mr. Ducaine himself," he said drily, "I came to the conclusion that he was mistaken in his suggestion. I think that you will probably be inclined to agree with me."

These men had learnt well the art of masking their feelings. From Lord Chelsford's polite bow I could gather nothing.

"I am forced to admit," he said, "that no other conclusion seems possible. Now, Mr. Ducaine, with regard to the execution of your work. It is carried out altogether, I believe, at the 'Brand'?"

"Entirely, sir."

"Your only servant is the man Grooton, for whom the Duke and I myself are prepared to vouch. You are also watched by detectives residing in the village, as I dare say you know. I also understand that you have no private correspondence, and receive practically no visitors. Now tell me the only persons who, to your knowledge, have entered the 'Brand' since you have been engaged in this work."

I answered him at once.

"Colonel Ray, Lady Angela Harberly, Lord Blenavon, the Prince of Malors, and a young lady called Blanche Moyat, the daughter of a farmer in Braster at whose house I used sometimes to visit."

Lord Chelsford referred to some notes in his hand. Then he leaned back in his chair, and looked at me steadfastly.

"Is there any one," he asked, "whom you suspect to have visited you for the purpose, either direct or indirect, of gaining information as to your work?"

"Yes, sir," I answered promptly.

A little exclamation escaped from the Commander-in-Chief. Lord Chelsford never removed his eyes from my face, the Duke had still the appearance of a tolerant but slightly bored listener.

"Who?" Lord Chelsford asked.

"The Prince of Malors," I answered.

There was a moment's silence. Lord Chelsford turned again to his notes.
Then he looked up at me.

"Your reasons?" he asked.

I told them the story carefully and circumstantially. When I had finished Colonel Ray left his seat and whispered something in Lord Chelsford's ear. The Duke interposed.

"I wish," he said, "to add a brief remark to the story which you have just heard. I have known Malors since he was a boy, my father knew his father, and, as you may know, our families have been frequently connected in marriage. I do not wish to impugn the good faith of this young man, but the Prince of Malors was my guest, and the accusation against him is one which I cannot believe."

"The story, as I have told it, sir, is absolutely true," I said to Lord Chelsford. "There was no room for any mistake or misapprehension on my part. I am afraid that I haven't been a great success as your secretary. Colonel Ray gave me to understand, of course, that your object in engaging an utterly unknown person was to try and stop this leakage of information. It is still going on, and I cannot stop it. I am quite prepared to give up my post at any moment."

Lord Chelsford nodded towards the door.

"Will you be so good as to step into the next room for a few minutes, Mr. Ducaine?" he said. "We will discuss this matter together."

I departed at once, and found my way into a bare waiting-room, hung with a few maps, and with uncarpeted floor. The minutes dragged along slowly. I hated the thought of dismissal, I rebelled against it almost fiercely. I had done my duty, I had told the truth, there was nothing against me save this obstinate and quixotic loyalty of the Duke to an old family friend. Yet I scarcely dared hope that there was a chance for me.

At last I heard the door open, and the sound of friendly adieux in the passage. Lord Chelsford came in to me alone. He took up a position with his back to the fire, and looked at me thoughtfully.

"Well, Mr. Ducaine," he said, "we have discussed this matter thoroughly, and we are all practically agreed that there is no reason why we should ask you to give up your position."

I was almost overcome. It was a wonderful relief to me.

"But surely the Duke—" I faltered.

"The Duke is very loyal to his friends, Mr. Ducaine," he said, "but he is also a man with a nice sense of justice. You and he regard two incidents from entirely different points of view, but he does not for a moment suggest that your account of them is not an honest one. He looks upon you as a little nervous and overstrung by your responsibilities and disposed to be imaginative. He will not hear anything against the Prince of Malors."

"My story is as true as God's Word," I declared.

"I am inclined to believe in it myself, Mr. Ducaine," said Lord Chelsford. "There are indications of a strong revival of Royalist sentiment amongst the French people, and it is very possible that the Prince of Malors may wish to ingratiate himself by any means with the French army. This sort of thing scarcely sounds like practical politics, but one has to bear in mind the peculiar temperament of the man himself, and the nation. I personally believe that the Prince of Malors would consider himself justified in abusing the hospitality of his dearest friend in the cause of patriotism. At any rate, this is my view, and I am acting upon it. All danger from that source will now be at an end, for in an hour's time the Prince will be under the surveillance of detectives for the remainder of his stay in England."

I breathed a sigh of relief.

"I am to go back to Braster, then?" I asked.

"To-night, if possible," Lord Chelsford answered. "Go on living as you have been living. And, listen! If you should have further cause to suspect the Prince of Malors or anybody else, communicate with me or with Ray. The Duke is, of course, a man of ability and an honourable man, but he is prejudiced in favour of his friends. Some of us others have had to learn our lessons of life, and men, in a sharper school. You understand me, Mr. Ducaine, I am sure."

"I perfectly understand, sir," I answered.

"There is nothing more which you wish to ask me?"

"There is a suggestion I should like to make, sir, with regard to the disposal of my finished work," I told him.

"Go on, Mr. Ducaine. I shall be glad to listen to it."

There was a knock at the door. Lord Chelsford held up his finger.

"Send it me in writing," he said in a low tone, "to-morrow.— Come in!"

Ray entered.

CHAPTER XIX
MRS. SMITH-LESSING

Ray and I left the building together. As we turned into Pall Mall he glanced at his watch.

"You have missed the six o'clock train," he remarked. "I suppose you know that there is nothing now till the nine-twenty. Will you come to the club with me, and have some dinner?"

It was less an invitation than a command. I felt a momentary impulse of rebellion, but the innate masterfulness of the man triumphed easily. I found myself walking, a little against my will, down Pall Mall by his side. A man of some note, he was saluted every minute by passers-by, whom, however, he seemed seldom to notice. In his town clothes, his great height, his bronzed face, and black beard made him a sufficiently striking personality. I myself, though I was little short of six feet, seemed almost insignificant by his side. Until we reached the club he maintained an unbroken silence. He even ignored some passing comment of mine; but when once inside the building he seemed to remember that he was my host, and his manner became one of stiff kindness. He ordered an excellent dinner and chose the wine with care. Then he leaned a little forward across the table, and electrified me by his first remark.

"Ducaine," he said, "what relatives have you with whom you are in any sort of communication?"

"None at all!" I answered.

"Sir Michael Trogoldy was your mother's brother," he remarked. "He is still alive."

"I believe so," I admitted. "I have never approached him, nor has he ever taken any notice of me."

"You did not write to him, for instance, when Heathcote absconded, and you had to leave college?"

"Certainly not," I answered. "I did not choose to turn beggar."

"How much," he asked, "do you know of your family history?"

"I know," I told him, "that my father was cashiered from the army for misconduct, and committed suicide. I know, too, that my mother's people treated her shamefully, and that she died alone in Paris and almost in poverty. It was scarcely likely, therefore, that I was going to apply to them for help." Ray nodded.

"I thought so," he remarked grimly. "I shall have to talk to you for a few minutes about your father."

I said nothing. My surprise, indeed, had bereft me of words. He sipped his wine slowly, and continued.

"Fate has dealt a little hardly with you," he said. "I am almost a stranger to you, and there are even reasons why you and I could never be friends. Yet it apparently falls to my lot to supplement the little you know of a very unpleasant portion of your family history. That rascal of a lawyer who absconded with your money should have told you on your twenty-first birthday."

"A pleasant heritage!" I remarked bitterly; "yet I always wanted to know the whole truth."

"Here goes, then," he said, filling my glass with wine. "Your father was second in command at Gibraltar. He sold a plan of the gallery forts to the French Government, and was dismissed from the army."

I started as though I had been stung. Ray continued, his stern matter-of-fact tone unshaken.

"He did not commit suicide as you were told. He lived, in Paris, a life of continual and painful degeneration. Your mother died of a broken heart. There was another woman, of course, whose influence over your father was unbounded, and at whose instigation he committed this disgraceful act. This woman is now at Braster."

My brain was in a whirl. I was quite incapable of speech.

"Her real name," he continued coolly, "God only knows. For the moment she calls herself Mrs. Smith-Lessing. She is a Franco-American, a political adventuress of the worst type, living by her wits. She is ugly enough to be Satan's mistress, and she's forty-five if she's a day, yet she has but to hold up her finger, and men tumble the gifts of their life into her lap, gold and honour, conscience and duty. At present I think it highly probable that you are her next selected victim."

For several minutes Ray proceeded with his dinner. I did my best to follow his example, but my appetite was gone. I could scarcely persuade myself that the whole affair was not a dream—that the men who sat all round us in little groups, the dark liveried servants passing noiselessly backwards and forwards, were not figures in some shadowy nightmare, and that I should not wake in a moment to find myself curled up in a railway carriage on my way home. But there was no mistaking the visible presence of Colonel Mostyn Ray. Strong, stalwart, he sat within a few feet of me, calmly eating his dinner as though my agony were a thing of little account. He, at least, was real.

"This woman," he continued, presently, "either is, or would like to be, mixed up with the treachery that is somewhere close upon us. Sooner or later she will approach you. You are warned."

"Yes," I repeated vaguely, "I am warned."

"I have finished," Colonel Ray remarked. "Go on with your dinner and think. I will answer any question presently."

There were only two I put to him, and that was when my hansom had been called and I was on the point of leaving.

"Is he—my father—alive now?" I asked.

"I have reason to believe," Ray answered, "that he may be dead."

"How is it," I asked, "that you are so well acquainted with these things? Were you at any time my father's friend?"

"I was acquainted with him," Ray answered. "We were at one time in the same regiment. My friendship was—with your mother."

The answer was illuming, but he never winced.

"Indirectly," I said, "I seem to have a good deal to thank you for. Why do you say that you can never be my friend?"

"You are your father's son," he answered curtly.

"I am also my mother's son," I objected.

"For which reason," he said, "I have done what I could to give you a start in life."

And with these words he dismissed me.

* * * * *

I received Ray's warning concerning Mrs. Smith-Lessing, the new tenant of Braster Grange, somewhere between seven and eight o'clock, and barely an hour later I found myself alone in a first-class carriage with her, and a four hours' journey before us. She had arrived at King's Cross apparently only a few minutes before the departure of the train, for the platform was almost deserted when I took my seat. Just as I had changed my hat for a cap, however, wrapped my rug around my knees, and settled down for the journey, the door of my carriage was thrown open, and I saw two women looking in, one of whom I recognized at once. Mrs. Smith-Lessing, although the night was warm, was wearing a heavy and magnificent fur coat, and the guard of the train himself was attending her. Behind stood a plainly dressed woman, evidently her maid, carrying a flat dressing-case. There was a brief colloquy between the three. It ended in dressing-case, a pile of books, a reading lamp, and a formidable array of hat-boxes, and milliner's parcels being placed upon the rack and vacant seats in my compartment, and immediately afterwards Mrs. Smith-Lessing herself entered. I heard her tell her maid to enter the carriage behind. The door was closed and the guard touched off his hat. A minute later and we were off.

I was alone with the adventuress. I had no doubt but that she had chosen my carriage with intent. I placed my dispatch-box on the rack above my head, and opened out a newspaper, which I had no intention of reading. She, for her part, arranged her travelling light and took out a novel. She did not apparently even glance in my direction, and seemed to become immersed at once in her reading. So we travelled for half an hour or so.

At the end of that time I was suddenly conscious that she had laid down her book, and was regarding me through partially-closed eyes. I too laid down my paper. Our eyes met, and she smiled.

"Forgive me," she said, "but did I not see you one day last week upon the sands at Braster with Lady Angela Harberly?"

"I believe so," I answered. "You were riding, I think, with her brother."

"How fortunate that I should find myself travelling with a neighbour!" she murmured. "I rather dreaded this night journey. I just missed the six o'clock, and I have been at the station ever since."

I understood at once one of the charms of this woman. Her voice was deliciously soft and musical. The words seemed to leave her lips slowly, almost lingeringly, and she spoke with the precision and slight accent of a well-educated foreigner. Her eyes seemed to be wandering all over me and my possessions, yet her interest, if it amounted to that, never even suggested curiosity or inquisitiveness.

"It is scarcely a pleasant journey at this time of night," I remarked.

"Indeed, no," she assented. "I wonder if you know my name? I am Mrs. Smith-Lessing, of Braster Grange. And you?"

"My name is Guy Ducaine," I told her. "I live at a small cottage called the 'Brand.'"

"That charming little place you can just see from the sands?" she exclaimed. "I thought the Duke's head-keeper lived there."

"It was a keeper's lodge before the Duke was kind enough to let it to me," I told her.

She nodded.

"It is a very delightful abode," she murmured.

She picked up her book, and after turning over the pages aimlessly for a few minutes, she recommenced to read. I followed her example; but when a little later on I glanced across in her direction, I found that her eyes were fixed upon me, and that her novel lay in her lap.

"My book is so stupid," she said apologetically. "I find, Mr. Ducaine," she added with sudden earnestness, "the elements of a much stranger story closer at hand."

"That," I remarked, laying down my own book, and looking steadily across at her, "sounds enigmatic."

"I think," she said, "that I am very foolish to talk to you at all about it. If you know who I am, you are probably armed against me at all points. You will weigh and measure my words, you will say to yourself, 'Lies, lies, lies!' You will not believe in me or anything I say.

And, again, if you do not know, the story is too painful a one for me to tell."

"Then let us both avoid it," I said, reaching again for my paper. "We shall stop at Ipswich in an hour. I will change carriages there."

She turned round in her seat towards the window, as though to hide her face. My own attempt at reading was a farce. I watched her over the top of my paper. She was looking out into the darkness, and she seemed to me to be crying. Every now and then her shoulders heaved convulsively. Suddenly she faced me once more. There were traces of tears on her face; a small lace handkerchief was knotted up in her nervous fingers.

"Oh, I cannot," she exclaimed plaintively. "I cannot sit here alone with you and say nothing. I know that I am judged already. It does not matter. I am your father's wife, Guy. You owe me at least some recognition of that fact."

"I never knew my father," I said, "except as the cause of my own miserable upbringing and friendless life."

"You never knew him," she answered, "and therefore you believe the worst. He was weak, perhaps, and, exposed to a terrible temptation, he fell! But he was not a bad man. He was never that."

"Do you think, Mrs. Smith-Lessing," I said, struggling to keep my voice firm, though I felt myself trembling, "that this is a profitable discussion for either of us?"

"Why not?" she exclaimed almost fiercely. "You have heard his story from enemies. You have judged him from the report of those who were never his friends. He sinned and he repented. Better and worse men than he have done that. If he were wholly bad, do you believe that after all these years I should care for him still?"

I held my peace. The woman was leaning over towards me now. She seemed to have lost the desire to attract. Her voice had grown sharper and less pleasant, her carefully arranged hair was in some disorder, and the telltale blue veins by her temples and the crow's feet under her eyes were plainly visible. Her face seemed suddenly to have become pinched and wan, the flaming light in her strangely coloured eyes was a convincing assertion of her earnestness. She was not acting now, though what lay behind the storm I could not tell.

"You seem afraid to talk to me," she exclaimed. "Why? I have done you no harm!"

"Perhaps not," I answered, "yet I cannot see what we gain by raking up this miserable history. It is both painful and profitless."

"I will say no more," she declared, with a sudden note of dignity in her tone. "I can see that I am judged already in your mind. After all, it does not really matter. No one likes to be thought worse of than they deserve, and women are all—a little foolish. But at least you must answer me one question. I have the right to ask it. You must tell me where he is."

"Where who is?" I asked.

Again her eyes flamed upon inc. Her lips parted a little, and I could see the white glimmer of her teeth.

"Oh, you shall not fence with me like a baby!" she exclaimed. "Tell me, or lie to me, or refuse to tell me! Which is it?"

"Upon my honour," I said, looking at her curiously, "I have no idea whom you mean!"

She looked at inc steadily for several moments, her lips parted, her breath seeming to come sharply between her teeth.

"I mean your father," she said. "Whom else should I mean?"

CHAPTER XX
TWO TO ONE

I looked across at the woman, who was waiting my answer with every appearance of feverish interest.

"What should I know about him?" I said slowly. "I have been told that he is dead. I know no more than that."

She started as though my words had stung her.

"It is not possible!" she exclaimed. "I must have heard of it. When he left me—it was less than three months ago—he seemed better than I had known him for years."

"All my life," I said, "I have understood that my father died by his own hand after his disgrace. To-night for the first time I was told that this was not the fact. I understood, from what my informant said, that he had died recently."

She drew a sharp breath between her teeth, and suddenly struck the cushioned arm of the carriage by her side with her clenched hand.

"It is a lie!" she declared. "Whoever told you so, it is a lie!"

"Do you mean that he is not dead?" I exclaimed. "Do you mean that you have not seen him yourself—within the last few months?" she demanded fiercely. "He left me to come to you on the first day of the New Year."

"I have never seen him to my knowledge in my life," I answered.

She leaned back in her seat, murmuring something to herself which I could not catch. Past-mistress of deceit though she may have been, I was convinced that her consternation at my statement was honest. She did not speak or look at me again for some time. As for me, I sat silent with the horror of a thought. Underneath the rug my limbs were cold and lifeless. I sat looking out of the rain-splashed window into the darkness, with fixed staring eyes, and a hideous fancy in my brain. Every now and then I thought that I could see it—a white evil face pressed close to the blurred glass, grinning in upon me. Every shriek of the engine—and there were many just then, for we were passing through a network of tunnels—brought beads of moisture on to my forehead, made me start and shake like a criminal. Surely that was a cry! I started in my seat, only to see that my companion, now her old self again, was watching me intently.

"I am afraid," she said softly, "that you are not very strong. The excitement of talking of these things has been too much for you."

"I have never had a day's illness in my life," I answered. "I am perfectly well."

"I am glad," she said simply. "I must finish what I was telling you. Your father was continually talking and thinking of you. He knew all about you at college. He knew about your degree, of your cricket and rowing. Lately he began to get restless. He lost sight of you after you left Oxford, and it worried him. There were reasons, as you know, why it was not well for him to come to England, but nevertheless he determined to brave it out. It was to find you that he risked so much. He left me on New Year's Day, and I have never heard a word from him since. That is why I came to England."

"The whole reason?" I asked, like a fool.

"The whole reason," she affirmed simply.

"I do not wish to see my father," I said. "If he comes to me I shall tell him so."

"He wants to tell you his story himself," she murmured.

"I would never listen to it," I answered. She sighed.

"You are very young," she said. "You do not know what temptation is. You do not know how badly he was treated. You have heard his history, perhaps, from his enemies. He is getting old now, Guy. I think that if you saw him now you would pity him."

"My pity," I answered, "would never be strong enough to suffer me to open the door to him—if he should come. He has left me alone all these years. The only favour I would ever ask of him would be that he continues to do so."

"You will believe the story of strangers?"

"No one in the world could be a greater stranger to me than he." She sighed.

"You will not even let me be your friend," she pleaded. "You are young, you are perhaps ambitious. There may be many ways in which I could help you."

"As you helped my father, perhaps," I answered bitterly. "Thank you, I have no need of friends—that sort of friends."

Her eyes seemed to narrow a little, and the smile upon her lips was forced.

"Is that kind of you?" she exclaimed. "Your father was in a position of great trust. It is different with you. You are idle, and you need a career. England has so little to offer her young men, but there are other countries—"

I interrupted her brusquely.

"Thank you," I said, "but I have employment, and such ambitions as I have admit of nothing but an honest career."

Again I saw that contraction of her eyes, but she never winced or changed her tone.

"You have employment?" she asked, as though surprised.

"Yes. As you doubtless know, I am in the service of the Duke of Rowchester," I told her.

"It is news to me," she replied. "You will forgive me at least for being interested, Guy. But when you say in the service of the Duke of Rowchester you puzzle me. In England what does that, mean?"

"I am one of the Duke's secretaries," I answered.

"Is the Duke, then, a politician?" she asked, "that he needs secretaries?"

"Not at all," I answered drily. "His Grace is President of the Society for the Prevention of Cruelty to Animals, or Children, whichever you like. We have a large correspondence."

She picked up her book.

"I am afraid that I understand you," she said. "You have a good deal of the brutality of youth, Guy, and, I might add, of its credulity also. Whose word is it, I wonder, that you have taken so abjectly—

with such an open mouth? If I have enemies I have not deserved them. But, after all, it matters little."

We did not speak again until we neared the junction. Then she began to gather up her things.

"How are you getting home?" she asked. "It is two o'clock, and raining."

"I am going to walk," I answered.

"But that is absurd," she protested. "I have a closed carriage here. I insist that you let me drive you. It is only common humanity; and you have that great box too."

I buttoned up my coat.

"Mrs. Smith-Lessing," I said, "you perhaps wish to force me into seeming ungracious. You have even called me brutal. It is your own fault. You give me no chance of escape. You even force me now to tell you that I do not desire — that I will not accept — any hospitality at your hands."

She fastened her jacket with trembling fingers. Her face she kept averted from me.

"Very well," she said softly, "I shall not trouble you any more."

At the junction I fetched the sleepy-looking porter to see to her luggage, and then left her. My rug I left in the station-master's office, and with the dispatch-box in my hand I climbed the steps from the station, and turned into the long straight road which led to Braster. I had barely gone a hundred yards when a small motor brougham, with blazing lights and insistent horn, came flying past me and on into the darkness. I caught a momentary glimpse of Mrs. Smith-Lessing's pale face as the car flashed by, a weird little silhouette, come and gone in a second. Away ahead I saw the mud and rain from the pools fly up into the air in a constant stream caught in the broad white glare of the brilliant search-lamps. Then the car turned a corner and vanished.

I was tired, yet I found the change from the close railway carriage, and the tension of the last few hours, delightful. The road along which I trudged ran straight to the sea, the distant roar of which was already in my ears, and the wet wind which blew in my face was salt and refreshing. It was a little after two in the morning, and the darkness would have been absolute, but for a watery moon, which every now and then gave a fitful light. For a mile or more I walked with steady, unflagging footsteps. Then suddenly I found myself slackening my pace. I walked slower and slower. At last I stopped.

About fifty yards farther on my left was Braster Grange. It stood a little way back from the road. Its gardens were enclosed by a thin storm-bent hedge, just thick enough to be a screen from the road. The entrance was along a lane which branched off here from the main road, and led on to the higher marshes, and thence on to the road from Braster village to Rowchester and my cottage. Straight on, the road which I was following led into Braster, but the lane to the left round past the Grange saved me fully half a mile. In an ordinary way I should never have hesitated for a moment as to my route. I knew every inch of the lane, and though it was rough walking, there were no creeks or obstacles of any sort to be reckoned with. And yet, as I neared the corner, I came to a full stop. As I stood there in the road I felt my heart beating, I seemed possessed by a curious nerve failure. My breath came quickly. I felt my heart thumping against my side. I stood still and listened. Down on the shingles I could hear the sea come thundering in with a loud increasing roar, dying monotonously away at regular intervals. I could hear the harsh grinding of the pebbles, the backward swirl of long waves thrown back from the land. I heard the wind come booming across the waste lands, rustling and creaking amongst the few stunted trees in the grounds of Braster Grange. Of slighter sounds there seemed to be none. The village ahead was dark and silent, the side of the house fronting the road was black and desolate. It was a lonely spot, a lonely hour. Yet as I stood there shivering with nameless apprehensions, I felt absolutely certain that I was confronted by some hidden danger.

In a moment or two, I am thankful to say, my courage returned. I struck a match and lit a cigar, one of a handful which Ray had forced upon me. Then I crossed stealthily to the other side of the road, and felt for the hedge. I pricked my hands badly, but after feeling about for some moments I was able to cut for myself a reasonably thick stick. With this in my right hand, and the dispatch-box under my left arm I proceeded on my way.

I walked warily, and when I had turned into the lane which passed the entrance to Braster Grange I walked in the middle of it instead of skirting the wall which enclosed the grounds. I passed the entrance gates, and had only about twenty yards farther to go before I emerged upon the open marshland. Here the darkness was almost impenetrable, for the lane narrowed. The hedge on the left was ten or twelve feet high, and on the right were two long barns. I clasped my stick tightly, and walked almost stealthily. I felt that if I could come safely to the end of these barn buildings I could afford to laugh at my fears.

Suddenly my strained hearing detected what I had been listening for all the time. There was a faint but audible rustling in the shrubs overgrowing the wall on my left. I made a quick dash forward, tripped against some invisible obstacle stretched across the lane, and went staggering sideways, struggling to preserve my balance. Almost at the same moment two dark forms dropped from the shelter of the shrubs on to the lane by my side. I felt the soft splash of a wet cloth upon my cheeks, an arm round my neck, and the sickening odour of chloroform in my nostrils. But already I had regained by balance. I wrenched myself free from the arm, and was suddenly blinded by the glare of a small electric hand-light within a foot of my face. I struck a sweeping blow at it with my stick, and from the soft impact it seemed to me that the blow must have descended upon the head of one of my assailants. I heard a groan, and I saw the shadowy form of the second man spring at me. What followed was not, I believe, cowardice on my part, for my blood was up and my sense of fear gone. I dashed my stick straight at the approaching figure, and I leaped forward and ran. I had won the hundred yards and the quarter of a mile at Oxford, and I was in fair training. I knew how to get off fast, and after the first dozen yards I felt that I was safe. The footsteps which had started in pursuit ceased in a few minutes. Breathless, but with the dispatch-box safe under my arm, I sprinted across the marsh, and never paused till I reached the road. Then I looked back and listened. I could see or hear nothing, but from one of the top rooms in the Grange a faint but steady light was shining out.

CHAPTER XXI
LADY ANGELA APPROVES

It was the only breath of fresh air which I had allowed myself all the morning, though the dazzling sunlight and the soft west wind had tempted me all the time. And now, as ill luck would have it, I had walked straight into the presence of the one person in the world whom I wished most earnestly to avoid. She was standing on the edge of the cliff, her hands behind her, gazing seawards, and though I stopped short at the sight of her, and for a moment entertained wild thoughts of flight, it was not possible for me to carry them out. A dry twig snapped beneath my feet, and, turning quickly round, she had seen me. She came forward at once, and for some reason or other I knew that she was glad. She smiled upon me almost gaily.

"So this sunshine has even tempted you out, Sir Hermit," she exclaimed.
"Is it not good to feel the Spring coming?"

"Delightful," I answered.

She looked at me curiously.

"How pale you are!" she said. "You are working too hard, Mr. Ducaine."

"I came down from London by the mail last night," I said. "I saw Colonel Ray—had dinner with him, in fact."

She nodded, but asked me no questions.

"I think," she said abruptly, "that they are all coming down here in a few days. I heard from my father this morning."

I sighed.

"I have been very unfortunate, Lady Angela," I said. "Your father is displeased with me. I think that but for Colonel Ray I should have been dismissed yesterday."

"Is it about—the Prince of Malors?" she asked in a low tone.

"Partly. I was forced to tell what I knew." She hesitated for a moment, then she turned impulsively toward me.

"You were right to tell them, Mr. Ducaine," she said. "I have hated myself ever since the other night when I seemed to side against you. There are things going on about us which I cannot fathom, and sometimes I have fears, terrible fears. But your course at least is a clear one. Don't let yourself be turned aside by any one. My father has prejudices which might lead him into grievous errors. Trust Colonel Ray—no one else. Yours is a dangerous position, but it is a splendid one. It means a career and independence. If there should come a time even—"

She broke off abruptly in her speech. I could see that she was agitated, and I thought that I knew the cause.

"Lady Angela," I said slowly, "would it not be possible for you and Colonel Ray to persuade Lord Blenavon to go abroad?"

She swayed for a moment as though she would have fallen, and her eyes looked at me full of fear.

"You think—that it would be better?"

"I do."

"It would break my father's heart," she murmured, "if ever he could be brought to believe it."

"The more reason why Lord Blenavon should go," I said. "He is set between dangerous influences here. Lady Angela, can you tell me where your brother was last night?"

"How should I?" she answered slowly. "He tells me nothing."

"He was not at home?"

"He dined at home. I think that he went out afterwards."

I nodded.

"And if he returned at all," I said, "I think you will find that it was after three o'clock."

She came a little nearer to me, although indeed we were in a spot where there was no danger of being overheard.'

"What do you know about it?"

"Am I not right?" I asked.

"He did not return at all," she answered. "He is not home yet."

I had believed from the first that Blenavon was one of my two assailants. Now I was sure of it.

"When he does come back," I remarked grimly, "you may find him more or less damaged."

"Mr. Ducaine," she said, "you must explain yourself."

I saw no reason why I should not do so. I told her the story of my early morning adventure. She listened with quivering lips.

"You were not hurt, then?" she asked eagerly.

"I was not hurt," I assured her. "I was fortunate."

"Tell me what measures you are taking," she begged.

"What can I do?" I asked. "It was pitch dark, and I could identify no one. I am writing Colonel Ray. That is all."

"That hateful woman," she murmured. "Mr. Ducaine, I believe that if Blenavon is really concerned in this, it is entirely through her influence."

"Very likely," I answered. "I have heard strange things about her. She is a dangerous woman."

We were both silent for a moment. Then Lady Angela, whose eyes were fixed seawards, suddenly turned to me.

"Oh," she cried, "I am weary of all these bothers and problems and anxieties. Let us put them away for one hour of this glorious morning. Dare you play truant for a little while and walk on the sands?"

"I think so," I answered readily, "if you will wait while I go and put Grooton in charge."

"I will be scrambling down," she declared. "It is not a difficult operation."

I joined her a few minutes later, and we set our faces toward the point of the bay. Over our heads the seagulls were lazily drifting and wheeling, the quiet sea stole almost noiselessly up the firm yellow sands. Farther over the marshes the larks were singing. Inland, men like tiny specks in the distance were working upon their farms. We walked for a while in silence, and I found myself watching my companion. Her head was thrown slightly back, she walked with all the delightful grace of youth and strength, yet there was a cloud which still lingered upon her face.

"These," I said abruptly "should be the happiest days of your life, Lady Angela. After all, is it worth while to spoil them by worrying about other people's doings?"

"Other people's doings?" she murmured.

I shrugged my shoulders.

"Selfishness, you know, is the permitted vice of the young — and of lovers."

"Blenavon can scarcely rank amongst the other people with me," she said.
"He is my only brother."

"Colonel Ray is to be your husband," I reminded her, "which is far more important."

She turned upon me with flaming cheeks.

"You do not understand what you are talking about, Mr. Ducaine," she said, stiffly. "Colonel Ray and I are not lovers. You have no right to assume anything of the sort."

"If you are not lovers," I said, "what right have you to marry?"

She seemed a little staggered, as indeed she might be by my boldness.

"You are very mediaeval," she remarked.

"The mediaeval sometimes survives. It is as true now as then that loveless marriages are a curse and a sin," I answered. "It is the one thing which remains now as it was in the beginning."

She looked at me furtively, almost timidly.

"I should like to know why you are speaking to me like this," she said. "I do not want to seem unkind, but do you think that the length of our acquaintance warrants it?"

"I do not know how long I have known you," I answered. "I do not remember the time when I did not know you. You are one of those people to whom I must say the things which come into my mind. I think that if you do not love Colonel Ray you have no right to marry him."

She looked me in the face. Her cheeks were flushed with walking, and the wind had blown her hair into becoming confusion.

"Mr. Ducaine," she said, "do you consider that Colonel Ray is your friend?"

"He has been very good to me," I answered.

"There is something between you two. What is it?"

"It is not my secret," I told her.

"There is a secret, then," she murmured. "I knew it. Is this why you do not wish me to marry him?"

"I have not said that I do not wish you to marry him," I reminded her.

"Not in words. You had no need to put it into words."

"You are very young," I said, "to marry any one for any other reason save the only true one. Some day there might be some one else."

She watched the flight of a seagull for a few moments — watched it till its wings shone like burnished silver as it lit upon the sun-gilded sea.

"I do not think so," she said, dreamily. "I have never fancied myself caring very much for any one. It is not easy, you know, for some of us."

"And for some," I murmured, "it is too easy."

She looked at me curiously, but she had no suspicion as to the meaning of my words.

"I want you to tell me something," she said, in a few minutes. "Have you any other reason beyond this for objecting to my marriage with Colonel Ray?"

"If I have," I answered slowly, "I cannot tell it you. It is his secret, not mine."

"You are mysterious!" she remarked.

"If I am," I objected, "you must remember that you are asking me strange questions."

"Colonel Ray is too honest," she said, thoughtfully, "to keep anything from me which I ought to know."

I changed the conversation. After all I was a fool to have blundered into it. We talked of other and lighter things. I exerted myself to shake off the depression against which I had been struggling all the morning. By degrees I think we both forgot some part of our troubles. We walked home across the sandhills, climbing gradually higher and higher, until we reached the cliffs. On all sides of us the coming change in the seasons seemed to be vigorously asserting itself. The plovers were crying over the freshly-turned ploughed fields, a whole world of wild birds and insects seemed to have imparted a sense of movement and life to what only a few days ago had been a land of desolation, a country silent and winterbound. Colour was asserting itself in all manner of places—in the green of the sprouting grass, the shimmer of the sun upon the sea-stained sands, in the silvery blue of the Braster creeks. Lady Angela drew a long breath of content as we paused for a moment at the summit of the cliffs.

"And you wonder," she murmured, "that I left London for this!"

"Yes, I still wonder," I answered. "The beauties of this place are for the lonely—I mean the lonely in disposition. For you life in the busy places should just be opening all her fascinations. It is only when one is disappointed in the more human life that one comes back to Nature."

"Perhaps then," she said, a little vaguely, "I too must be suffering from disappointments. I have never realized—"

We had taken the last turn. My cottage was in sight. To my surprise a man was standing there as though waiting. He turned round as we approached. His face was very pale, and the back of his head was bandaged. He carried his arm, too, in a sling. It was Colonel Mostyn Ray!

CHAPTER XXII
MISS MOYAT MAKES A SCENE

Ray was smoking his customary enormous pipe, which he deliberately emptied as Lady Angela and I approached. The sight of him and the significance of his wounds reduced me to a state of astonishment which could find no outlet in words. I simply stood and stared at him. Lady Angela, however, after her first exclamation of surprise, went up and greeted him.

"Why, my dear Mostyn," she exclaimed, "wherever have you sprung from, and what have you been doing to yourself?"

"I came from London—newspaper train," he answered.

"And your head and arm?"

"Thrown out of a hansom last night," he said grimly.

We were all silent for a moment. So far as I was concerned, speech was altogether beyond me. Lady Angela, too, seemed to find something disconcerting in Ray's searching gaze.

"My welcome," he remarked quietly, "does not seem to be overpowering."

Lady Angela laughed, but there was a note of unreality in her mirth.

"You must expect people to be amazed, Mostyn," she said, "if you treat them to such surprises. Of course I am glad to see you. Have you seen Blenavon yet?"

"I have not been to the house," he answered. "I came straight here."

"And your luggage?" she asked.

"Lost," he answered tersely. "I only just caught the train, and the porter seems to have missed me."

"You appear to have passed through a complete chapter of mishaps," she remarked. "Never mind! You must want your lunch very badly, or do you want to talk to Mr. Ducaine?"

"Nexttothewalkuptothehousewithyou,"heanswered,"Ithinkthat I want my lunch more than anything in the world."

Lady Angela smiled her farewells at me, and Ray nodded curtly. I watched them pass through the plantation and stroll across the Park. There was nothing very loverlike in their attitude. Ray seemed scarcely to be glancing towards his companion; Lady Angela had the air of one absorbed in thought. I watched them until they disappeared, and then I entered my own abode and sat down mechanically before the lunch which Grooton had prepared. I ate and drank as one in a dream. Only last night Ray had said nothing about coming to Braster. Yet, there he was, without luggage, with his arm and head bound up. Just like this I expected to see the man whom I had struck last night.

Now though Ray's attitude towards me was often puzzling, an absolute faith in his honesty was the one foundation which I had felt solid beneath my feet during these last few weeks of strange happenings. This was the first blow which my faith had received, and I felt that at any cost I must know the truth. After lunch I finished the papers which, when complete, it was my duty to lock away in the library safe up at the house, and secured them in my breast-pocket. But instead of going at once to the house I set out for Braster Junction.

There was a porter there whom I had spoken to once or twice. I called him on one side.

"Can you tell me," I asked, "what passengers there were from London by the newspaper train this morning?"

"None at all, sir," the man answered readily.

"Are you quite sure?" I asked.

The man smiled.

"I'm more than sure, sir," the man answered, "because she never stopped. She only sets down by signal now, and we had the message 'no passengers' from Wells. She went through here at forty miles an hour."

"I was expecting Colonel Ray by that train," I remarked, "the gentleman who lectured on the war, you know, at the Village Hall."

The man looked at me curiously.

"Why, he came down last night, same train as you, sir. I know, because he only got out just as the train was going on, and he stepped into the station master's house to light his pipe."

"Thank you," I said, giving the man a shilling. "I must have just missed him, then."

I left the station and walked home. Now, indeed, all my convictions were upset. Colonel Ray had left me outside his clubhouse last night, twenty minutes before the train started, without a word of coming to Braster. Yet he travelled down by the same train, avoided me, lied to Lady Angela and myself this morning, and had exactly the sort of wounds which I had inflicted upon that unknown assailant who attacked me in the darkness. If circumstantial evidence went for anything, Ray himself had been my aggressor.

I avoided the turn by Braster Grange and went straight on to the village. Coming out of the post office I found myself face to face with Blanche Moyat. She held out her hand eagerly.

"Were you coming in?" she asked.

"Well, not to-day," I answered. "I am on my way to Rowchester, and I am late already."

She kept by my side.

"Come in for a few moments," she begged, in a low tone. "I want to talk to you."

"Not the old subject, I hope," I remarked.

She looked around with an air of mystery.

"Do you know that some one is making inquiries about — that man?"

"I always thought it possible," I answered, "that his friends might turn up some time or other."

We were opposite the front of the Moyats' house. She opened the door and beckoned me to follow. I hesitated, but eventually did so. She led the way into the drawing-room, and carefully closed the door after us.

"Mr. Ducaine," she said, "I mean it, really. There is some one in the village making inquiries — about — the man who was found dead."

"Well," I said, "that is not very surprising, is it? His friends were almost certain to turn up sooner or later."

"His friends! But do you know who it is?" she asked.

I sank resignedly into one of Mrs. Moyat's wool-work covered chairs. An absurd little canary was singing itself hoarse almost over my head. I half closed my eyes. How many more problems was I to be confronted with during these long-drawn-out days of mystery?

"Oh, I do not know," I declared. "I am sure I do not care. I am sorry that I ever asked you for one moment to keep your counsel about the fellow. I never saw him, I do not know who he was, I know nothing about him. And I don't want to, Miss Moyat. He may have been prince or pedlar for anything I care."

"Well, he wasn't an ordinary person, after all," she declared, with an air of mystery. "Have you heard of the lady who's taken Braster Grange? She's a friend of Lord Blenavon's. He's always there."

"I have heard that there is such a person," I answered wearily.

"She's been making inquiries right and left — everywhere. There's a notice in yesterday's Wells Gazette, and a reward of fifty pounds for any one who can give any information about him sufficient to lead to identification."

"If you think," I said, "that you can earn the pounds, pray do not let me stand in your way."

She looked at me with a fixed intentness which I found peculiarly irritating.

"You don't think that I care about the fifty pounds," she said, coming over and standing by my chair.

"Then why take any notice of the matter at all?" I said. "All that you can disclose is that he came from the land and not from the sea, and that he asked where I lived. Why trouble yourself or me about the matter at all? There really isn't any necessity. Some one else probably saw him besides you, and they will soon find their way to this woman."

"It was only to me," she murmured, "that he spoke of you."

"Do you believe," I asked, "that I murdered him?"

She shuddered.

"No, of course I don't," she declared.

"Then why all this nervousness and mystery?" I asked. "I have no fear of anything which might happen. Why should you be afraid?"

"I am not afraid," she said slowly, "but there is something about it which I do not understand. Ever since that morning you have avoided me."

"Nonsense!" I exclaimed.

"It is not nonsense," she answered. "It is the truth. You used to come sometimes to see father — and now you never come near the place. It is — too bad of you," she went on, with a little sob. "I thought that after that morning, and my promising to do what you asked, that we should be greater friends than ever. Instead of that you have never been near us since. And I don't care who knows it. I am miserable."

She was leaning against the arm of my chair. It was clearly my duty to administer the consolation which the situation demanded. I realized, however, that the occasion was critical, and I ignored her proximity.

"Miss Moyat," I said, "I am sorry if asking you to tell that harmless little fib has made you miserable. I simply desired — "

"It isn't altogether that," she interrupted. "You know it isn't."

"You give me credit for greater powers of divination than I possess," I answered calmly. "Your father was always very kind to me, and I can assure you that I have not forgotten it. But I have work to do now, and I have scarcely an hour to spare. Mr. Moyat would understand it, I am sure."

The door was suddenly opened. Mrs. Moyat, fat and comely, came in. She surveyed us both with a friendly and meaning smile, which somehow made my cheeks burn. It was no fault of mine that Blanche had been hanging over my chair.

"Come," she said, "I'm sure I'm very glad to see you once more, Mr. Ducaine. Such a stranger as you are too! But you don't mean to sit in here without a fire all the afternoon, I suppose, Blanche. Tea is just ready in the dining-room. Bring Mr. Ducaine along, Blanche."

I held out my hand.

"I am sorry that I cannot stop, Mrs. Moyat," I said. "Good-afternoon, Miss Moyat."

She looked me in the eyes.

"You are not going," she murmured.

"I am afraid," I answered, "that it is imperative. I ought to have been at Rowchester long ago. We are too near neighbours, though, not to see something of one another again before long."

"Well, I'm sure there's no need to hurry so," Mrs. Moyat declared, backing out of the room. "Blanche, you see if you can't persuade Mr. Ducaine. Father'll be home early this evening, too."

"I think," Blanche said, "that Mr. Ducaine has made up his mind."

She walked with me to the hall door, but she declined to shake hands with me. Her appearance was little short of tragic. I think that at another time I might have been amused, for never in my life had I spoken more than a few courteous words to the girl. But my nerves were all on edge, and I took her seriously. I walked down the street, leaving her standing in the threshold with the door open as though anxious to give me a chance to return if I would. I looked back at the corner, and waved my hand. There was something almost threatening in the grim irresponsive figure, standing watching me, and making no pretence at returning my farewell — watching me with steady eyes and close-drawn brows.

CHAPTER XXIII
MOSTYN RAY EXPLAINS

I walked straight to the House, and locked up my papers in the great safe. I had hoped to escape without seeing either Ray or Lady Angela, but as I crossed the hall they issued from the billiard-room. Lady Angela turned towards me eagerly.

"Mr. Ducaine," she exclaimed, "have you seen anything of Lord Blenavon to-day?"

I shook my head.

"I have not seen him for several days, Lady Angela," I answered.

Ray said something to her which I could not hear. She nodded and left us together.

"It seems," he said, "that this amiable young gentleman is more or less in the clutches of our siren friend at Braster Grange. I think that you and I had better go and dig him out."

"Thank you," I answered, "but I had all I wanted of Braster Grange last night."

"Pooh!" he answered lightly, "you are not even scratched. They are clumsy conspirators there. I think that you and I are a match for them. Come along!"

"You must excuse me, Colonel Ray," I said, "but I have no desire to visit Braster Grange, even with you."

Lady Angela, whose crossing the hall had been noiseless, suddenly interposed.

"You are quite right, Mr. Ducaine," she said; "but this is no visit of courtesy, is it? I am sure that my brother would never stay there voluntarily. Something must have happened to him."

"We will go and see," Ray declared. "Come along, Ducaine."

I hesitated, but a glance from Lady Angela settled the matter. For another such I would have walked into hell. Ray and I started off together, and I was not long before I spoke of the things which were in my mind.

"Colonel Ray," I said, "when I saw you this morning you made two statements, both of which were false."

Ray brought out his pipe and began to fill it in leisurely fashion.

"Go on," he said. "What were they?"

"The first was that you had come down from London by the newspaper train this morning, and the second was that you had received your injuries in a hansom cab accident."

His pipe was started, and he puffed out dense volumes of smoke with an air of keen enjoyment.

"Worst of having a woman for your hostess," he remarked, "one can't smoke except a sickly cigarette or two. You should take to a pipe, Ducaine."

"Will you be good enough to explain those two misstatements, Colonel
Ray?"

"Lies, both of them!" he answered, with grim cheerfulness. "Rotten lies, and I hate telling 'em. The hansom cab accident must have sounded a bit thin."

"It did," I assured him.

He removed his pipe from his teeth, and pushed down the tobacco with the end of his finger.

"I came down from town by the same train that you did," he said, "and as for my broken head and smashed arm, you did it yourself."

"I imagined so," I answered. "Perhaps you will admit that you owe me some explanation." He laughed, a deep bass laugh, and looked down at me with a gleam of humour in his black eyes.

"Come," he said, "I think that the boot is on the other leg. My head is exceedingly painful and my leg is very stiff. For a young man of your build you have a most surprising muscle."

"I am to understand, then, that it was you who committed an unprovoked assault upon me—who planned to have me waylaid in that dastardly fashion?"

"Do you think," Ray asked quietly, "that I should be such a damned fool?"

"What am I to think, then, what am I to believe?" I asked, with a sudden anger. "You found me starving, and you gave me employment, but ever since I started my work life has become a huge ugly riddle. Are you my friend or my enemy? I do not know. There is a drama being played out before my very eyes. The figures in it move about me continually, yet I alone am blindfolded. I am trusted to almost an incredible extent. Great issues are confided to me. I have been given such a post as a man might work for a lifetime to secure. Yet where a little confidence would give me zest for my work — would take away this horrible sense of moving always in the darkness — it is withheld from me."

Ray smoked on in silence for several moments.

"Well," he said, "I am not sure that you are altogether unreasonable. But, on the other hand, you must not forget that there is method, and a good deal of it, in the very things of which you complain. There are certain positions in which a man may find himself where a measure of ignorance is a blessed thing. Believe me, that if you understood, your difficulties would increase instead of diminish."

I shrugged my shoulders.

"But between you and me at least, Colonel Ray," I said, "there is a plain issue. You can explain the events of last night to me."

"I will do that," he answered, "since you have asked it. Briefly, then, I parted from you on the steps of my club at a few minutes past nine last night."

"Yes!"

"I saw from the moment we appeared that you were being watched. I saw the man who was loitering on the pavement lean over to hear the address you gave to the cabman, and you were scarcely away before he was following you. But it was only just as he drove by, leaning a little forward in his hansom, that I saw his face. I recognized him for one of that woman's most dangerous confederates, and I knew then that some villainy was on foot. To cut a long story short, I came down unobserved in your train, followed you to Braster Grange, and was only a yard or two behind when this fellow, who acts as the woman's chauffeur, sprang out upon you. I was unfortunately a little two quick to the rescue, and received a smash on the head from your stick. Then you bolted, and I found myself engaged with a pair of them. On the whole I think that they got the worst of it."

"The other one — was Lord Blenavon!" I exclaimed.

"It was."

"Then he is concerned in the plots which are going on against us," I continued. "I felt certain of it. What a blackguard!"

"For his sister's sake," Colonel Ray said softly, "I want to keep him out of it if I can. Therefore I hit him a little harder than was necessary. He should be hors de combat for some time."

"But why didn't you cry out to me?" I said. "I should not have run if I had known that I had an ally there."

"To run was exactly what I wanted you to do," Ray answered. "You had the dispatch-box, and I wanted to see you safe away."

I glanced at his bandaged head and arm.

"I suppose that I ought to apologize to you," I said.

"Under the circumstances," he declared, "we will cry quits."

Then as we walked together in the glittering spring sunshine, this big silent man and I, there came upon me a swift, poignant impulse, the keener perhaps because of the loneliness of my days, to implore him to unravel all the things which lay between us. I wanted the story of that night, of my concern in it, stripped bare. Already my lips were opened, when round the corner of the rough lane by which Braster Grange was approached on this side came a doctor's gig. Ray shaded his eyes and gazed at its occupant.

"Is this Bouriggs, Ducaine?" he asked, "the man who shot with us?"

"It is Dr. Bouriggs," I answered.

Ray stopped the gig and exchanged greetings with the big sandy-haired man, who held a rein in each hand as though he were driving a market wagon. They chatted for a moment or two, idly enough, as it seemed to me.

"Any one ill at the Grange, doctor?" Ray asked at length.

The doctor looked at him curiously.

"I have just come from there," he answered. "There is nothing very seriously wrong."

"Can you tell me if Lord Blenavon is there?" Ray asked.

The doctor hesitated.

"It was hinted to me, Colonel Ray," he said, "that my visit to the Grange was not to be spoken of. You will understand, of course, that the etiquette of our profession —"

"Quite right," Ray interrupted. "The fact is, Lady Angela is very anxious about her brother, who did not return to Rowchester last night, and she has sent us out as a search party. Of course, if you were able to help us she would be very gratified."

The doctor hesitated.

"The Duke and, in fact, all the family have always been exceedingly kind to me," he remarked, looking straight between his horse's ears. "Under the circumstances you mention, if you were to assert that Lord Blenavon was at Braster Grange I do not think that I should contradict you."

Ray smiled.

"Thank you, doctor," he said. "Good morning."

The doctor drove on, and we pursued our way.

"It was a very dark night," Ray said, half to himself, "but if Blenavon was the man I hit he ought to have a cracked skull."

After all, our interrogation of the doctor was quite unnecessary. We were admitted at once to the Grange by a neatly-dressed parlour-maid. Mrs. Smith-Lessing was at home, and the girl did not for a moment seem to doubt her mistress's willingness to receive us. As she busied herself poking the fire and opening wider the thick curtains, Ray asked her another question.

"Do you know if Lord Blenavon is here?"

"Yes, sir," the girl answered promptly. "He was brought in last night rather badly hurt, but he is much better this morning. I will let Mrs. Smith-Lessing know that you are here, sir."

She hurried out, with the rustle of stiff starch and the quick light-footedness of the well-trained servant. Ray and I exchanged glances.

"After all, this is not such a home of mystery as we expected," I remarked.

"Apparently not," he answered. "The little woman is playing a bold game."

Then Mrs. Smith-Lessing came in.

CHAPTER XXIV
LORD BLENAVON'S SURRENDER

She came in very quietly, a little pale and wan in this cold evening light. She held out her hand to me with a subdued but charming smile of welcome.

"I am so glad that you have come to see me," she said softly. "You can help me, too, about this unfortunate young man who has been thrown upon my hands. I—"

Then she saw Ray, and the words seemed to die away upon her lips. I had to steel my heart against her to shut out the pity which I could scarcely help feeling. She was white to the lips. She stood as one turned to stone, with her distended eyes fixed upon him. It was like a trapped bird, watching its impending fate. She faltered a little on her feet, and—I could not help it—I hurried to her side with a chair. As she sank into it she thanked me with a very plaintive smile.

"Thank you," she said, simply. "I am not very strong, and I did not know that man was with you."

Ray broke in. His voice sounded harsh, his manner, I thought, was unnecessarily brutal.

"I can understand," he said, "that you find my presence a little unwelcome. I need scarcely say that this is not a visit of courtesy. You know very well that willingly I would never spend a moment under the same roof as you. I am here to speak a few plain words, to which you will do well to listen."

She raised her eyes to his. Her courage seemed to be returning at the note of battle in his tone. Her small, well-shaped head was thrown back. The hands which grasped the sides of her chair ceased to tremble.

"Go on," she said.

"We will not play at cheap diplomacy," he said, sneeringly. "I know you by a dozen names, which you alter and adopt to suit the occasion. You are a creature of the French police, one of those parasitical creatures who live by sucking the honesty out of simpler persons. You are here because the more private meetings of the English Council of Defence are being held at Rowchester. It is your object by bribery, or theft, or robbery, or the seductive use of those wonderful charms of yours, to gain possession of copies of any particulars whatever about the English autumn manoeuvres, which, curiously enough, have been arranged as a sort of addendum to those on your side of the Channel. You have an ally, I regret to say, in the Duke's son, you are seeking to gain for yourself a far more valuable one in the person of this boy. You say to yourself, no doubt, Like father, like son. You ruined and disgraced the one. You think, perhaps, the other will be as easy."

"Stop!" she cried.

He looked at her curiously. Her face was drawn with pain. In her eyes was the look of a being stricken to death.

"It is terrible!" she murmured, "that men so coarse and brutal as you should have the gift of speech. I do not wish to ask for any mercy from you, but if I am to stay here and listen, you will speak only of facts."

He shrugged his shoulders contemptuously.

"You should be hardened by this time," he said, "but I forgot that we had an audience. It is always worth while to play a little to the gallery, isn't it? Well, facts, then. The boy is warned against you, and from to-day this house is watched by picked detectives. Blenavon can avail you nothing, for he knows nothing. Such clumsy schemes as last night's are foredoomed to failure, and will only get you into trouble. You will waste your time here. Take my advice, and go!"

She rose to her feet. Smaller and frailer than ever she seemed, as she stood before Ray, dark and massive.

"Your story is plausible," she said coldly. "It may even be true. But, apart from that, I had another and a greater reason for coming to England, for coming to Braster. I came to seek my husband — the father of this boy. I am even now in search of him."

I held my breath and gazed at Ray. For the moment it seemed as though the tables were turned. No signs of emotion were present in his face, but he seemed to have no words. He simply looked at her.

"He left me in January," she continued, "determined at least to have speech with his son. He heard then for the first time of the absconding trustee. He came to England, if not to implore his son's forgiveness, at least to place him above want. And in this country he has never been heard of. He has disappeared. I am here to find him. Perhaps," she added, leaning a little over towards Ray, and in a slightly altered tone, "perhaps you can help me?"

Again it seemed to me that Ray was troubled by a certain speechlessness. When at last he found words, they and his tone were alike harsh, almost violent.

"Do you think," he said, "that I would stretch out the little finger of my hand to help you or him? You know very well that I would not. The pair of you, in my opinion, were long since outside the pale of consideration from any living being. If he is lost, so much the better. If he is dead, so much the better still."

"It is because I know how you feel towards him," she said, slowly, "that I wondered — yes, I wondered!"

"Well?"

"Whether you could not, if you chose, solve for me the mystery of his disappearance."

There was as much as a dozen seconds or so of tense silence between them. She never once flinched. The cold question of her eyes seemed to burn its way into the man's composure. A fierce exclamation broke from his lips.

"If he were dead," he said, "and if it were my hand which had removed him, I should count it amongst the best actions of my life."

She looked at him curiously — as one might regard a wild beast.

"You can speak like this before his son?"

"I veil my words at no time and for no man," he answered. "The truth is always best."

Then the door opened, and Blenavon entered. His arm and head were bandaged, and he walked with a limp. He was deathly pale, and apparently very nervous. He attempted a casual greeting with Ray, but it was a poor pretence. Ray, for his part, had evidently no mind to beat about the bush.

"Lord Blenavon," he said, "this house is no fit place for your father's son. I have warned you before, but the time for advice is past. Your hostess here is a creature of the French police, and her business here is to suborn you and others whom she can buy or cajole into a treasonable breach of confidence. It is very possible that you know all this, and more. But I appeal to you as an Englishman and the representative of a great English family. Are you willing to leave at once with us and to depart altogether from this part of the country, or will you face the consequences?"

Blenavon was a coward. He shook and stammered. He was not even master of his voice.

"I do not understand you," he faltered. "You have no right to speak to me like this."

"Right or no right, I do," Ray answered. "If you refuse I shall not spare you. Last night was only one incident of many. I break my faith as a soldier by giving you this opportunity. Will you come?"

"I am waiting now for a carriage," Blenavon answered. "I have sent to the house for one."

"You will not return to the house," Ray said shortly. "You will leave here for the station, the station for London, and London for the Continent. You do this, and I hold my peace. You refuse, and I see Lord Chelsford and your father to-night."

From the first I knew that he would yield, but he did it with an ill grace.

"I don't see why I should go," he said, sulkily.

"Either you and I together, or I alone, are going to catch the six o'clock train to London," Ray said. "If I go alone you will be an exile from England for the rest of your life, your name will be removed from every club to which you belong, and you will have brought irreparable disgrace upon your family. The choice is yours."

Blenavon turned towards the woman as though for aid. But she stood with her back to him, pale and with a thin scornful smile upon her lips.

"The choice," Ray repeated, glancing at his watch, "is yours, but the time is short."

"I will go," Blenavon said. "I was off in a day or two, anyway. Of what you suspect me I don't know, and I don't care. But I will go."

Ray put his watch into his pocket. He turned to Mrs. Smith-Lessing.

"Better come too," he said quietly. "You have no more chance here. Every one knows now who and what you are."

She looked at him with white expressionless face.

"It does not suit me to leave the neighbourhood at present," she said calmly.

If she had been a man Ray would have struck her. I could see his white teeth clenched fiercely together.

"It does not suit me," he said, in a low tone vibrate with suppressed passion, "to have you here. You are a plague spot upon the place. You have been a plague spot all your life. Whatever you touch you corrupt."

She shrank away for a moment. After all, she was a woman, and I hated Ray for his brutality.

"What a butcher you are!" she said, looking at him curiously. "If ever you should marry — God help the woman."

"There are women and women," he answered roughly. "As for you, you do not count in the sex at all."

She turned away from him with a little shudder, and for the first time during the interview she hid her face in her hands. It was all I could do to avoid speech.

"Come," he said, "do you agree? Will you leave this place? I promise you that your schemes here at any rate are at an end."

She turned to me. Perhaps something in my face had spoken the sympathy which I could not wholly suppress.

"Guy," she said, "I want to be rid of this man, because every word he speaks — hurts. But I cannot even look at him any more. At this war of words he has won. I am beaten. I admit it. I am crushed. I am not going away. I spoke truthfully when I said that I came to England in search of your father. We may both of us be the creatures that man would have you believe, but we have been husband and wife for eighteen years, and it is my duty to find out what has become of him. Therefore I stay."

I could see Ray's black eyes flashing. He almost gripped my arm as he drew me away. We three left the house together. At the bottom of the drive we met a carriage sent down from Rowchester. Ray stopped it.

"Blenavon and I will take this carriage to the station," he said. "Will you, Ducaine, return to Lady Angela and tell her exactly what has happened?"

"Oh, come, I'm not going to have that," Blenavon exclaimed.

"It will not be unexpected news," Ray said sternly. "Your sister suspects already."

"I'm not going to be bundled away and leave you to concoct any precious story you think fit," Blenavon declared, doggedly. "I—"

Ray opened the carriage door and gripped Blenavon's arm. "Get in," he said in a low, suppressed tone. There was something almost animal in the fury of Ray's voice. I looked away with a shudder. Blenavon stepped quietly into the carriage. Then Ray came over to me, and as he looked searchingly into my face, he pointed up the carriage drive.

"Boy," he said, "you are young, and in hell itself there cannot be many such as she. You think me brutal. It is because I remember— your mother!"

He stepped into the carriage. I turned round and set out for Rowchester.

CHAPTER XXV
MY SECRET

There followed for me another three days of unremitting work. Then midway through one morning I threw my pen from me with a great sense of relief. They might come or send for me when they chose. I had finished. My eyes were hot and my brain weary. Instinctively I threw open my front door, and it seemed to me that the sun and the wind and the birds were calling.

So I walked northwards down on the beach, across the grass-sprinkled sandhills and the mud-bottomed marshes. I walked with my cap stuffed in my pocket, my head bared to the freshening wind, and all the way I met no living creature. As I walked, my thoughts, which had been concentrated for these last few days upon my work, went back to that terrible half-hour at Braster Grange. I thought of Ray. I realized now that for days past I had been striving not to think of him. The man's sheer brutality appalled me. I believed in him now wholly, I believed at least in his honesty, his vigorous and trenchant loyalty. But the ways of the man were surely brutal to torture even vermin caught in the trap, and that woman, adventuress though she might be, had flinched before him in agony, as though her very nerves were being hacked out of her body. And Blenavon, too! Surely he might have remembered that he was her brother. He might have helped him to retain just a portion of his self-respect. Was he as severe on every measure of wrong-doing? I fancied to myself the meeting on that lonely road between the poor white-faced creature who had looked in upon my window, and this strong merciless man. Warmed with exercise as I was, I shivered. Ray reminded me of those grim figures of the Old Testament. An eye for an eye, a life for a life, were precepts with him indeed. He was as inexorable as Fate itself. I feared him, and I knew why. I feared him when I thought of Angela, almost over-sensitive, so delicate a flower to be held in his strong, merciless grasp. I walked faster and faster, for thoughts were crowding in upon me. Such a tangled web, such bitter sweetness as they held for me. These were the thoughts which in those days it was the struggle of my life to keep from coming to fruition. I knew very well that, if once I gave way to them, flight alone could save me. For the love of her was in my nerves, in every beat of my pulse, a wild and beautiful dream, against which I was fighting always a hopeless battle.

Far away, coming towards me along the sands, I saw her. I stopped short. For a moment my heart was hot with joy, then I looked wildly around, thinking of flight. It was not possible. Already she had seen me. She waved her hand and increased her pace, walking with the swift effortless grace of her beautiful young limbs, her head thrown back, a welcoming smile already parting her lips. I set my teeth and prepared myself for the meeting. Afterwards would come the pain, but for the present the joy of seeing her, of being with her, was everything! I hastened forward.

"I could not stay indoors," she said, as she turned by my side, "although I have an old aunt and some very uninteresting visitors to entertain. Besides, I have news! My father is coming down to-day, and I think some of the others. We have just had a telegram."

"I am glad," I answered. "I have just finished my work, and I want some more."

"You are insatiable," she declared, smiling. "You have written for three days, days and nights too, I believe, and you look like a ghost. You ought to take a rest now. You ought to want one, at any rate."

Then the smile faded from her lips, and the anxiety of a sudden thought possessed her.

"I have not heard a word from Colonel Ray," she said. "It terrifies me to think that he may have told my father about Blenavon."

"You must insist upon it that he does not," I declared. "Your brother has left England, has he not?"

"He is at Ostend."

"Then Colonel Ray will keep his word," I assured her. "Besides, you have written to him, have you not?"

"I have written," she answered. "Still, I am afraid. He will do what he thinks right, whatever it may be."

"He will respect your wishes," I said.

She smiled a little bitterly.

"He is not an easy person to influence," she murmured. "I doubt whether my wishes, even my prayers, would weigh with him a particle against his own judgment. And he is severe — very severe."

I said nothing, and we walked for some time in silence.

"Next week," she said abruptly, "I must go back to London."

It was too sudden! I could not keep back the little exclamation of despair. She walked for some time with her head turned away from me, as though something on the dark clear horizon across the waters had fascinated her, but I caught a glimpse of her face, and I knew that my secret had escaped me. Whether I was glad or sorry I could not tell. My thoughts were all in hopeless confusions. When she spoke, there was a certain reserve in her tone. I knew that things would never again be exactly the same between us. Yet she was not angry! I hugged that thought to myself. She was startled and serious, but she was not angry.

"One season is very much like another," she said, "but it is not possible to absent oneself altogether. Then afterwards there is Cowes and Homburg, and I always have a plan for at least three weeks in Scotland. I believe we shall close Rowchester altogether."

"The Duke?" I asked.

"He never spends the summer here," she answered. "We are generally together after July, so perhaps," she added, "you may have to endure more of my company than you think."

She looked at me with a faint, provoking smile. How dare she? I was master of myself now, and I answered her coldly.

"I shall be very sorry to leave here," I said. "I hope if my work lasts so long that I shall be able to go on with it at the 'Brand.'"

She made no answer to that, but in a moment or two she turned and looked at me thoughtfully.

"You are rather a surprising person," she remarked, "in many ways. And you certainly have strange tastes."

"Is it a strange taste to love this place?" I asked.

"Of course not. But, on the other hand, it is strange that you should be content to remain here indefinitely. Solitude is all very well at times, but at your age I think that the vigorous life of a great city should have many attractions for you. Life here, after all, must become something of an abstraction."

"It contents me," I declared shortly.

"Then I am not sure that you are in an altogether healthy frame of mind," she answered, coolly. "Have you no ambitions?"

"Such as I have," I muttered, "are hopeless. They were built on sand — and they have fallen."

"Then reconstruct them," she said. "You are far too young to speak with such a note of finality."

"Some day," I answered, "I suppose I shall. At present I am content to live on, amongst the fragments. One needs only imagination. The things one dreams about are always more beautiful and perhaps more satisfying than the things one does."

Again our eyes met, and I fancied that this time she was looking a little frightened. At any rate she knew. I was sure of that.

"What an ineffective sort of proceeding!" she murmured.

A creek separated us for a few minutes. When we came together again I asked her a question.

"There is something, Lady Angela," I said, "which, if you would forgive the impertinence of it, I should very much like to ask you."

She moved her head slowly, as though giving a tacit consent. But I do not think that she was quite prepared for what I asked her.

"When are you going to marry Colonel Ray?"

She looked at me quickly, almost furtively, and I saw that her cheeks were flushed. There was a look in her eyes, too, which I could not fathom.

"The date is not decided yet," she said. "You know there is some talk of trouble in Egypt, and if so he might have to leave at a moment's notice."

"It will not be, at any rate, before the autumn, then?" I persisted.

"No!"

I drew a little breath of relief. I was reckless whether she heard it or not. Suddenly she paused.

"Who is that?" she asked.

I recognized him at once — a small grey figure, standing on the top of a sandhill a little way off, and regarding us steadily. It was the Duke.

"Your father!" I said.

We quickened our pace. If Lady Angela was in any way discomposed she showed no signs of it. She waved her hand, and the Duke solemnly removed his hat.

"I am so glad that he has come down before the others," she said. "I am longing to have a talk with him. And I don't believe he knows anything about Blenavon. No, he's far too cheerful."

She went straight up to him and passed her arm through his. He greeted me stiffly, but not unkindly.

"I am so glad that you have come," she said. "If I had not heard I should have telegraphed to you. I've seen it in all the papers."

"You approve?" I heard him ask quietly.

"Approve is not the word," she declared eagerly. "It is magnificent."

"I wonder," he asked, "if you realize what it means?"

"It simply doesn't matter," she answered, with a delightful smile. "I can make my own dresses, if you like. Annette is a shocking nuisance to me."

"I am afraid," he remarked, with an odd little smile, "that Blenavon will scarcely regard the matter in the same light."

"Bother Blenavon!" she answered lightly. "I suppose you know that he's gone off abroad somewhere?"

"I had a hurried line from him with information to that effect," the Duke answered. "I think that it would have been more respectful if he had called to see me on his way through London."

I heard her sigh of relief.

"Now, tell me," she begged, "where shall we begin? Cowes, Homburg, town house, or Annette? I'm ready."

The Duke looked at her for a moment as I had never seen him look at any living person.

"You must not exaggerate to yourself the importance of this affair, Angela," he said. "I do not think we need interfere for the present with any existing arrangements."

She took his arm, and they walked on ahead to the clearing in front of my. cottage, talking earnestly together. I had no clue to the meaning of those first few sentences which had passed between them. And needless to say, I now lingered far enough behind to be out of earshot. When they reached the turn in the path they halted and waited for me.

"I am anxious for a few minutes' conversation inside with you, Ducaine," the Duke said. "Angela, you had better perhaps not wait for me."

She nodded her farewell, a brief imperious little gesture, it seemed to me, with very little of kindliness in it. Then the Duke followed me into my sitting-room. I waited anxiously to hear what he had to say.

CHAPTER XXVI
"NOBLESSE OBLIGE"

The Duke selected my most comfortable easy chair and remained silent for several minutes, looking thoughtfully out of the window. Notwithstanding the fresh colour, which he seldom lost, and the trim perfection of his dress, I could see at once that there was a change in him. The lines about his mouth were deeper, his eyes had lost much of their keen brightness. I found myself wondering whether, after all, some suspicion of Lord Blenavon's doings had found its way to him.

"You are well forward with your work, I trust, Mr. Ducaine?" he said at last.

"It is completed, your Grace," I answered.

"The proposed subway fortifications as well as the new battery stations?"

"Yes, your Grace."

"What about the maps?"

"I have done them also to the best of my ability, sir," I answered. "I am not a very expert draughtsman, I am afraid, but these are at least accurate. If you would care to look them over, they are in the library safe."

"And the code word?"

In accordance with our usual custom I scribbled it upon a piece of paper, and held it for a moment before his eyes. Then I carefully destroyed it.

"To-morrow," he said, "perhaps to-night, we have some railway men coming down to thoroughly discuss the most efficient method of moving troops from Aldershot and London to different points, and to inaugurate a fresh system. You had better hold yourself in readiness to come up to the house at any moment. They are business men, and their time is valuable. They will probably want to work from the moment of their arrival until they go."

"Very good, your Grace," I answered.

He turned his head and looked at me for a moment reflectively.

"You remember our conversation at the War Office, Mr. Ducaine?"

"Yes, your Grace."

"I do not wish you to have a false impression as to my meaning at that time," he said coldly. "I do not, I have never, doubted your trustworthiness. My feeling was, and is, that you are somewhat young and of an impetuous disposition for a post of such importance. That feeling was increased, of course, by the fact that I considered your story with reference to the Prince of Malors improbable to the last degree. In justice to you," he continued more slowly, "I must now admit the possibility that your description of that incident may after all be in accordance with the facts. Certain facts have come to my knowledge which tend somewhat in that direction. I shall consider it a favour, therefore, if you will consider my remarks at that interview retracted."

"I thank your Grace very much," I answered.

"With reference to the other matter," he continued, "there my opinion remains unaltered. I do not believe that the papers in the safe were touched after you yourself deposited them there, and I consider your statement to the contrary a most unfortunate one. But the fact remains that you have done your work faithfully, and the Council is satisfied with your services. That being so, you may rely upon it that any feeling I may have in the matter I shall keep to myself."

I would have expressed my gratitude to him, but he checked me.

"There is," he said, "one other, a more personal matter, concerning which I desired a few words with you. I have had a visit from a relative of yours who is also an old friend of my own. I refer to Sir Michael Trogoldy."

I looked at him in amazement. I was, in fact, so surprised that I said nothing at all.

"Sir Michael, it seems, has been making inquiries about you, and learned of your present position," the Duke continued. "He asked me certain questions which I was glad to be able to answer on your behalf. He also entrusted me with a note, which I have here in my pocket."

He produced it and laid it upon the table. I made no movement to take it.

"The details of your family history," the Duke said, "are unknown to me. But if the advice of an old man is in any way acceptable to you, I should strongly recommend you to accept any offer of friendship which Sir Michael may make. He is an old man, and he is possessed of considerable wealth. Further, I gather that you are his nearest relative."

"Sir Michael was very cruel to my mother, sir," I said slowly.

"You have nothing to gain by the harbouring of ancient grievances," the Duke replied. "I have always known Sir Michael as a just if a somewhat stern man. Please, however, do not look upon me in any way as a would-be mediator. My interest in this matter ceases with the delivery of that letter."

The Duke rose to his feet. I followed him to the door.

"In any case, sir," I said, "I am very much obliged to you for your advice and for bringing me this letter."

"By-the-bye," the Duke said, pausing on the threshold, "I fear that we may lose the help of Colonel Ray upon the Council. There are rumours of serious trouble in the Soudan, and if these are in any way substantiated, he will be certainly sent there. Good afternoon, Mr. Ducaine."—

"Good afternoon, your Grace."

So he left me, stiff, formal, having satisfied his conscience, though I felt in my heart that his opinion of me, once formed, was not likely to be changed. Directly I was alone I opened my uncle's letter.

"**127, GROSVENOR SQUARE,**

"**LONDON, W.**

"DEAR Guy,—

"It has been on my mind more than once during the last few years—ever since, in fact, I heard of you at college—to write· and inform myself as to your prospects in life. You are the son of my only sister, although I regret to say that you are the son also of a man who disgraced himself and his profession. You have a claim upon me which you have made no effort to press. Perhaps I do not think the worse of you for that. In any case, I wish you to accept an allowance of which my lawyers will advise you, and if you will call upon me when you are in town I shall be glad to make your acquaintance. I may say that it was a pleasure to me to learn that you have succeeded in obtaining a responsible and honourable post.

"I am, yours sincerely,

"MICHAEL TROGOLDY."

I took pen and paper, and answered this letter at once.

"My DEAR SIR MICHAEL, —

"As I am your nephew, and I understand, almost your nearest relative, I see no reason why I should not accept the allowance which you are good enough to offer me. I shall also be glad to come and see you next time I am in London, if it is your wish.

"Yours sincerely,

"GUY DUCAINE."

Grooton brought in my tea, also a London morning paper which he had secured in the village.

"I thought that you might be interested in the news about the Duke, sir," he said respectfully.

"What news, Grooton?" I asked, stretching out my hand for the paper.

"You will find a leading article on the second page, sir, and another in the money news. It reads quite extraordinary, sir."

I opened the paper eagerly. I read every word of the leading article, which was entitled "Noblesse Oblige," and all the paragraphs in the money column. What I read did not surprise me in the least when once I had read the circumstances. It was just what I should have expected from the Duke. It seemed that he had lent his name to the prospectus of a company formed for the purpose of working some worthless patent designed to revolutionize the silk weaving trade. The Duke's reason for going on the Board was purely philanthropic. He had hoped to restore an ancient industry in a decaying neighbourhood. The whole thing turned out to be a swindle. One angry shareholder stated plainly at the meeting that he had taken his shares on account of the Duke's name upon the prospectus, and hinted ugly things. The

Duke had risen calmly in his place. He assured them that he fully recognized his responsibilities in the matter. If the person who had last spoken was in earnest when he stated that the Duke's name had induced him to take shares in this company, then he was prepared to relieve him of those shares at the price which he had paid for them. Further, if there was any other persons who were able honestly to say that the name of the Duke of Rowchester upon the prospectus had induced them to invest their money in this concern, his offer extended also to them.

There were roars of applause, wild enthusiasm. It was magnificent, but the lowest estimate of what it would cost the Duke was a hundred thousand pounds.

I put down the paper, and my cheeks were flushed with enthusiasm. I think that if the Duke had been there at that moment I could have kissed his hand. I passed with much less interest to the letter which Grooton had brought in with the paper. It was from a firm of solicitors in Lincoln's Inn, and it informed me, in a few precise sentences, that they had the authority of their client, Sir Michael Trogoldy, to pay me yearly the sum of five hundred pounds.

CHAPTER XXVII
FRIEND OR ENEMY?

There came no summons from Rowchester, and I dined alone. I must have dozed over my after-dinner cigarette, for at first that soft rapping seemed to come to me from a long way off. Then I sat up in my chair with a start. My cigarette had burnt out, my coffee was cold. I had been asleep, and outside some one was knocking at my' front door.

I had sent Grooton to the village with letters, and I was alone in the place. I sprang from my chair just as the handle of the door was turned and a woman stepped quietly in. She was wrapped from head to foot in a long cloak, and she was thickly veiled. But I knew her at once. It was Mrs. Smith-Lessing.

My first impulse was one of anger. It seemed to me that she was taking advantage of the sympathy which Ray's brutality during our last interview had forced from me. I spoke to her coldly, almost angrily.

"Mrs. Smith-Lessing," I said, "I regret that I cannot receive you here. My position just now does not allow me to receive visitors."

She simply raised her veil and sank into the nearest chair. I was staggered when I saw her face. It was positively haggard, and her eyes were burning. She looked at me almost with horror.

"I had to come," she said. "I could not keep away a moment longer. Tell me the truth, Guy Ducaine. The truth, mind!" she repeated, fearfully.

"What do you mean?" I asked, bewildered. "I do not understand you."

"Tell me the truth about that man who came to see you on the seventh of January."

I shook my head.

"I have nothing to tell you," I said firmly. "When I found him on the marshes he was dead. I did not hear till afterwards that he had ever asked for me."

"This is the truth?" she asked eagerly.

"It is the truth!" I answered.

I could see the relief shine in her face. She was still anxious, however.

"Is it true," she asked, "that you told a girl in the village, Blanche Moyat, to keep secret the fact that this man inquired in the village for the way to your cottage?"

"That also is true," I admitted. "She did not tell me until afterwards, and I saw no purpose in publishing the fact that the man had been on his way to see me."

"You have been very foolish," she said. "You have quarrelled with the girl. She is telling this against you, and there will be trouble."

"I cannot help it," I answered. "I never spoke to the man. I saw nothing of him until I found him dead."

"Guy!" she cried, "this is an awful thing. I am not sure, but I believe that the man was your father!"

As often as the thought had comae to me I had thrust it away. This time, however, there was no escape. The whole hideous scene spread itself out again before my eyes. I saw the doubled-up body, limp and nerveless. I felt again the thrill of horror with which one looks for the first time on death. The mockery of the sunlight filling the air, gleaming far and wide upon the creek-riven marshes and wet sands, the singing of the birds, the slow tramp of the wagon horses. All these things went to fill up that one terrible picture. I looked at the woman opposite to me, and in her face was some reflection of the horror which I as surely felt.

"For your sake," she murmured, "we must find out how he met with his death."

"The verdict was Found drowned," I murmured.

"People will change their opinion now," she answered. "Besides, you and
I know that he was not drowned."

"You are sure of that?" I asked.

"Quite," she answered. "He had letters with him, I know, and papers for you. Besides, he carried always with him a number of trifles by which he could have been identified. When he was searched at the police station his pockets were empty. He had been robbed. Guy, he had, as I have had, one unflinching, relentless enemy. Tell me, was Colonel Ray in Braster at the time?"

"No," I answered hoarsely. "I cannot tell you. I will have no more to do with it. The matter is over — let it rest,"

"But, my poor boy," she said quietly, "it will not be allowed to rest. Can't you see that this girl's statement does away with the theory that he was washed up from the sea? He met with his death there on the sands. He left Braster to visit you, and he was found within a few yards of your cottage dead, and with marks of violence upon him. You will be suspected, perhaps charged. It is inevitable. Now tell me the truth. Was Mostyn Ray in Braster at the time?"

"He lectured that night in the village," I answered.

Her eyes gleamed with a strange fire.

"I knew it!" she exclaimed. "I have him at last, then. I saw him falter when I spoke of your father. Guy, I will save you, but I would give the rest of my days to bring this home to Mostyn Ray."

I shook my head.

"You will never do it," I declared. "There might be suspicion, but there will never be any proof. If there was any murder done at all, it was done without witnesses."

"We shall see about that," she muttered. "There is what you call circumstantial evidence. It has hanged people before now."

We remained silent for several moments. All this time she was watching me.

"Guy," she said softly, "you are very like what he was — at your age."

Her cloak had fallen back. She was wearing a black evening gown with a string of pearls around her neck. The excitement had given her a faint colour, and something like tears softened her eyes as she looked across at me. But the more I looked at her the more anxious I was to see her no more. Her words reminded me of the past.

I remembered that it was she who had been my father's evil genius, she who had brought this terrible disgrace upon him, and this cloud over my own life. I rose to my feet.

"I do not wish to ask for any favours from you," I said, "but I will ask you to remember that if you are seen here I shall certainly lose my post."

"What does it matter?" she answered contemptuously. "I am not a rich woman, Guy, but I know how to earn money. Mostyn Ray would not believe it, perhaps, but I loved your father. Yours has been a miserable little life. Come with me, and I promise that I will show you how to make it great. You have no relatives or any ties. I promise you that I will be a model stepmother."

I looked at her, bewildered.

"It is not possible for me to do anything of the sort," I told her. "I do not wish to seem unkind, but nothing in this world would induce me to consider such a thing for a moment. I have chosen my life and the manner of it. Do you think that I can ever forget that you and my father between you broke my mother's heart, and made it necessary for me to be brought up without friends, ashamed of my name and of my history? One does not forget these things. I bear you no ill will, but I wish that you would go away."

She sat there quite quietly, listening to me.

"Guy," she said, when I had finished, "all that you speak of happened many years ago. There is forgiveness for everybody, isn't there? You and I are almost alone in the world. I want to be your friend. You might find me a more powerful one than you think. Try me! I will make your future mine. You shall have your own way in all things. I know the hills and the valleys of life, the underneath and the matchless places. If you accept my offer you will never regret it. I can be a faithful friend or a relentless enemy. Between you and me, Guy, there can be no middle course. I want to be your friend. Don't make me your enemy."

The woman puzzled me. She had every appearance of being in earnest.
Yet the things which she proposed were absurd.

"This is folly," I answered her. "I cannot count it anything else. Do you suppose that I want to creep through life at a woman's apron-strings? I am old enough, and strong enough, I hope, to think and act for myself. My career is my own, to make or to mar. I do not wish for enmity from any one, but your friendship I cannot accept. Our ways lie apart—a long way apart."

"Do not be too sure of that," she said quietly. "I think that you and I may come together again very soon, and it is possible that you may need my help."

"All that I need now," I answered impatiently, "is your absence."

She rose at once from her chair.

"Very well," she said, "I will go. Only let me warn you that I am a persistent woman. I think that it will not be very long before you will see things differently. Will you shake hands with me, Guy?"

Her small white fingers came hesitatingly out from under her cloak. I did not stop to think to what my action might commit me, whether indeed it was seemly that I should accept any measure of friendship from this woman. I took her hand and held it for a moment in mine.

"You cannot go back alone," I said, doubtfully, as I opened the door.

"I have a servant waiting close by," she answered, "and I am not at all afraid. Think over what I have said to you—and good-bye."

She drew her cloak around her and flitted away into the darkness.

CHAPTER XXVIII
A WOMAN'S TONGUE

Grooton returned a few minutes later from the village. He begged the favour of a few words with me. He was a man of impassive features and singular quietness of demeanour. Yet it was obvious that something had happened to disturb him.

"I think it only right, sir, that you should know of the reports which are circulating in the neighbourhood," he said, fixing his dark grave eyes respectfully upon me. "I called for a few minutes at the inn, and made it my business to listen."

"Do these reports concern me, Grooton?" I asked.

"They do, sir."

"Go ahead, then," I told him.

"They refer also, sir," he said, "to the man who was found dead near the cottage where you used to live in January last. He was supposed to have been washed up from the sea, but it has recently been stated that he was seen, on the evening of the day before his body was found, in the village, and it is also stated that he inquired from a certain person as to the whereabouts of your cottage. He set out with the intention of calling upon you, and he was found dead in the morning by you, sir, within a hundred yards of where you were living."

"Anything else, Grooton?"

"There is a lot of foolish talk, sir. He is said to have been a relative of yours with whom you were not on good terms, and the young lady who has just given this information to the police through her father states that she has remained silent up to now at your request."

"I am supposed, then," I said, "to be concerned in this fellow's death?"

"I have heard that opinion openly expressed, sir," Grooton assented, respectfully.

I nodded.

"Thank you, Grooton," I said. "I shall be prepared then for anything that may happen. If you hear anything further let me know."

"I shall not fail to do so, sir," he answered.

He bowed and withdrew. Then as I lit my pipe and resumed my seat it suddenly occurred to me that the man who was chiefly concerned in this matter should at least be warned. I sat down at my desk and wrote to Ray. I had scarcely finished when I heard footsteps outside, followed by an imperious knocking at my front door. I opened it at once. The Duke and Lady Angela entered. I saw at once from her disturbed expression that something had happened.

The Duke wore a long cape over his dinner clothes, and he had evidently walked fast. He looked at me sharply as I rose to my feet.

"Mr. Ducaine," he said, "I have come to ask you to explain the sudden departure of my son for abroad."

I was taken aback, and I dare say I showed it.

"I have already told Lady Angela — all that I know," I said.

"My daughter's story," the Duke answered, "is incoherent. It tells me only enough to make me sure that something is being concealed."

I glanced at Lady Angela. She was looking white and troubled.

"I have told my father," she said, "all that I know."

"Then I must discover the rest for myself," the Duke replied. "I know that Blenavon is uncertain and unstable to a degree. When I heard that he had left for the Continent, I was not particularly surprised or interested. I have only just discovered the manner of his leaving. It puts an entirely different complexion upon the affair. I understand that he left with Colonel Ray without luggage or explanations of any sort. His own servant had no warning, and was left behind. My daughter informs me that such information as she has she gained from you. I require you to supplement it."

"I am afraid that the only person who can enlighten you further, sir, is Colonel Ray," I answered. "I understood you to say, I believe, that he would be here shortly."

"I insist upon it," the Duke said sternly, "that you tell me what you know at once and without further prevarication."

I was in a dilemma from which there seemed to be no escape. Lady Angela had seated herself in my easy chair and was keeping her face averted from me. The Duke stood between us.

"I know very little, sir, except what I overheard," I declared. "Colonel Ray was, I believe, responsible for Lord Blenavon's abrupt departure, and I would rather that your information came from him."

"Colonel Ray is not here, and you are," the Duke answered. "Remember that I am no trifler with words. I have said that I insist. I repeat it!"

There seemed to be no escape for me. Lady Angela remained silent, the Duke was plainly insistent. I did not dare to trifle with him.

"Very good, your Grace," I said, "I will tell you what I know. It dates from last Monday, when you will remember that I was in London to attend a meeting of the Council."

"Go on!"

"I returned here by the last train, bringing with me the notes and instructions taken at that meeting. Outside Braster Grange an attack was made upon me, evidently with the intention of securing these. I escaped, with the assistance of Colonel Ray, who had come down from London by the same train unknown to me."

"Well?"

"The attack was made from the grounds of Braster Grange. It seems that Lord Blenavon spent the night there. The next morning Colonel Ray insisted upon my accompanying him to Braster Grange. Lord Blenavon was still there, and we saw him. He was suffering from wounds such as in the darkness I had inflicted upon my assailant of the night before."

It seemed to me that even then the Duke would not, or could not, understand. His brows were knitted into a heavy frown, and he was evidently following my story with close attention. But exactly where I was going to lead, he seemed to have no idea.

"The tenant of Braster Grange," I continued, "is a Mrs. Smith-Lessing, whom Colonel Ray has told me is a servant of the French secret police. I am afraid that Lord Blenavon has been a good deal under her influence."

Then the Duke blazed out, which was very much what I expected from him. Horror, amazement, and scornful disbelief were all expressed in his transfigured face and angry words.

"Blenavon! My son! The confederate of a French spy! What nonsense! Who dares to suggest such a thing? Angela — I — I beg your pardon."

He stopped short, making an effort to regain his self-control. He continued in a more collected manner, but his voice still shook with inexpressible scorn.

"Angela," he said, turning to her, "is it within your knowledge that Blenavon had any acquaintance with this person?"

I think that her face might well have answered him: very white it was, and very sorrowful.

"Blenavon met Mrs. Smith-Lessing, I believe, at Bordighera," she said.
"I have seen them together several times."

"Here?" the Duke asked sharply.

"Yes, I have seen them riding on the sands, and Blenavon dined there on the night — Mr. Ducaine has been speaking of."

"Blenavon is a fool!" the Duke said. "This is to my mind convincing proof that he was ignorant of the woman's antecedents. At the worst he probably regarded her as an ordinary adventuress. As for the rest, I look upon it as the most extraordinary mare's nest which the mind of man could possibly conceive. Do you mean to tell me, Mr. Ducaine, that Colonel Ray went so far as to charge Blenavon to his face with being in league with this person?"

"He certainly did, sir."

"And Blenavon? Oh, Ray is mad, stark mad!"

"Your son denied it, sir," I answered.

"Denied it! Of course he did. What followed?"

"Colonel Ray was very forcible and very imperative, sir," I answered. "He insisted upon Lord Blenavon leaving England at once."

"Well?"

"Lord Blenavon consented to do so, sir," I said quietly.

I saw the veins in the Duke's forehead stand out like whipcord. He began a sentence and left it unfinished. He was in that condition when words are impotent.

"Can you tell me, Mr. Ducaine," he asked, "what possible argument Colonel Ray could have made use of to induce my son to consent to this extraordinary proceeding?"

"I know no more about the matter, your Grace," I answered. "Perhaps Lord Blenavon felt that his intimacy with Mrs. Smith-Lessing had compromised him — that appearances were against him — "

"Pshaw!" the Duke interrupted. "Blenavon's intrigues are foolish enough, but they are beside the mark.. I want to know what further argument or inducement Colonel Ray used. I understand neither why Ray desired to get rid of my son, nor why my son obeyed his ridiculous request."

"Colonel Ray will doubtless have some further explanation to offer you, sir," I said.

"He had better," the Duke answered grimly. "I shall wire him to come here at once. With your permission, Mr. Ducaine, I will sit down for a moment. This affair has shaken me."

Indeed, as the excitement passed away, I could see that he was looking ill and worn. Lady Angela made him take the easy chair, and he accepted a liqueur glass full of brandy which I poured out. He remained for several minutes sipping it and looking thoughtfully into the fire. He seemed to me to have aged by a dozen years. The brisk alertness of his manner had all departed. He was an old man, limp and querulous.

"This unfortunate affair, Mr. Ducaine," he said, looking up at last, "remains of course between ourselves and Ray — and the woman."

"It is unnecessary for you to ask me that, sir," I answered quietly. "Colonel Ray will doubtless have some explanation. He is a man of vigorous temper, and I fancy that Lord Blenavon was not quite himself."

The Duke rose to his feet.

"If you are ready, Angela," he said, "we will not detain Mr. Ducaine further."

"You will allow me to walk with you to the house, sir," I begged.

He shook his head.

"I am quite recovered, I thank you," he said. "My daughter will give me her arm."

I let them out myself and held the lamp over my head to light them on their way. With slow uncertain steps, and leaning heavily upon Lady Angela's arm, I watched him disappear in the blackness of the plantation.

CHAPTER XXIX
THE LINK IN THE CHAIN

Practically for three days and three nights the Council sat continually. There was no pretence now at recreation, no other guests. We worked, all of us, from the Duke downwards, unflaggingly and with very little respite. When at last the end came, my padlocked notebook, with its hundreds of pages of hieroglyphics, held the principal material for three schemes of coast defence, each one considered separately and supported by a mass of detail as to transport, commissariat, and many minor points.

The principal members of the Council departed by special train early on Monday morning. I myself, a little dizzy and hot-eyed, walked across the park an hour after dawn, and flung myself upon my bed with a deep sigh of relief. Before I had closed my eyes, however, Grooton appeared with apologies for his dishabille.

"I have been up to the house twice, sir," he said, "but they would not let me see you or even send in a message. I thought it only right to let you know at once, sir, that the police have been here rummaging about. They had what they called a search warrant, I believe. I came up to the house immediately, but I could not induce any of the servants to bring word in to you. Mr. Jesson, the Duke's own man, told me that it was as much as his place was worth to allow any one to enter the library."

"All right, Grooton," I muttered. "Hang the police!"

I believe he said something else, but I never heard it. I was already fast asleep.

* * * * *

About mid-day I was awakened by the dazzling sunshine which seemed to fill the room. I called for a bath, dressed, and made an excellent breakfast. Then I brought out my notebook and prepared for work. I had scarcely dipped my pen in the ink, however, when a shadow darkened the window. I looked up quickly. It was Ray.

He entered without knocking, and I saw at once that he was in a strange condition. He scarcely greeted me, but sank into my easy chair, and drawing out his pipe began to fill it. Then I saw, too, what I had never seen before. His fingers were shaking.

"Boy," he said, "have you any wine?"

"The Duke sent me some claret," I answered. "Will that do?"

I summoned Grooton and ordered the wine and some biscuits. Ray was a man who ate and drunk sparingly. Yet he filled a tumbler and drank it straight off.

"You and I," he remarked, "are the only two who sat the whole show out.
It was a grind, wasn't it?"

"It was," I answered, "but I have slept, and I feel none the worse for it. Lord Chelsford carried us on splendidly. There is solid work here," I said; "something worth the planning."

I touched my notebook almost affectionately, for the work was fascinating now that it had attained coherent form. Ray smoked on and said nothing for several minutes. Then he looked up at me.

"Have you a spare bedroom, Ducaine?"

"One or two," I answered. "They are not all furnished, but one at any rate is decent."

"Will you put me up for a day — perhaps two?"

"Of course," I answered, "but —"

He answered my unspoken question.

"The Duke has turned me out," he said grimly. "Who would have suspected the old man of such folly? He believes in Blenavon. I told him the plain truth, and he told me that I was a liar."

"I thought that he would be difficult to convince," I remarked.

"He has all the magnificent pig-headedness of his race," Ray answered. "Blenavon is Blenavon, and he can do no wrong. He would summon him home again, but fortunately the young man himself is no fool. He will not come. You told Lady Angela?"

"Everything."

"She believed you?"

"I think that she did," I answered.

His face softened.

"The Duke showed me from the door himself," he said. "You will not object to my sending a note to Lady Angela by your servant?"

"Make whatever use of him you choose," I answered. "There are pen and ink and notepaper upon the table."

Then I settled down to my work. Ray wrote his note, and went upstairs to sleep. In an hour's time he was down again. There were black rims under his eyes, and I could see at once that he had had no rest. Grooton had brought his bag from the house, and a note from Lady Angela. He read it with unchanging face, and placed it carefully in his breast coat-pocket.

"I am off to the village to send some telegrams," he said, "and afterwards I shall go on for a walk." "What about lunch?" I asked, glancing at the clock. "None for me," he answered. "Some tea at four o'clock, if I may have it. I will be back by then." He swung off, and I was thankful, for my work demanded my whole attention and very careful thought. At a few minutes after four he returned, and Grooton brought us some tea. Directly we were alone Ray looked across at me with a black frown upon his face.

"You know what they are saying in the village about you, young man?"

"I can guess," I answered.

"Who is this girl, Blanche Moyat?"

"A farmer's daughter," I answered. "It seems that I paid her too much or too little, attention, I am not sure which. At any rate, she has an imaginary grievance against me, and this is the result."

"She tells the truth?"

"I have not heard her story," I answered, "but it is true that I encouraged her to suppress the fact that she bad seen the man in the village, and that he had asked for me."

"What folly!"

"Perhaps," I answered. "You see, I thought that a verdict of 'found drowned' would save trouble."

"This accursed woman at the Grange is in it, I know," Ray remarked, slowly filling his pipe. "I wonder if she knew that I was about? That would give her a zest for the job."

"She knows that you were at Braster at the time," I said. "It was the night of your lecture."

Ray began to blow out dense clouds of smoke.

"We're safe," he said thoughtfully, "both of us. There's just a link in the chain missing."

"The police have been here with a warrant in search of that link," I remarked.

"They'll never find it, for it's in my pocket," he remarked grimly.

"Colonel Ray," I said, suddenly nerving myself to risk his anger, "there is a question which I must ask you."

I saw his lips come firmly together. He neither encouraged nor checked me.

"Who was that man?"

"You are better ignorant."

"Was it my father?"

If he did not answer my question, it at least seemed to suggest something to him.

"Has that woman been here?" he asked.

"Yes."

"She believes that it was your father?"

"She does."

He removed his pipe from his teeth and looked at it thoughtfully.

"Ah!" he said.

"You have not answered my question," I reminded him.

"Nor am I going to," he replied coolly. "You know already as much as is good for you."

He rose and threw open the door of my cottage. For several moments he stood bareheaded, looking up towards the house, looking and listening. He glanced at his watch, and walked several times backwards and forwards from the edge of the cliff to my door. Then he came in for his hat and stick.

"I am going down to the sea," he said. "If Lady Angela comes, will you call me? I shall not be out of hearing."

"You are expecting her?" I asked, looking down at my work.

"Yes. It was necessary for me to see her somewhere, so I asked her to come here. Perhaps the Duke has found out and stopped her. Anyhow, call me if she comes."

He stepped outside, and I heard him scrambling down the cliff. I set my teeth and turned to my work. It was a hard thing to have my little room, with its store of memories, turned into a meeting-place for these two. I at least would take care to be far enough away. And then I began wondering whether she would come. I was still wondering when I heard her footsteps.

She came in unaccustomed garb to me. She wore a grey dress of some soft material, and a large black hat with feathers. Her skirts were gathered up in her hand, and I heard the jingling of harness at the corner of the avenue where her carriage was waiting. I opened the door, and she entered with a soft swish of silk and a gentle rustling. The room seemed instantly full of perfume of Neapolitan violets, a great bunch of which were in her bosom.

She looked swiftly around, and I fancied that it was a relief to her to find me alone.

"Is Colonel Ray here?" she asked.

"He is waiting for you," I answered, "on the sands. I promised to call him directly you came."

I moved toward the door, but she checked me with an imperative gesture.

"Wait," she said.

I came slowly back and stood by my table. She was sitting with her hands clasped together, looking into the fire. She looked very girlish and frail.

"I want to think—for a moment," she said. "Everything seems confusion.
My father has commanded me to break my
engagement with Colonel Ray."

I remained silent. What was there, indeed, for me to say?

"In my heart," she went on slowly, "I know that my father is wrong and that Colonel Ray is right. He has simply done his duty. Blenavon was being sorely tempted. He is better away — out of the country. Oh, I am sure of that."

"Colonel Ray has done what he believed to be his duty," I said slowly. "It is hard that he should suffer for that."

"Often," she murmured, "one has to suffer for doing the right thing. My father has made himself a poor man because of his sense of what was right. I do not know what to do."

I glanced out of the window. For many reasons I did not wish to prolong this interview.

"He is waiting," I reminded her.

"I must do one of two things," she murmured. "I must break my faith with my father — or with him."

Then she lifted her eyes to mine.

"Tell me what you think, Mr. Ducaine?" she asked.

I opened my lips to speak, but I could not. Was it fair that she should ask me? My little room was peopled with dreams of her, with delightful but impossible visions. My very nerves were full of the joy of her presence. It was madness to ask for my judgment, when the very poetry of my life was an unreasoning and hopeless love for her.

"I cannot!" I muttered. "You must not ask me."

She seemed surprised. After all, I had guarded my secret well, then?

"You will not refuse to help me," she pleaded.

I set my teeth hard. I longed for Ray, but there were no signs of him.

"Your father has ordered you to break your engagement with Colonel Ray," I said, "but he has done so under a misapprehension of the facts. You owe obedience to your father, but you owe more — to — the man whose wife you have promised to be. I do not think you should give him up."

She listened eagerly. Was it my fancy, or was she indeed a little paler? Her eyes seemed to gleam with a strange softness in the twilight. Her head drooped a a little as she resumed her former thoughtful attitude.

"Thank you," she said, simply. "I believe that you are right."

I caught up a bundle of papers from my desk and stole softly from the room. Ray was close at hand, and I called to him.

"She is in there waiting for you," I said. "I have some transcribed matter, which I am taking up to the safe."

Ray nodded abruptly, and I heard the door of my cottage open and close behind him.

CHAPTER XXX
MOSTYN RAY'S LOVE STORY

In a dark corner of the library, sitting motionless before a small writing-desk, I found the Duke. The table was littered all over with papers, a ledger or two and various documents. I had met Mr. Hulshaw, the agent to the estates, in the drive, so I judged that the two had had business together.

The Duke had not greeted me on my entrance, and he seemed to be asleep in his chair. But at the sound of the electric bell, which announced the opening of the safe, he turned sharply round.

"Is that you, Ducaine?"

"Yes, your Grace," I answered.

"What are you doing there?"

"I have brought up the first batch of copy, sir," I answered.

"You have sealed it properly?"

"With Lord Chelsford's seal, sir," I told him.

He turned round in his chair sharply.

"What's that?" he asked.

"Lord Chelsford gave me an old signet ring before he left, sir," I said, "with a very peculiar design. I wear it attached by a chain to an iron bracelet round my arm."

"Let me see it," the Duke ordered.

I took off my coat, and baring my arm, showed him the ring hanging by a few inches of strong chain from the bracelet. He examined the design curiously.

"How do you detach it?" he asked.

"I cannot detach it, sir," I answered. "The bracelet has a Bramah lock, and Lord Chelsford has the key. He used to wear it many years ago when he was Queen's messenger."

The Duke examined the ring long and searchingly. Then he looked from it into my face.

"You mean to say that you cannot take that off?"

"A locksmith might, sir. I certainly could not."

The Duke shrugged his shoulders.

"Chelsford's methods seem to me to savour a little of opera bouffe," he remarked drily. "For my own part I believe that these marvellous documents would be perfectly safe in the unlocked drawer of my desk. I do not believe any of these stories which come from Paris about copies of our work being in existence. I do not wish you to be careless, of course, but don't overdo your precautions. This place is scarcely so much a nest of conspirators as faddists like Chelsford and Ray would have us believe."

"I am glad to hear that you think so, sir," I answered. "Our precautions do seem a little elaborate, but it is quite certain that the Winchester papers were disturbed."

"I do not choose to believe it, Ducaine," the Duke said irritably. "Kindly remember that!"

"Very good, sir," I answered. "There is nothing else you wish to say to me?"

"There is something else," the Duke answered coldly. "I understand that the police yesterday, on a sworn affidavit, were granted a search warrant to examine your premises for stolen property. What the devil is the meaning of this?"

"I think, sir," I answered, "that the stolen property was a pretext. It seems that during the last few days has come to light that the man whose body I found on the sands was not washed in from the sea, but was a stranger, who had arrived in Braster the previous evening, and had made inquiries as to where I lived. It seems to be the desire of the police, therefore, to connect me in some way with the affair."

The Duke looked at me searchingly.

"I presume," he said, "that they had something in the nature of evidence, or they would scarcely have been able to swear the affidavit for the search warrant."

"They have nothing more direct, sir, than that the body was found close to my cottage, that he had presumably left Braster to see me, and that I was foolish enough to persuade the person, of whom the dead man made these inquiries in Braster, not to come forward at the inquest."

"Stop! Stop!" the Duke said irritably. "You did what?"

"The young woman of whom he inquired was close at hand when I discovered the body of the man," I said. "She told me about him. I was a little upset, and I suggested that there was no necessity for her to disclose the fact of having seen him."

"It was a remarkably foolish thing of you to do," the Duke said.

"I am realizing it now, sir," I answered.

"Did this person call on you at all?" the Duke asked.

"No, sir. You may remember that it was the night of Colonel Ray's lecture. He called to see me on his way back and found me ill. I believe that this person looked in at the window and went away. I saw no more of him alive after this."

"You have some idea, I presume, as to his identity?"

"I have no definite information, your Grace," I answered.

The Duke did not look at me for several moments.

"I am afraid," he said, stiffly, "that you may experience some inconvenience from this most ill-advised attempt of yours to suppress evidence which should most certainly have been given at the inquest. However, I have no doubt that your story is true. I have some inquiries now before me from the police station. I will do what I can for you. Good-evening, Ducaine."

"Good-evening, sir," I answered. "I am much obliged to you."

I walked homewards across the park. The carriage had gone from the private road, and Ray was alone when I entered. It was impossible to tell what had happened from his expression. He sat stretched out in my easy chair, smoking furiously, and his face was impassive. Grooton served us with dinner, and he ate and drank with only a few curt remarks. But afterwards, when I was deep in my work, he suddenly addressed me.

"Boy," he then said, "turn round and listen to me."

I obeyed him at once.

"Listen well," he said, "for I am not given to confidences. Yet I am going to speak to you of the secret places of my life."

I laid down the pen which I had been holding between my fingers, and turned my chair. I judged that it was not necessary for me to speak, nor apparently did he think so.

"I have been soldiering all my days," he said, "since I was a child almost. It is a glorious life. God knows I have never grudged a single month of it. But when one comes back once more to dwell amongst civilians one realizes that there is another side to life. It is so with me. I am not given to doubts or to asking advice from any man. But the time has come when I have the one and need of the other."

He paused, knocked out some ashes from his pipe, and relighted it.

"I have loved two women in my life, Guy," he went on slowly. "The first was your mother."

I started a little, but I still held my peace. He looked hard into the ashes of the fire, and continued.

"I tried my best," he said, "to be a friend to her after her marriage, and I hope, I think, that I succeeded. I even did my best to fight that woman's influence with your father at Gibraltar. There I failed. I was foredoomed to failure! She had the trick of playing what tune she cared to on a man's heartstrings. After it was all over, and your father and she had left the place, I spent years trying to persuade your mother to get a divorce and marry me. But she was the daughter of a Bishop, a High Churchwoman, and a holy woman. She died with your father's name upon her lips."

I shuddered! The words were spoken so deliberately, and yet with such vibrant force.

"After that," Ray continued, "came Egypt, then India, and afterwards Khartoum. I came home before the last war, and I met Lady Angela. I am so little of a woman's man that I suppose the girl whom I thought of at all became like an angel, a creature altogether apart from that sex of whom I know so little. However that may be, she was the second woman to hold any place in my — heart — as she most surely will be the last. Then the war broke out, luck came my way, and I returned with a greater reputation than I deserved. The very night of my return I asked Lady Angela to marry me, and she consented."

He puffed vigorously at his pipe, but he seemed wholly ignorant of the fact that it was out. His face was set in its grimmest lines. He looked steadily at a certain spot in the fire, and went on.

"There are things," he said, "which troubled me little at the time, but which just lately have been on my mind. The first is that I am nearly fifty, and Lady Angela is twenty-one. The second is that I came home with all the tinsel and glamour of a popular hero. Heaven knows I loathed it, but the fact remains. The King's reception, the V.C., and all that sort of thing, I suppose, accounted for it. Anyhow, I am troubled with this reflection. Lady Angela was very young, and I fear that her imagination was touched. She accepted my offer, and she has been very loyal. Until to-night no word of disagreement has passed between us. But there have been times lately when I have fancied that I have noticed a change. A time has come now when I could give her back her freedom without reproach on either side. I want to know whether it is my duty to give it her back."

Then Ray looked straight into my face, and the colour flamed there, for I saw now why he had made me his confidant.

"What do you think, Guy? You are only a boy, but you are of her age, and you have seen a little of her lately. You are only a boy, but then only boys and novelists understand women. Speak up and tell me what is in your mind."

"I will tell you this," I answered hotly. "If I were you, and Lady Angela had promised to be my wife, I would not sit and hatch scruples about marrying her. I would marry her first, and make her happy afterwards, and as for the rest — for the questions which you have asked me, and yet not put into words — I have never heard or seen in Lady Angela the slightest sign that you were not her lover as well as the man whom she was engaged to marry. As for my own folly, since you seem to have noticed it, no one knows better than I that it is the rankest, most absurd presumption. But with me it begins and ends. That is a most absolute and certain fact."

Ray rapped his pipe upon the table.

"Listen," he said. "I found you nameless and practically lost. Yet you have powerful relatives, and your family is equal to the Duke's. There may be money too some day. Bear these things in mind. Can you repeat what you have said?"

It was a wild dream—a wonderful one. But, before me I saw the stern white face of the man, eager for his share of happiness after all these magnificent years of dauntless service. I forgot my own distrust of him, his coldness, his brutality. I remembered only those other and greater things.

"Even were I in such a position," I said, "it would make no difference. I am sure that Lady Angela is loyal. She has no idea—and it is not worth while that she should have."

"You would have me marry her, then?" he asked slowly.

"There is only one thing," I said, taking my courage into my hands.

"And that?" he asked sharply.

"That," I answered, "lies between you and your conscience."

He rose to his feet.

"Wait here," he said, "and I will show you my justification."

CHAPTER XXXI
MY FATHER'S LETTER

I heard Ray's heavy footsteps ascending the stairs to his room. In a few moments he returned, bearing in his hand a letter.

"Guy," he said thoughtfully, "I am a man who is slow to place trust in any one. For that reason, and perhaps because ignorance was better for you, I have told you little of the events of that night. Now my first opinion of you has undergone some modifications. You are stronger than I thought, you have shown faith in me too, or I should not be here practically a guest under your roof to-night. Listen! The man whom you found dead in the marshes was not your father!"

I was not surprised. Always I had doubted it.

"Who was he, then?" I asked calmly.

"When your father went mad at Gibraltar," Ray said, "he needed help. This man, Clery by name, supplied it. When I knew them both he was your father's valet. Since then he has been his confederate in many schemes. Your father on many occasions manifested the remnants of a sense of honour. This creature set himself deliberately and successfully to corrupt it. He was a parasite, a nerveless, bloodless thing without a single human attribute. He and that woman were alike responsible for your father's ruined life."

"Once before," Ray continued, after a moment's pause, "I had told him that if ever we should meet where his life would cost me nothing, I would kill him as I would set my heel upon an adder—and he only smiled as though I had paid him some delicate compliment. And that night, Guy, a hundred yards from your cottage, he sidled up to me in that lonely road, and bade me direct him to the abode of Mr. Guy Ducaine. A moment after he recognized me."

A grim smile parted Ray's lips, but I could not repress a shudder. Invariably at any reference to that awful night the old fear came back.

"He seemed at first paralyzed with fear," Ray continued. "He tried to slip away into the marshes, but I caught him easily, and held him so that he could not escape. He admitted that he had come to find you with a message from your father. He denied at first having a letter, but I searched him until I found it. As you see, it is addressed to you. Nevertheless I struck matches, opened it, and with some difficulty managed to read it. All the time this creature was doubling about like an eel trying to get away. Read the letter."

I drew it from the envelope. It was dated from the Savoy Hotel.

"My DEAR SON, — I do not deserve that you should read beyond these three words. I have as little right to call you my son as you can have desire to claim me for your father. I am here, however, purely on an errand of justice. I have learned that you have been robbed of the sum set aside to give you a start in life. I am here to endeavor to replace it, for which purpose I desire that you will grant me a business interview within the next few days. I beg your reply by Clery, my faithful companion and servant. I am known here as

"RICHARD DREW FOSTER."

I laid the letter down without remark. Ray had filled his pipe whilst I had been reading, and was sitting now on the arm of his easy chair, facing me.

"I understood the letter and its meaning," he continued. "I knew that the whole neighbourhood was under the observation of the French Secret Service, and the man who signed himself Richard Drew Foster saw in you an excellent tool ready to his hand. It is very certain also that the matter would probably have presented itself to you in a wholly different light. Accordingly, I placed the letter in my own pocket, and I released my hold of Clery.

"'You can go back to your master,' I said, 'and tell him that you have seen me, and that I have his letter. It will be sufficient. And you can tell him that I shall be in London to-morrow night, and if any such person as Mr. Drew Foster is staying at the Savoy Hotel, he will know the inside of a military prison before midnight.'

"The man slunk away. I suppose he realized that with me in the way their game was up. But afterwards he must have hesitated, and then made up his mind to attempt what was probably the bravest action of his life. He followed me, stole up softly behind, and with an old trick which they teach them on the other side of the Seine, he as nearly as possible throttled me. However, I got my finger inside the slipknot, and I held him by the throat. When I could breathe, I lifted him up and threw him into the marshes. There I left him. It seems the fall killed him. That is the whole story. It was absolutely God's justice, but I am quite aware that the laws of the country do not exactly favour such summary treatment. Accordingly I held my peace. I am sorry for it now."

"And Mr. Drew Foster?"

"Had left the Savoy Hotel when I reached there," Ray said drily, "and had omitted to leave an address."

"You might have trusted me," I remarked, thoughtfully.

"If I had known you as well then as I do now," Ray answered, "I would have risked it."

Then as we sat in silence there came a low tapping at the door. Ray looked at me keenly.

"Who visits you at this hour?" he asked.

"We will see," I answered.

I had meant to be careful whom I admitted, but I had scarcely withdrawn the latch when the door was pushed open, and a slim, thickly-cloaked figure glided past me into the room. I knew her by the supple swiftness of her movements. Ray sat still, and smoked with the face of a Sphinx.

I think that at first she did not see him. She swept round upon me and raised her veil.

"Guy," she cried, "forgive me, but I could not help it. I have made a mummy of myself, and I have walked along those awful sands that I might not be seen; but there is a question—"

She saw Ray. The words died from her lips. She stood and shivered like a trapped bird. He removed his pipe from his teeth.

"Go on," he said mildly. "Don't mind me. Perhaps I can help Mr. Ducaine to answer it."

She sank into a chair. Her eyes seemed to implore me to protect her. I heard Ray's little snort of contempt; but I answered her kindly. I could not help it.

"I am sorry that you came," I said, "but, of course, I will answer any question you want to ask me. Don't hurry! You are out of breath. Let me give you some wine."

My own untasted liqueur was on the table by the side of my empty coffee cup. I made her drink it, and her teeth ceased to chatter. She was rather a pathetic object. One of her little black satin slippers was cut to shreds, and the other was clogged with wet sand. The fear of Ray, too, was in her white face. She caught hold of my hand impulsively.

"The man," she murmured, "whom you found—what was he like?"

"He was a small dark man."

She laughed hysterically.

"He," she exclaimed, "was over six feet, and broad! It was not he. It may have been some one whom he sent, but it was not he. Guy, have you heard from him? Do you know where he is?"

I shook my head. Ray interposed.

"I think," he said roughly, "that you'll find him at home when you get there, madam, wherever that may be. If he were in this country it would be within the four walls of a prison."

She looked across at him.

"You have set them on—the police—then?" she said. "You would hunt him down still? After all these years?"

"Ay!" he answered.—"Tell me where he is hiding in this country, and I will promise you that his days of freedom are over."

She pointed to me.

"His father?"

"Ay, were he his father a hundred times over."

She turned to me as though in protest, but my face gave her no encouragement. She rose wearily to her feet.

"I will go," she muttered. "Guy," she added, turning to me, "you are honest. You will always be honest. You have nothing to fear, so you do not hesitate to speak if necessary to those whom nevertheless you do not trust. But there are other things in the world to fear besides dishonesty. There is animal brutality, coarse indifference to pain in others. There is the triumph of the beast over the man. There he sits, he who can teach you these things," she added, pointing to Ray. "Do not choose him for your friend, Guy. You will grow to see life, to judge others, through his eyes-and then God help you."

Ray laughed, and again to me there seemed to be a note of coarseness in his strident and unconcealed contempt of the woman. She took no notice of him whatever. She opened the door and passed out so quickly that though I tried to intercept her, and called out after her, I was powerless to prevent her going. She had flitted away into the shadows. I could not even hear her retreating footsteps.

CHAPTER XXXII
A PAINFUL ENCOUNTER

More work. A week of it, ceaseless and unremitting. The police seemed to have abandoned their watch over my cottage, and I heard a whisper that a statement by the Duke had at any rate partially cleared me from suspicion. Ray had declined to leave England. I knew quite well that it was on my account. He, with the others, was now in London.

Then came my own summons thither. I was told to report myself immediately on arrival at Rowchester House, and to my surprise was informed by the servant who answered my inquiries that a room was reserved for me there. I had no sooner reached it than Lady Angela's own maid arrived with a message. Her ladyship would be glad if I could spare her a few moments in the drawing-room as soon as possible.

Lady Angela was standing upon the hearthrug. I stepped a little way across the threshold and stopped short. She held out her hand to me with a quiet laugh.

"Have you forgotten me?" she asked, "or am I so alarming?"

I set my teeth and moved towards her.

"You took my breath away," I said, with an ease which I was very far from feeling. "Remember that I have come from Braster."

I do not know what she wore. Her gown seemed to me to be of some soft crepe or silk, and the colour of it was a smoky misty blue. There were pearls around her neck, and her hair, arranged with exquisite simplicity, seemed to be drawn back from her face and arranged low down on the back of her neck. She had still the fresh delightful colour which had been in her cheeks when she left Braster, and the smile with which she welcomed me was as delightful as ever.

"This is a charming arrangement," she declared. "You know that you are such an important person, and have to be watched so closely, that you are to stay here. I went up myself with the housekeeper to see to your rooms. I do hope that you will be comfortable."

"Comfortable is not the word," I answered. "I have never been used to such luxury."

She laughed.

"Dear me!" she said. "I have so much to tell you, and the carriage is waiting already. Thank goodness we dine alone to-morrow night. But there is one thing which I must tell you at once. Sir Michael Trogoldy is in town, you know. He took me in to dinner at Amberley House last night, and we talked about you."

"I had a letter from Sir Michael a few days ago," I answered. "He made a proposition to me — and asked me to call and see him."

Something in my voice, I suppose, betrayed my feelings. She laid her hand upon my arm.

"Mr. Ducaine," she said, "I do hope that you mean to be reasonable. Sir Michael is a dear old man."

"He is my mother's brother," I answered, "and he left me to starve."

"He had not the least idea," she declared, "that you were not reasonably well off. He is most interested in hearing about you, and he was delighted to have you accept the allowance he offered you. You will go and see him?"

"Yes, I shall go," I promised. "I scarcely see the use of it, but I will go."

"You must not be foolish," she said softly. "Sir Michael is very rich> and you are his only near relative. Besides, you have had such a lonely time, and it is quite time that you saw a little of the other side of life. Sir Michael is a particular friend of mine, and I promised him that I would talk to you about this. I am most anxious to hear that you get on well together. You can be amiable if you like, you know, and you can be very much the other thing."

"I will try," I assured her, "not to be the other thing." She smiled.

"And tell me all about Braster."

"There is not much to tell," I answered. "I have been hard at work all the time, and I have scarcely seen a soul."

"The woman—Mrs. Smith-Lessing?"

"She left Braster before you. I have not seen her since the evening of the day I saw her last."

She appeared relieved.

"May I ask you a question?" I asked. She nodded. "About Colonel Ray. Has the Duke forgiven him?"

"On the contrary, he is more bitter than ever," Lady Angela answered. "I have seen him once or twice only. He does not come here." "I saw in the paper," I said, "that your engage—"

"It is not true," she interrupted. "Everything is as it was. But it is shockingly indefinite, of course. I scarcely know whether I am to consider myself an engaged person or not. Colonel Ray offered to release me, but we agreed to wait for a little time."

"Lady Angela!"

She looked at me with a soft flush upon her cheeks. But my words were never spoken. The Duke entered the room, brilliant in sash and orders.

"Good evening, Ducaine," he said, looking at me with slightly lifted eyebrows.

"Good evening, your Grace," I answered in some embarrassment.

"I sent for Mr. Ducaine," Lady Angela remarked, stooping that her maid, who had followed the Duke, might arrange her cloak. "I wanted to hear all about Braster, and I had a message for him from Sir Michael Trogoldy."

The Duke made no remark.

"I shall require you, Ducaine, at ten o'clock to-morrow morning in my study," he said. "Afterwards we go over to the War Office. You have brought all the papers with you?—If you are quite ready, Angela."

The Duke, without saying a word, had managed to make me feel that he considered my presence in the drawing-room with Lady Angela superfluous, but her smile and farewell were quite sufficient recompense for me. Still, I knew that this living together under the same roof was to be no unmixed blessing for me. I shut myself in the dainty little sitting-room which I was told was mine, and turned the key in the door. I felt the need of solitude.

* * * * *

Later in the evening I became mundane again. I remembered that I had sent dinner away, and though I had only to ring the bell and order something, I felt the need of fresh air. So I took up my hat and stick and left the house.

After a while I found my way into Piccadilly. I knew very little of London, but after my solitary evening walks at Braster along the sandhills and across the marshes, the contrast was in itself suggestive and almost exciting. I watched the people, the stream of carriages. I listened to the low ceaseless hum of this wonderful life, and I found it fascinating. The glow in the sky was marvellous to me—the faces of the passers-by, the laughter and the whining, the tears and the cursing, the pleasure-seekers and the pleasure-satiated, how they all told their story as they swept by in one unceasing stream! For a while I forgot even my appetite. The sight of a restaurant, however, at last reminded me that I was desperately hungry.

I knew it by name—a huge cosmopolitan place of the lower middle class, and entering I found a quiet seat, where my country clothes were not conspicuous. There were few people about me, and those few uninteresting, so I kept my attention divided between my dinner and the evening paper. But just as I was drawing towards the close of my meal, something happened to change all that.

A woman, followed by a man, passed my table, and the two seated themselves diagonally opposite to me. Something in the woman's light footsteps, her free movements, and the graceful carriage of her head, struck me instantly as being familiar. She was dressed very plainly, and she was closely veiled. Their entrance, too, had been unobtrusive, almost furtive. But when she raised her veil and took the carte-du-jour in her hand, I knew her at once. It was Mrs. Smith-Lessing.

She had not seen me, and my first impulse was to pay my bill and step quietly out. Then by chance I glanced at her companion, and my heart stood still. He was a tall man, over six feet, but he stooped badly, and his walk had been almost the walk of an invalid. He had the appearance of a man who had once been stout and well built, but who was now barely recovered from a long illness. The flesh hung in little bags underneath his bloodshot eyes, his mouth twitched continually, and the hand which rested on the table trembled. He wore a scanty grey moustache, which failed to hide a weak thin mouth, and a very obvious wig concealed his baldness. His clothes had seen plenty of service and his linen was doubtful. He had evidently ordered some brandy immediately on his entrance, and his eyes met mine just as he was in the act of raising the glass to his lips. I am convinced that he had no idea then who I was, but the earnestness of my gaze seemed to disturb him. He set down his glass with shaking fingers, and directed his companion's attention towards me.

They talked together earnestly for several moments. I fancied that she was reproving him for showing alarm at my notice. Very soon, however, she herself, after giving an order to a waiter, turned slightly round in her chair, and glanced with well-affected carelessness across at me. I saw her start and look apprehensively at her companion. He took the alarm at once, and I heard his eager question.

"Who is it? Who is it, Maud?"

She made him some reassuring answer, and, rising to her feet, came over to my table. I rose to greet her, and she slipped quietly into the chair opposite to me.

"What are you doing here?" she asked quickly.

"I have just arrived from Braster," I answered. "I came here by accident to get something to eat. Is that—"

I could not go on, but she finished the sentence for me.

"Yes!"

I set my teeth hard and looked steadily down at the tablecloth. I felt rather than saw that her regard was compassionate.

"I am sorry," she murmured. "I would not have brought him here if I had known. You two are better apart. Talk to me as naturally as you can. He has no idea who you are."

"Has he been ill?" I asked.

"Very. I found him in a hospital. He has been ill, and the rest you can guess."

Even while we were talking I saw him toss off another glass of brandy which the waiter had brought him. And all the time his eyes never left my face.

"I thought," I said, "that he had money."

"It has all gone," she answered, "and — well, things are not very flourishing with him. Our mission over here has been unsuccessful, and they have stopped sending us money from Paris. How queer that I should be telling you this!" she added, with a hard little laugh, "you, of all people in the world. Guy, take my advice. Get up and go. If he guesses who you are he will come and speak to you — and you are better apart."

It was too late. With fascinated eyes I watched him leave his place and come towards us. I was absolutely powerless to move. Mrs. Smith-Lessing had left the outside chair vacant. He sank into it and leaned across the table towards me.

"It is Guy," he said in a shaking voice. "I am sure that it is Guy. She has told you who I am. Eh?"

"Yes," I answered. "I know who you are."

He extended a shaking hand across the table. I could not take it.

"Well, well," he said nervously, "perhaps you are right. But I came to England to see you. Yes, Guy, that is the truth! I have been a bad father, but I may be able to make amends. I think I know a way. — Waiter, a glass of brandy."

"I am afraid," I said, rising to my feet, "that you must excuse me. — If you have anything to say to me, sir, we can meet another time."

He almost dragged me down.

"Stop, stop!" he said irritably. "You do not seem to understand. I had an important matter of business to discuss with you. I may make your fortune yet, my boy! I have powerful friends abroad, very powerful."

I looked at him steadily.

"Well?"

She laid her hand upon his arm, and whispered in his ear. He only shook his head angrily.

"Nonsense, Maud!" he exclaimed. "You do not understand. This is my son Guy. Of course we must talk together. It is a wonderful meeting—yes, a wonderful meeting."

"Well?" I repeated.

"I am glad to hear," he continued, "that you are holding such an important position. Clerk to the Military Defence Board, eh? Quite an important position, of course; but it might be made—yes, with care, it might be made," he added, watching me with nervous alertness, "a very lucrative one."

"I am quite satisfied with my salary," I remarked calmly.

"Pooh! my dear boy, that is nonsense," he continued. "You do not understand me. It is an open secret. Maud, are we overheard here, do you think? Is it safe to discuss an important matter with Guy here?"

I rose to my feet and took up my hat. Again she whispered in his ear, and this time he seemed to assent.

"Quite right! Quite right!" he said, nodding his head. "Guy, my boy, you shall come and see us. No. 29, Bloomsbury Street—poor rooms, but our remittances have gone astray, and I have been ill. To-morrow, eh? or the next day? We shall expect you, Guy. We do not go out except in the evenings. You will not fail, Guy?"

I looked down into his flushed face. His lips were shaking, and his eyes were fixed anxiously upon mine. I was miserably ashamed and unhappy.

"I do not think that I shall care to hear what you have to say," I answered. "But I will come to see you."

I left them there. As I went out she was gently countermanding his order for more brandy.

CHAPTER XXXIII
THE DUKE'S MESSAGE

It was late, but I felt that I must see Ray. I went to his house, little expecting to find him there. I was shown, however, into the study, where he was hard at work with a pile of correspondence. He wore an ancient shooting jacket, and his feet were encased in slippers. As usual, his pipe was between his teeth, and the tobacco smoke hung about him in little clouds.

"Well," he said gruffly. "What do you want of me? I am busy. Speak to the point."

"I have come to ask your advice," I said. "I am afraid that I must resign my post."

"Why?"

"My father is in London. I have seen and spoken with him."

"With that woman?"

"Yes."

"And you have spoken to him in a public place, perhaps?"

Ray was silent for a moment. Then he looked at me keenly.

"Do you want to give it up?" he asked.

"No," I answered. "But do you suppose Lord Chelsford and the others would be willing for me to continue — under the circumstances?"

"Probably not," he admitted. "The Duke would not, at any rate."

"Then what am I to do?" I asked.

"I don't know!" he answered shortly. "It requires consideration. I will see Lord Chelsford. You shall hear from me in the morning."

That was all the consolation I had from Colonel Mostyn Ray.

At ten o'clock the next morning the Duke came to me in the study, where I was already at work. He was looking, even for him, particularly trim and smart, and he wore a carefully-selected pink rosebud in his buttonhole. His greeting was almost cordial. He gave me a few instructions, and then lit a cigarette.

"What is this about your resignation, Ducaine?" he asked.

"I do not wish to resign, sir," I answered. "I have explained certain circumstances to Colonel Ray, which it seemed to me might make my resignation necessary. He promised to confer with Lord Chelsford, and let me know the result."

The urbanity slowly faded from the Duke's face.

"I am your employer," he said coldly. "I do not understand why you thought it necessary to go to Colonel Ray."

"It was entirely owing to Colonel Ray, sir," I answered, "that I received the appointment, and he has practically made himself responsible for me."

"You are mistaken," the Duke answered. "The responsibility is shared by all of us. Your unfortunate family history was known to the whole Board."

"Then I am less indebted to Colonel Ray, sir, than I imagined," I answered. "I am very glad, however, that it is known. Perhaps Lord Chelsford may not consider my resignation necessary?"

"The circumstances being — ?"

"I have seen and spoken with my father in London," I answered.

The Duke was silent.

"I presume," he said, after a short pause, "that you must yourself realize the indiscretion of this."

"I went at once to Colonel Ray and offered my resignation," I answered.

The Duke nodded.

"Your father," he said slowly, "is in London?" "Yes, sir."

"Alone?"

I hesitated. Yet perhaps the Duke had a right to know the truth.

"He is with the lady who occupied Braster Grange, sir, until last week," I answered. "She passed under the name of Mrs. Smith-Lessing, but I believe that she is in reality my stepmother."

The Duke stood a few paces from me, looking out of the window. He held his cigarette between his fingers, and he stood sideways to me. Nothing about his attitude or face was unusual. Yet I felt myself watching him curiously. There was something about his manner which seemed to me to suggest some powerful emotion only kept in check by the exercise of a strong will.

"This is the person, I believe," he said in a slow measured tone, "with whom my son, Lord Blenavon, was said to have been intimate?"

"Lord Blenavon was certainly a constant visitor at Braster Grange," I answered.

"You know her address in London?" the Duke asked.

"Yes."

He turned and faced me. He was certainly paler than he had been a few minutes ago.

"I should be glad," he said, "if you would arrange for me to have an interview with her."

"An interview with Mrs. Smith-Lessing!" I repeated incredulously.

The Duke inclined his head.

"There are a few questions," he said, "which I wish to ask her."

"I can give you her address," I said.

"I wish you to see her and arrange for the interview personally," the. Duke answered.

"You will see that my visiting her does not prejudice me further with the Board, sir?" I ventured to say. "You can take that for granted," the Duke said. So that afternoon I called at No. 29, Bloomsbury Street, and in a shabby back room of a gloomy, smoke-begrimed lodging-house I found my father and Mrs. Smith-Lessing. He was lying upon a horsehair sofa, apparently dozing. She was gazing negligently out of the window, and drumming upon the window pane with her fingers. My arrival seemed to act like an electric shock upon both of them. It struck me that to her it was not altogether welcome, but my father was nervously anxious to impress upon me his satisfaction at my visit.

"Now," he said, drawing his chair up to the table, "we can discuss this little matter in a business-like way. I am delighted to see you, Guy, quite delighted."

"What matter?" I asked quietly.

My father coughed and looked towards my stepmother, as though for guidance. But her face was a blank.

"Guy," he said, "I am sure that you are a young man of common sense. You will prefer that I speak to you plainly. There are some fools at our end—I mean at Paris—who think they will be better off for a glance at the doings of your Military Board. Up to now we have kept them supplied with a little general information. Lord Blenavon, who is a remarkably sensible young man, lent us his assistance. I tell you this quite frankly. I believe that it is best."

He was watching me furtively. I did my best to keep my features immovable.

"With Lord Blenavon's assistance," my father continued, "we did at first very well. Since his—er—departure we have not been so fortunate. I will be quite candid. We have not succeeded at all. Our friends pay generously, but they pay by results. As a consequence your stepmother and I are nearly penniless. This fact induces me to make you a special—a very special—offer."

My stepmother seemed about to speak. She checked herself, however.

"Go on," I said.

My father coughed. There was a bottle upon the table, and he helped himself from it.

"My nerves," he remarked, "are in a shocking state this morning. Can I offer you anything?"

I shook my head. My father poured out nearly a glass full of the raw spirit, diluted it with a little, a very little, water, and drank it off.

"Your labours, my dear boy," he continued, "I refer, of course, to the labours of the Military Council, are, I believe, concentrated upon a general scheme of defence against any possible invasion on the part of France. Quite a scare you people seem to be in. Not that one can wonder at it. These military manoeuvres of our friends across the water are just a little obvious even to John Bull, eh? You don't answer.

Quite right, quite right! Never commit yourself uselessly. It is very good diplomacy. Let me see, where was I? Ah! The general scheme of defence is, of course, known to you?"

"Naturally," I admitted.

"With a list of the places to be fortified, eh? The positions to be held and the general distribution of troops? No doubt, too, you have gone into the railway and commissariat arrangements?"

"All these details," I assented, "have gone through my hands."

He dabbed his forehead with a corner of his handkerchief. There was a streak of purple colour in his checks. He kept his bloodshot eyes fixed upon me.

"I will tell you something, Guy," he said, "which will astonish you. You realize for yourself, of course, that such details as you have spoken of can never be kept altogether secret? There are always leakages, sometimes very considerable leakages. Yes, Guy," he added, "there are people, friends of mine in Paris, who are willing to pay a very large sum of money — such a large sum of money that it is worth dividing, Guy — for just a bare outline of the whole scheme. Foolish! Of course it is foolish. But with them money is no object. They think they are getting value for it. Absurd! But, Guy, what should you say to five thousand pounds?"

"It is a large sum," I answered.

He plucked me by the sleeve. His eyes were hungering already for the gold.

"We can get it," he whispered hoarsely. "No trouble to you — no risk. I can make all the arrangements. You have only to hand me the documents."

"I must think it over," I said.

He leaned back in his chair.

"Why?" he asked. "What need is there to hesitate? The chance may slip by. There are many others on the look out."

"There is no one outside the Military Board save myself who could give these particulars," I said slowly.

"But my friends," he said sharply. "Theirs is a foolish offer. They may change their minds. Guy, my boy, I know the world well. Let me give you a word of advice. When a good thing turns up, don't play with it. The men who decide quickly are the men who do things."

I thrust my hand into my breast-pocket and drew out a roll of papers.

"Supposing I have already decided," I said.

His eyes gleamed with excitement. He almost snatched at the papers, but I held them out of his reach. Then with a sharp little cry the woman stood suddenly between us. There was a look almost of horror on her pale strained face, as she held out her hand as though to push me away.

"Guy, are you mad?" she cried.

The veins stood out upon my father's forehead. He regarded her with mingled anger and surprise.

"What do you mean, Maud?" he exclaimed. "How dare you interfere? Guy, give me the papers."

"He shall not!" she exclaimed fiercely. "Guy, have you lost your senses? Do you want to ruin your whole life?"

"Do you mean," I asked incredulously, "that you do not wish me to join you?"

"Join us! For Heaven's sake, no!" she answered fiercely. "Look at your father, an outcast all his life. Do you want to become like him? Do you want to turn the other way whenever you meet an Englishman, to skulk all your days in hiding, to be the scorn even of the men who employ you? Guy, I would sooner see you dead than part with those papers."

"You damned fool!" my father muttered. "Take no notice of her, Guy. Five thousand pounds! I will see it paid to you, every penny of it. And not a soul will ever know!"

My father stood over her, and there was a threat in his face. She did not shrink from him for a moment. She laid her white hands upon my shoulders, and she looked earnestly into my eyes.

"Guy," she said, "even now I do not believe that you meant to be so very, very foolish. But I want you to go away at once. You should never have come. It is not good for you to come near either of us."

I rose obediently. I think that if I had not been there my father would have struck her. He was almost speechless with fury. He poured himself out another glass of brandy with shaking fingers.

"Thank you," I said to her, simply. "I do not think that these papers are worth five thousand. Let me tell you what I came here for. I am a messenger from the Duke of Rowchester."

My father dropped his glass. Mrs. Smith-Lessing looked bewildered.

"The Duke," I said to her, "desires to see you. Can you come to Cavendish Square this afternoon?"

"The Duke?" she murmured.

"He wishes to see you," I repeated. "Shall I tell him that you will call at four o'clock this afternoon, or will you go back with me?"

"Do you mean this?" she asked in a low tone. "I do not understand it. I have never seen the Duke in my life."

"I understand no more than you do," I assured her. "That is the message."

"I do not promise to come," she said. "I must think it over."

My father pushed her roughly away.

"Come, there's been enough of this fooling," he declared roughly. "Guy, sit down again, my boy. We must have another talk about this matter."

I turned upon him in a momentary fit of passion.

"I have no more to say, sir," I declared. "It seems that you are not content with ruining your own life and overshadowing mine. You want to drag me, too, down into the slough."

"You don't understand, my dear boy!"

The door opened and Ray entered. My bundle of papers slipped from my fingers on to the floor in the excitement of the moment.

CHAPTER XXXIV
MYSELF AND MY STEPMOTHER

I Saw then what a man's face may look like when he is stricken with a sudden paralysing fear. I saw my father sit in his chair and shake from head to foot. Ray's black eyes seemed to be flashing upon us all the most unutterable scorn.

"What is this pleasant meeting which I seem to have interrupted, eh?" he asked, with fierce sarcasm. "Quite a family reunion!"

My stepmother, very pale, but very calm, answered him.

"To which you," she said, "come an uninvited guest."

He laughed harshly.

"You shall have others, other uninvited guests, before many hours are past," he declared. "You remember my warning, Ducaine."

My father seemed to me to be on the eve of a collapse. His lips moved, and he mumbled something, but the words were wholly unintelligible. Ray turned to my stepmother.

"When that man," he continued, "had the effrontery to return to this country, he sent his cursed jackal with letters to his son. I intercepted those letters, and I burned them; but I came straight to London, and I found him out. I told him then that I spared him only for the sake of his son. I told him that if ever again he attempted in any way to communicate with him, personally or by letter, nothing should stay my hand. He had a very clear warning. He has chosen to defy me. I only regret, madam, that the law has no hold upon you also."

She turned from him scornfully and laid her hand upon my father's shoulder. Her very touch seemed to impart life to him. His words were not very coherent, but they were comprehensible.

"I kept my word, Ray. Yes, I kept my word," he said. "I never sent for him. Ask him; ask her. We met by accident. I told him my address. That is all. He came here this afternoon with a message from the Duke."

Ray laughed bitterly. There was about his manner a cold and singular aloofness. We were all judged and condemned.

"An invitation to dinner, I presume," he remarked.

"The Duke sent for me," my stepmother said, quietly.

She did not for a moment quail before the scornful disbelief which Ray took no pains to hide.

"You can see for yourself if you like," she continued, "that in a few minutes I shall leave this house, with you, if you are gallant enough to offer me your escort, and I shall go straight to Cavendish Square. You have no imagination, Colonel Ray, or you would not be so utterly surprised. Think for a moment. Does no reason occur to you why the Duke might wish to see me?"

It obviously did. He frowned heavily.

"If this absurd story is true," he said, "and the Duke has really sent to ask news of Blenavon from you — well, he is a bigger fool than I took him for. But there remains something else to be explained. What are those papers?"

My father laid his trembling hands upon them.

"They have nothing to do with you," he explained; "nothing at all! It is a little family matter-between Guy and me. Nothing more. They belong to me. Damn you, Ray, why are you always interfering in my concerns?"

Ray turned to me. There was a look in his eyes which I readily understood. At that moment I think that I hated him.

"What are those papers?" he asked.

"Take them and see," I answered. "If I told you you would not believe me."

He moved a few steps towards them, and then paused. I saw that my father was leaning forward, and in his shaking hand was a tiny gleaming revolver. A certain desperate courage seemed to have come to him.

"Ray," he cried hoarsely, "touch them at your peril!"

There was a moment's breathless silence. Then with an incredibly swift movement my stepmother stepped in between and snatched up the little roll. She glanced behind at the grate, but the fire was almost extinct. With a little gesture of despair she held them out to me. "Take them, Guy," she cried.

Ray stood by my side, and I felt his hand descend like a vice upon my shoulder.

"Give me those papers," he demanded.

I hesitated for a moment. Then I obeyed him. I heard a little sob from behind. The pistol had fallen from my father's shaking fingers, his head had fallen forwards upon his hands. A tardy remorse seemed for a moment to have pierced the husk of his colossal selfishness.

"It is all my fault, my fault!" he muttered.

My stepmother turned upon him, pale to the lips, with blazing eyes.

"You are out of your senses," she exclaimed. "Guy, this man is a bully. All his life it has been his pleasure to persecute the weak and defenceless. The papers are yours. I do not know what they are, nor does he," she added, pointing to where my father still crouched before the table. "Don't let him frighten you into giving them up. He is trying to drag you into the mesh with us. Don't let him! You have nothing to do with us, thank Heaven!"

She stopped suddenly, and snatched the pistol from my father's nerveless grasp. Then her hand flashed out. Ray was covered, and her white fingers never quivered. Even Ray took a quick step backwards.

"Give him back those papers," she commanded.

I intervened, stepping into the line of fire.

"I gave them to him willingly," I told her. "I do not wish to have them back. He is one of my employers, and he has a right to claim them."

I spoke firmly, and she saw that I was at any rate in earnest. Yet the look which she threw upon me was a strange one. I felt that she was disappointed, that a certain measure of contempt too was mingled with her disappointment. She threw the pistol on to the sofa and shrugged her shoulders.

"After all," she said, "I suppose you are right. The whole affair is not worth these heroics. I am ready to go with you to the Duke, Guy, unless Colonel Ray has any contrary orders for us."

Ray turned to me.

"You must come with me at once to my rooms," he said coldly. "This person can find the Duke by herself, if indeed the Duke has sent for her."

I understood then why people hated Ray. There was a vein of positive brutality somewhere in the man's nature.

"I am sorry," I answered him, "but I cannot come to your rooms at present. The Duke is my present employer, and I am here to take Mrs. Smith-Lessing to him. As long as she is willing to accept my escort I shall certainly carry out my instructions."

"Don't be a fool, boy," Ray exclaimed sharply. "I want to give you a last chance before I go to Lord Chelsford."

"I do not think," I answered, "that I care about accepting any favours from you just now, Colonel Ray. Nor am I at all sure that I need them," I added.

He turned on his heel, but at the door he hesitated again.

"Guy," he said in a low tone, "will you speak to me for a moment outside?"

I stood on the landing with him. He closed the door leading into the sitting-room.

"Guy," he said, "you know that if I leave you behind, you link your lot with—them. You will be an outcast and a fugitive all your days. You will have to avoid every place where the English language is spoken. You will never be able to recover your honour, you will be the scorn of all Englishmen and English—women. I speak to you for your mother's sake, boy. You have started life with a cursed heritage. I want to make allowance for it."

I looked him straight in the face.

"I am afraid, Colonel Ray," I said, "that you are not inclined to give me credit for very much common sense. Take those papers to Lord Chelsford. I will come round to your rooms as soon as possible."

He looked at me with eager, searching gaze.

"You mean this?"

"Certainly!" I answered.

He seemed about to say something, but changed his mind. He left me without another word. I stepped back into the sitting-room. My father, with an empty tumbler in his hand, was crouched forward over the table, breathing heavily. My stepmother, with marble 'face and hard set eyes, was leaning forward in her chair, looking into the dying fire. She scarcely glanced at me as I entered.

"Has he gone?" she asked.

"Yes," I answered. "Will you get ready, please? I want to take you to the Duke."

She rose to her feet at once, and moved towards the door. I was left alone with my father, but he never stirred during her absence, nor did I speak to him. She returned in a few minutes, dressed very quietly, and wearing a veil which completely obscured her features. We walked to the corner of the square, and then I called a hansom.

"I know nothing about Lord Blenavon," she said, a little wearily. "I suppose the Duke will not believe that, but it is true."

"You can do no more than tell the truth," I remarked.

"Tell me what he is like—the Duke?" she asked abruptly.

"He is a typical man of his class," I answered. "He is stiff, obstinate, punctilious, with an extreme sense of honour, to gratify which, by-the-bye, he has just deliberately pauperized himself. He will not remind you in the least of Lord Blenavon."

"I should imagine not," she answered.

Then there was a short silence, and I could see that she was crying under her veil. I laid my hand upon hers.

"I am afraid," I said gently, "that I have misled you a little. You are worrying about me, and it isn't half so necessary as you imagine. You thought me mad to listen to my father's offer, and a coward to give up those papers to Ray. Isn't that so?"

My words seemed to electrify her. She pushed up her veil and looked at me eagerly.

"Well? Go on!" she exclaimed.

"There are some things," I said, "which I have made up my mind to tell no one. But at least I can assure you of this. I am not nearly in so desperate a position as you and Colonel Ray seem to think."

She caught hold of my hand and grasped it convulsively. The hard lines seemed to have fallen away from her face. She smiled tremulously.

"Oh, I am glad!" she declared. "I am glad!"

Just then a carriage passed us, and I saw Lady Angela lean a little forward in her seat as though to gain a better view of us.

CHAPTER XXXV
ANGELA'S CONFESSION

The Duke was in his study awaiting our arrival. I saw him rise and bow stiffly to my stepmother. Then I closed the door and left them alone.

I wandered through the house, a little at a loss to know what to do with myself. It was too soon to go to Ray, and the work on which I was engaged was all in the study. Just as I passed the drawing-room door, however, it opened suddenly, and Lady Angela came out, talking to a white-haired old gentleman, who carried a stick on which he leaned heavily. He looked at me rather curiously, and then began to hobble down the hall at a great pace. But Lady Angela laid her hand upon his arm.

"Why, Sir Michael," she exclaimed, "this won't do at all. You can't look him in the face and run. Mr. Ducaine, this is Sir Michael Trogoldy."

He swung round and held out his hand. His eyes searched my face eagerly.

"Nephew," he said, "I wanted to meet you, and I didn't want to meet you. God bless my soul! you've got Muriel's eyes and mouth. Come and dine with me one night next week-any night: let me know. Good-bye, good-bye, Lady Angela. God bless you. Here, James, give me your arm down the steps, and whistle for my fellow to draw up. There he is, in the middle of the road, the blockhead."

Lady Angela and I exchanged glances. I think that we should both have laughed but for the tears which we had seen in his eyes.

"Poor old man," she murmured. "He is very nervous and very sensitive. I know that he dreaded seeing you, and yet he came this afternoon for no other purpose. Will you come into the drawing-room for a moment?"

There was a certain stiffness in her manner, which was new to me. She remained standing, and her soft dark eyes were full of grave inquiry.

"Mr. Ducaine," she said, "I passed you just now driving in a hansom with a person—of whom I disapprove. May I know—is it any secret why you were with her?"

"It is no secret at all, Lady Angela," I answered. "I was sent to fetch her by your father."

"By my father?" she repeated incredulously. "Do you mean that she is in this house?"

"Certainly," I answered. "Your father is anxious, I believe, about Lord Blenavon. It occurred to me that he perhaps hoped to get news of him from Mrs. Smith-Lessing. At any rate he sent me for her."

She seemed to me to be trembling a little. Her eyes sought mine almost pathetically. She was afraid of something. In the half-lights she appeared to me then so frail and girlish that a great wave of tenderness swept in upon me. I longed to take her into my arms—even to hold her hands and try to comfort her. Surely to do these things was the privilege of the man who loved her. And I loved her—loved her so that the pain and joy of it were woven together like live things in my heart, fighting always against the grim silence which lay like a seal upon my lips. But there were moments when I was sorely tried, and this was one of them. My eyes fell from hers. I dared not look her in the face.

"Is this—all?" she asked falteringly.

"It is all that I know," I answered.

Then we were silent. With a little sigh she sank down in the corner of a high-backed easy chair. It seemed to me that she was thinner, that something of the delicate childishness of her appearance had passed away since her coming to London. I knew that she was in trouble, and I dared not ask her the cause of it.

"I wish that we were going back to Braster to-morrow," she said suddenly. "Everything and everybody is different here. You seem to spend most of your time trying to avoid me, and—Colonel Ray, I do not know what is the matter with him, but he has become like a walking tragedy."

"I have not tried to avoid you," I said. "I—"

Then I stopped short. Her eyes were fixed upon mine and the lie stuck in my throat. I went on desperately.

"I think," I said, "that if you fancy Colonel Ray is different you should ask him about it."

She shook her head dejectedly.

"I cannot," she said. "Sometimes I am frightened of Colonel Ray. It is like that just now."

"But you should try and get over it," I said gently. "He has strange moods, but you should always remember that he is the man whom you are going to marry. There ought to be every confidence between you, and I know—yes, I know that he is very fond of you."

She leaned a little forward. Her hair was a little dishevelled, her face was almost haggard. Her under lip was quivering like a child's.

"I am afraid of him," she sobbed out suddenly. "I am afraid of him, and I have promised to marry him. Can't somebody—help me?"

Her head fell suddenly forward and was buried in her hands. Her whole frame shook with convulsive weeping, and then suddenly a little white hand shot out towards me. She did not look up, but the hand was there, timid, yet inviting. I dropped on my knee by her side, and I held it in mine.

"Dear Lady Angela," I murmured. "You must not give way like this, you must not! Ray is not used to women, and you are very young. But he loves you, I know that he loves you."

"I don't—want him to love me," she sobbed. "Oh, I know that I am foolish and wicked and childish, but I am afraid of him."

I kept silence, for my own battle was a hard one. The little hand was holding fast to mine. She lay curled up in the corner of the chair, her face hidden, her slim delicate figure shaking every now and then with sobs. All the while I longed passionately to take her into my arms and comfort her.

"Don't!" I begged. "Oh, don't. Ray has told me his story. He has made me his confidant. He has told me how unhappy he has been, and how he loves you. Oh, Lady Angela, what is there I can say? What can I do?"

I was losing my head a little, I think, for her fingers were gripping mine convulsively, warm and tender little fingers which seemed to be drawing me all the while closer to her.

"I am so miserable," she murmured.

Then suddenly her other arm was around my neck, her wet tear-stained face was pressed to mine. I scarcely knew how it happened, but I knew that she was in my arms, and my lips were pressed to hers. A sudden, beautiful wave of colour flooded her cheeks; she smiled gladly up at me. She gave a delicious little sigh of satisfaction and then buried her face on my shoulder. Almost at the same moment Ray entered the room.

She did not at once raise her head, although she pushed me gently away from her at the sound of the opening door. But I, who was standing facing that direction, saw him from the first, a dark stern figure, standing as though rooted to the ground, with the doorhandle still in his hand. For the second time in one day he seemed to have intervened at the precise psychological moment. He did not speak to me, nor I to him. Lady Angela, as though wondering at the silence, turned her head at last, and a little gasping cry broke from her lips.

"Mostyn," she exclaimed. "Is that you?"

For answer he turned towards the wall and flooded the room with electric light. Then he looked at us both intently and mercilessly; only this time I saw that much of his wonderful self-control was wanting. He did not answer Lady Angela. He did not glance towards her.

"You cur!" he cried. "Twice in a day am I to be brought face to face with your cursed treachery? Twice in a day! Lady Angela, may I beg that you will leave us?"

She stood up and faced him, slim and white-faced, yet with her head thrown back and her voice steady.

"Mostyn," she said, "this is my fault. I do not ask for your forgiveness. I have behaved shamefully, but I was miserable, and I forgot. Mr. Ducaine is blameless. It was my fault."

"You will pardon the keenness of my observation," he answered, "but the attitude in which I was unfortunate enough to find you tells its own story. You will oblige me, Lady Angela, by leaving us alone."

I would have spoken, but she held out her hand.

"I think you forget, Colonel Ray," she said, "that this is my house. I am not disposed to leave you and Mr. Ducaine here together in your present mood."

He laughed harshly.

"Are you afraid for your lover?" he asked. "I promise you that I will hold his person sacred."

"Lady Angela," I begged. "Please leave us. I—"

Then came an interruption so unexpected and yet so natural that the whole scene seemed at once to dissolve into bathos. The door was thrown open, and a footman ushered in callers.

"Lady Chelsford and the Marchioness of Cardenne, your ladyship," he announced. "Mrs. and the Misses Colquhoun. Sir George Treherne!"

It was a transformation. The room, with its dull note of tragedy, was suddenly filled with faint perfumes, shaken from the rustling draperies of half a dozen women, a little chorus of light voices started the babel of small-talk, Lady Angela had taken her place behind the large round tea-table and was talking nonsense with the tall young guardsman who had drawn his chair up to her side, and I, with a plate of sandwiches in my hand, nearly ran into Ray, who was carrying a cup of tea. For a quarter of an hour or so we played our parts in the comedy. Then a servant entered the room and whispered in my ear.

"His Grace would be glad to see you in the library, sir."

I rose at once. Angela's eyes were fixed upon mine questioningly. As I passed the table I spoke to her, and purposely raised my voice so that Ray should hear.

"Your father has sent for me, Lady Angela. He is terribly industrious to-day."

She smiled back to me quietly. I lingered in the hall for a minute, and Ray joined me there. He did not speak a word, but he motioned me fiercely to precede him to the library. Directly we entered it was clear that something unusual had happened. The great safe door stood open. Lord Chelsford and the Duke were both awaiting our coming.

CHAPTER XXXVI
I LOSE MY POST

The Duke solemnly closed the door. "Ray," he said, "I am glad that you are here. Something serious has happened. Mr. Ducaine, Lord Chelsford and I desire to ask you a few questions."

I bowed. What was coming I could not indeed imagine, unless Ray had already made the disclosure.

"The word code for the safe to-day was Magenta, I believe?" the Duke asked.

"That is correct, sir," I answered.

"And it was known to whom?"

"To Lord Chelsford, yourself, Colonel Ray, and myself," I answered.

"And what was there in the safe?" the Duke asked.

"The plans for the Guildford Camp, the new map of Surrey pricked for fortifications, and one or two transport schemes," I answered.

"Exactly! Those documents are now all missing."

I strode to the safe and looked in. It was as the Duke had said. The safe was practically empty.

"They were there this morning," I said. "It was arranged that I should examine the contents of the safe the first thing, and take any finished work over to the War Office. Do you remember who has been in the room to-day, sir?"

"Yourself, myself, and the woman whom you brought here an hour or so ago."

"Mrs. Smith-Lessing?" I exclaimed.

"Precisely!" the Duke remarked, drily.

"Did you leave her alone here?" I asked.

"For two minutes only," the Duke answered. "I was called up on the telephone from the House of Lords. I did not imagine that there could be the slightest risk in leaving her, for without the knowledge of that word Magenta the safe would defy a professional locksmith."

"You will forgive my suggesting it, your Grace," I said, with some hesitation, "but you have not, I presume, had occasion to go to the safe during the day?"

"I have not," the Duke answered tersely.

"Then I cannot suggest any explanation of the opening of the safe," I admitted. "It was impossible for Mrs. Smith-Lessing to have opened it unless she knew the code word."

"The question is," the Duke said quietly, "did she know it?"

Then I realized the object of this cross-examination. The colour flared suddenly into my cheeks, and as suddenly left them. The absence of those papers was extraordinary to me. I utterly failed to understand it.

"I think I know what you mean, sir," I said. "It is true that Mrs. Smith-Lessing is my stepmother. I believe it is true, too, that she is connected with the French Secret Police. I was there this afternoon — you yourself sent me. But I did not tell Mrs. Smith-Lessing the code word, and I know nothing of the disappearance of those documents."

Then Ray moved forward and placed deliberately upon the table the roll of papers which I had given up to him a few hours ago.

"What about these?" he asked, with biting scorn. "Tell the Duke and Lord Chelsford where I found them! Let us hear your glib young tongue telling the truth for once, sir."

Both the Duke and Lord Chelsford were obviously startled. Ray had always been my friend and upholder. He spoke now with very apparent enmity.

"Perhaps you would prefer to tell the story yourself," I answered. "I will correct you if it is necessary."

"Very well," he answered. "I will tell the story, and a pitiful one it is. This boy is watched, as we all know, for, owing to my folly in ignoring his antecedents, a great trust has been reposed in him. News was brought to me that he had been seen with his father and Mrs.

Smith-Lessing in Gattini's Restaurant. Later, that he had found his way to their lodging. I followed him there. He may have gone there with an errand from you, Duke, but when I arrived he was doing a little business on his own account, and these papers were in the act of passing from him to his father."

"What are they?" Lord Chelsford asked.

"Your Lordship may recognize them," I answered quietly. "They are a summary of the schemes of defence of the southern ports. I was at that moment, the moment when Colonel Ray entered, considering an offer of five thousand pounds for them."

Even Ray was staggered at my admission, and the Duke looked as though he could scarcely believe his ears. Lord Chelsford was busy looking through the papers.

"You young blackguard," Ray muttered through his teeth. "After that admission, do you still deny that you told Mrs. Smith-Lessing, or whatever the woman calls herself, the code word for that safe?"

"Most certainly I deny it," I answered firmly. "The two things are wholly disconnected."

The Duke sat down heavily in his chair. I knew very well that of the three men he was the most surprised. Lord Chelsford carefully placed the papers which he had been reading in his breast-pocket. Ray leaned over towards him.

"Lord Chelsford," he said, "and you, Duke, you took this young man on trust, and I pledged my word for him. Like many a better man, I made a mistake. For all that we know he has secret copies of all the work he has done for us, ready to dispose of. What in God's name, are we going to do with him?"

"What do you suggest?" Lord Chelsford asked softly.

"My way would not be yours," Ray answered, with a hard laugh. "I am only half civilized, you know, and if he and I were alone in the desert at this moment I would shoot him without remorse. Such a breach of trust as this deserves death."

"We are, unfortunately," Lord Chelsford remarked, "not in a position to adopt such extreme measures. It would not even be wise for us to attempt to formulate a legal charge against him. The position is somewhat embarrassing. What do you suggest, Duke?"

I glanced towards the Duke, and I was surprised to see that his hands were shaking. For a man who rarely displayed feeling the Duke seemed to be wonderfully affected.

"I can suggest nothing," he answered in a low tone. "I must confess that I am bewildered. These matters have developed so rapidly."

Lord Chelsford looked thoughtful for a moment.

"I have a plan in my mind," he said slowly. "Duke, should I be taking a liberty if I asked to be left alone with this young man for five minutes?"

The Duke rose slowly to his feet. He had the air of one not altogether approving of the suggestion. Ray glowered upon us both, but offered no objection. They left the room together. Lord Chelsford at once turned to me.

"Ducaine," he said, "forgive me that I did not come to your aid. I will see that you do not suffer later on. But what in Heaven's name is the meaning of this last abstraction' from the safe?"

I shook my head.

"The woman could never have guessed the word!" I said.

"Impossible!" he agreed. "Ducaine, do you know why Lord Blenavon left
England so suddenly?"

"Colonel Ray knows, sir," I answered. "Ask him!"

Lord Chelsford became very thoughtful.

"Ducaine," he said, "we are in a fix. So far your plan has worked to perfection. Paris has plenty of false information, and your real copies have all reached me safely. But if you leave, how is this to be carried on? I do not know whom I mistrust, but if the day's work of the Board is really to be left in the safe, either here or at Braster—"

"You must choose my successor yourself, sir," I interrupted.

"The Duke has always opposed my selections. Besides, you have prepared your false copies with rare skill. Even I was deceived for a moment just now by your summary. You don't overdo it. Everything is just a little wrong. I am not sure even now whether I should not do better to tell Ray and the Duke the truth."

"I am in your hands, sir," I answered. "You must do as you think best."

"They will be back in a moment. It is absurd to doubt either of them, Ducaine. Yet I shall keep silent. I have an idea. Agree to everything I say."

The Duke and Ray returned together. Lord Chelsford turned to them.

"Mr. Ducaine," he said, coldly, "persists in his denial of any knowledge of to-day's affair. With regard to the future, I have offered him his choice of an arrest on the charge of espionage, or a twelve months' cruise on the Ajax, which leaves to-morrow for China. He has chosen the latter. I shall take steps of course to see that he is not allowed to land at any calling-place, or dispatch letters."

Ray smiled a little cruelly.

"The idea is an excellent one, Chelsford," he said. "When did you say that the Ajax sailed?"

"To-morrow," Lord Chelsford answered. "I propose to take Mr. Ducaine to my house to-night, and to hand him over to the charge of a person on whom I can thoroughly rely."

The Duke looked at me curiously.

"Mr. Ducaine consents to go?" he asked.

"It is a voyage which I have long desired to take," I answered coolly, "though I never expected to enjoy it at my country's expense."

The Duke rang the bell.

"Will you have Mr. Ducaine's things packed and sent across — did you say to your house, Lord Chelsford?"

"To my house," Lord Chelsford assented.

"To No. 19, Grosvenor Square," the Duke ordered. "Mr. Ducaine will not be returning."

Lord Chelsford rose. I followed his example. Neither the Duke nor Ray attempted any form of farewell. The former, however, laid some notes upon the table.

"I believe, Mr. Ducaine," he said, "that there is a month's salary due to you. I have added something to the amount. Until to-day I have always considered your duties admirably fulfilled."

I looked at the notes and at the Duke.

"I thank your Grace," I answered. "I will take the liberty of declining your gift. My salary has been fully paid."

For a moment I fancied I caught a softer gleam in Ray's eyes. He seemed about to speak, but checked himself. Lord Chelsford hurried me from the room, and into his little brougham, which was waiting.

"Do you really mean me to go to China, sir?" I asked him, anxiously.

"Not I!" he answered. "I am going to send you to Braster."

CHAPTER XXXVII
LORD CHELSFORD'S DIPLOMACY

I dined alone with Lord and Lady Chelsford. From the moment of our arrival at Chelsford House my host had encouraged nothing but the most general conversation. It happened that they were alone, as a great dinner party had been postponed at the last moment owing to some Royal indisposition. Lord Chelsford in his wife's presence was careful to treat me as an ordinary guest; but directly she had left the room and we were alone he abandoned his reticence.

"Mr. Ducaine," he said, "from the time of our last conversation at the War Office and our subsequent tete-a-tete I have reposed in you the most implicit confidence."

"I have done my best, sir," I answered, "to deserve it."

"I believe you," he declared. "I am going now to extend it. I am going to tell you something which will probably surprise you very much. Since the first time when you found your documents tampered with, every map and every word of writing entrusted to the safe, either at Braster House or Cavendish Square, has been got at. Exact copies of them are in Paris to-day."

I looked at him in blank amazement. The thing seemed impossible.

"But in very many cases," I protested, "the code word for opening the safe has been known only to Colonel Ray, the Duke, and myself."

"The fact remains as I have stated it," Lord Chelsford said slowly. "My information is positive. When you came to me and suggested that you should make two copies of everything, one correct, one a mass of incorrectness, I must admit that I thought the idea farfetched and unworkable. Events, however, have proved otherwise. I have safely received everything which you sent me, and up to the present, with the exception of that first plan of the Winchester forts, our secrets are unknown. But now we have come to a deadlock."

"If you do not mind telling me, Lord Chelsford, I should very much like to know why you did not explain the exact circumstances to Ray and the Duke this afternoon."

Lord Chelsford nodded.

"I thought that you would ask that," he said. "It is not altogether an easy question to answer. Remember this. The French War Office are to-day in possession of an altogether false scheme of our proposed defences — a scheme which, if they continue to regard it as genuine, should prove nothing short of disastrous to them. Only you and I are in the secret at present. Positively I did not feel that I cared to extend that knowledge to a single other person."

"But you might have told Colonel Ray and the Duke separately," I remarked. "The Duke has never been my friend, and Ray has other causes for being angry with me just at present; but between them they rescued me from something like starvation, and it is terrible for them to think of me as they are doing now."

Lord Chelsford poured himself out a glass of wine, and held it up to the light for a moment.

"Mr. Ducaine," he said, "a secret is a very subtle thing. Though the people who handle it are men of the most unblemished honour and reputation, still the fewer they are, the safer the life of that secret."

"But the Duke and Colonel Ray!" I protested.

"I might remind you," Lord Chelsford said, smiling, "that those are precisely the two persons who shared with you the knowledge of the word which opened the safe."

I laughed.

"I presume that you do not suspect either of them?" I remarked.

"The absurdity is obvious," Lord Chelsford answered. "But the force of my former remark remains. I like that secret better when it rests between you and me. It means, I know, that for a time — I promise you that it shall be only for a time — you must lose your friends, but the cause is great enough, and it should be within our power to reward you later on."

"Oh, I am willing enough," I answered. "But may I ask what you are going to do with me?"

Lord Chelsford smoked in silence for several moments.

"Mr. Ducaine," he said, "who is there in the household of the Duke who opens that safe and copies those papers? Who is the traitor?"

"God only knows!" I answered. "It is a hopeless mystery."

"Yet we must solve it," Lord Chelsford said, "and quickly. If a single batch of genuine maps and plans were tampered with, disparities would certainly appear, and the thing might be suspected. Besides, upon the face of it, the thing is terribly serious."

"You have a plan," I said.

"I have," Lord Chelsford answered calmly. "You remember Grooton?"

"Certainly! He was a servant at Braster."

"And the very faithful servant of his country also," Lord Chelsford remarked. "You know, I believe, that he was a secret service man. He is entirely safe, and I have sent for him. Now I imagine that the Duke will wish our new secretary to live still at the 'Brand'—he preferred it in your case, as you will remember. Our new secretary is going to be my nephew. He is very stolid and honest, and fortunately not a chatterbox. He is going to be the nominal secretary, but I want you to be the one who really does the work."

"I am afraid I don't understand!" I was forced to admit.

"It will mean," Lord Chelsford said, "some privation and a great deal of inconvenience for you. But I am going to ask you to face it, for the end to be gained is worth it. I want you also to be at the 'Brand,' but to lie hidden all the day time. You can have one of the upstair rooms fitted as a writing room. Then you and my nephew can do the transposition. And beyond all that I want you to think—to think and to watch."

My heart leaped with joy to think that after all I was not to go into exile. Then the quiet significance of Lord Chelsford's last words were further impressed upon me by the added gravity of his manner.

"Mr. Ducaine," he said, "you must see for yourself that I am running a very serious risk in making these plans with you behind the backs of the Duke of Rowchester and Colonel Ray. The Duke is a man of the keenest sense of honour, as his recent commercial transactions have shown. He has parted with a hundred thousand pounds rather than that the shadow of a stigma should rest upon his name. He is also my personal friend, and very sensitive of any advice or criticism. Then Ray — a V.C., and one of the most popular soldiers in England to-day — he also is quick tempered, and he also is my friend. You can see for yourself that in acting as I am, behind the backs of these men, I am laying myself open to very grave trouble. Yet I see no alternative. There is a rank traitor either on the Military Board or closely connected with the Duke's household. He does not know it, nor do they know it, but everyone of his servants has been vigorously and zealously watched without avail. The circle has been drawn closer and closer, Mr. Ducaine. Down in Braster you may be able to help me in narrowing it down till only one person is within it. Listen!"

Lady Chelsford entered, gorgeous in white satin and a flaming tiara. She looked at me, I thought, a little gravely.

"Morton," she said, "I want you to spare me a minute. Mr. Ducaine will excuse you, I am sure."

Lord Chelsford and she left the room together. I, feeling the heat of the apartment, walked to the window, and raising the sash looked out into the cool dark evening. At the door, drawn up in front of Lord Chelsford's brougham, was a carriage with a tall footman standing facing me. I recognized him and the liveries in a moment. It was the Rowchester carriage. Some one from Rowchester House was even now with Lord and Lady Chelsford.

Fresh complications, then! Had the Duke come to see me off, or had his suspicions been aroused? Was he even now insisting upon an explanation with Lord Chelsford? The minutes passed, and I began to get restless and anxious. Then the door opened, and Lord Chelsford entered alone. He came over at once to my side. He was looking perplexed and a little annoyed.

"Ducaine," he said, "Lady Angela Harberly is here."

I started, and I suppose my face betrayed me.

"Lady Angela — here?"

"And she wishes to see you," he continued. "Lady Chelsford is chaperoning her to-night to Suffolk House, but she says that she should have come here in any case. She believes that you are going to China."

"Did you tell her?" I asked.

"I have told her nothing," he answered. "The question is, what you are to tell her. I understand, Ducaine, that Lady Angela was engaged to be married to Colonel Ray."

"I believe that she is," I admitted.

"Then I do not understand her desire to see you," Lord Chelsford said. "The Duke of Rowchester is my friend and relative, Ducaine, and I do not see how I can permit this interview."

"And I," said a quiet thrilling voice behind his back, "do not know how you are going to prevent it."

She closed the door behind her. She was so frail and so delicately beautiful in her white gown, with the ropes of pearls around her neck, the simply parted hair, and her dark eyes were so plaintive and yet so tender, that the angry exclamation died away on Lord Chelsford's lips.

"Angela," he said, "Mr. Ducaine is here. You can speak with him if you will, but it must be in my presence. You must not think that I do not trust you — both of you. But I owe this condition to your father."

She came over to me very timidly. She seemed to me so beautiful, so exquisitely childish, that I touched the fingers of the hand she gave me with a feeling of positive reverence.

"You have come to wish me God-speed," I murmured. "I shall never forget it."

"You are really going, then?"

"I am going for a little time out of your life, Lady Angela," I answered. "It is necessary: Lord Chelsford knows that. But I am not going in disgrace. I am very thankful to be able to tell you that."

"It was not necessary to tell me," she answered. "Am I not here?"

I bent low over her hand, which rested still in mine.

"Mine is not a purposeless exile — nor altogether an unhappy one — now," I said. "I have work to do, Lady Angela, and I am going to it with a good heart. When we meet again I hope that it may be differently. Your coming — the memory of it will stand often between me and loneliness. It will sweeten the very bitterest of my days."

"You are really going — to China?" she murmured.

I glanced towards Lord Chelsford. His back was turned to us. If he understood the meaning of my pause he made no sign.

"I may not tell you where I am going or why," I answered. "But I will tell you this, Lady Angela. I shall come back, and as you have come to see me to-night, so shall I come to you before long. If you will trust me I will prove myself worthy of it."

She did not answer me with any word at all, but with a sudden little forward movement of both her hands, and I saw that her eyes were swimming in tears. Yet they shone into mine like stars, and I saw heaven there.

"I am sorry," Lord Chelsford said, gravely interposing, "but Lady Chelsford will be waiting for you, Angela. And I think that I must ask you to remember that I cannot sanction, or appear by my silence to sanction, anything of this sort."

So he led her away, but what did I care? My heart was beating with the rapture of her backward glance. I cared neither for Ray nor the Duke nor any living person. For with me it was the one supreme moment of a man's lifetime, come too at the very moment of my despair. I was no longer at the bottom of the pit. The wonderful gates stood open.

CHAPTER XXXVIII
A TERRIBLE DISCOVERY

I Called softly to Grooton from my room upstairs.

"Grooton!"

"Yes, sir."

"You are alone?"

"Yes, sir."

"Is Mr. Hill still up at the Court?"

"He will be there until midnight, sir."

A gust of wind came suddenly roaring through the wood, drowning even the muffled thunder of the sea below. The rain beat upon the window panes. The little house, strongly built though it was, seemed to quiver from its very foundations. I caught up my overcoat, and boldly descended the narrow staircase. Grooton stood at the bottom, holding a lamp in his hand.

"You are quite safe to-night, sir," he said. "There'll be no one about in such a storm."

I stood still for a moment. The raging and tearing of the sea below had momentarily triumphed over the north wind.

"The trees in the spinney are snapping like twigs, sir," Grooton remarked. "There's one lying right across the path outside. But you'll excuse me, sir — you're not going out!"

"I think so, Grooton," I answered, "for a few minutes. Remember that I have been a prisoner here for three days. I'm dying for some fresh air."

"I don't think it's hardly safe, sir," he protested, deprecatingly. "Not that there's any fear of your being seen: the wind's enough to carry you over the cliff."

"I shall risk it, Grooton," I answered. "I think that the wind is going down, and there won't be a soul about. It's too good a chance to miss."

I waited for a momentary lull, and then I opened the door and slipped out. The first breath of cold strong air was like wine to me after my confinement, but a moment later I felt my breath taken away, and I was lifted almost from my feet by a sudden gust. I linked my arm around the trunk of a swaying pine tree and hung there till the lull came. Up into the darkness from that unseen gulf below came showers of spray, white as snow, falling like rain all about me. It was a night to remember.

Presently I turned inland, and reached the park. I left the footpath so that I should avoid all risk of meeting any one, and followed the wire fencing which divided the park from the belt of fir trees bordering the road. I walked for a few hundred yards, and then stopped short.

I had reached the point where that long straight road from Braster turned sharply away inland for the second time. At a point about a quarter of a mile away, and rapidly approaching me, came a twin pair of flaring eyes. I knew at once what they were—the head lights of a motor car. Without a moment's hesitation I doubled back to the "Brand."

"Grooton!" I called sharply.

Grooton appeared.

"Is any one at Braster Grange?" I asked.

"Not that I have heard of, sir," he answered.

"You do not know whether Mrs. Smith-Lessing is expected back?"

"I have not heard, sir. They left no servants there—not even a caretaker."

I stepped back again into the night and took the shortest cut across the park to the house. As I neared the entrance gates I left the path and crept up close to the plantation which bordered the road. My heart gave a jump as I listened. I could hear the low level throbbing of a motor somewhere quite close at hand. The lights had been extinguished, but it was there waiting. I did not hesitate any longer. I kept on the turf by the side of the avenue and made my way up to the house.

The library alone and one small window on the ground floor were lit. I crept up on the terrace and tried to peer in, but across each of the library windows the curtains were too closely drawn. There remained the small window at the end of the terrace. I crept on tiptoe towards this, feeling my way through the darkness by the front of the house. Suddenly I came to a full stop. I flattened myself against the stonework and held my breath. Some one else was on the terrace. What I had heard was unmistakable. It was the wind blowing amongst a woman's skirts, and the woman was very close at hand.

I almost felt her warm breath as she stole past me. I caught a gleam of a pale face, sufficient to tell me who she was. She passed on and took up her stand outside that small end window.

I, too, crept nearer to it. — About a yard away there was a projection of the front. I stole into the deep corner and waited. A few feet from me I knew that she too was waiting.

Half an hour, perhaps an hour, passed. My ears became trained to all sounds that were not absolutely deadened by the roar of the wind. I heard the crash of falling boughs in the wood, the more distant but unchanging thunder of the sea, the sharp spitting of the rain upon the stone walk. And I heard the opening of the window by the side of which I was leaning.

I was only just in time. Through the raised sash there came a hand, holding a packet of some sort, and out of the darkness came another hand eagerly stretched out to receive it. I brushed it ruthlessly aside, tore the packet from the fingers which suddenly strove to retain it, and with my other hand I caught the arm a little above the wrist. I heard the flying footsteps of my fellow-watcher, but I did not even turn round. A fierce joy was in my heart. Now I was to know. The veil of mystery which had hung over the doings at Braster was to be swept aside. I stooped down till my eyes were within a few inches of the hand. I passed my fingers over it. I felt the ring —

Then I remember only that mad headlong flight back across the park, where the very air seemed full of sobbing, mocking voices, and the ground beneath my feet swayed and heaved. I could not even think coherently. I heard the motor go tearing down the road past me, and come to a standstill at the turn. Still I had no thought of any danger. It never occurred to me to leave the footpath and make my way back to the "Brand," as I might well have done, by a more circuitous route. I kept on the footpath, and just as I reached the little iron gate which led into the spinney, I felt a man's arm suddenly flung around my neck, and with a jerk I was thrown almost off my feet.

"He is here, madame," I heard a low voice say. "Take the papers from him. I have him safe."

I think that my desperate humour lent me more than my usual strength. With a fierce effort I wrenched myself free. Almost immediately I heard the click of a revolver. "If you move," a low voice said, "I fire!" "What do you want?" I asked. "The papers." I laughed bitterly. "Are they worth my life?" I asked. "The life of a dozen such as you," the man answered. "Quick! Hand them over."

Then I heard a little cry from the woman who had been standing a few feet off. In the struggle I had lost my cap, and a faint watery moon, half hidden by a ragged bank of black clouds, was shining weakly down upon us.

"Guy," she cried, and her voice was shaking as though with terror. "Guy, is that you?"

I lost my self-control. I forgot her sex, I forgot everything except that she was responsible for this unspeakable corruption. I said terrible things to her. And she listened, white—calm—speechless. When I had finished she signed to the man to leave us. He hesitated, but with a more peremptory gesture she dismissed him.

"Guy," she said, "you have not spared me. Perhaps I do not deserve it. Now listen. The whole thing is at an end. Those few papers are all we want. Your father is already in France. I am leaving at once. Give me those papers and you will be rid of us for ever. If you do not I must stay on until I have received copies of a portion of them, at any rate. You know very well now that I can do this. Give me those that you have. It will be safer—in every way."

"Give them to you?" I answered scornfully. "Are you serious?"

"Very serious, Guy. Do you not see that the sooner it is all over—the better—the safer—up there?"

She pointed towards the house. I could have struck the white fingers with their loathsome meaning.

"I shall take this packet to Lord Chelsford," I said. "I am down here as a spy—a spy upon spies. He is up at the house now, and to-morrow this packet will be in his hands. I shall tell him how I secured it. I think that after that you will not have many opportunities for plying your cursed trade."

"You know the consequences?"

"They are not my concern," I answered coldly.

She looked over her shoulder.

"If I," she said, "were as unwavering in my duty as you I should call Jean back."

"I am indifferent," I answered. "I do not value my life enough to shrink from fighting for it."

She turned away.

"You are very young, Guy," she said, "and you talk like a very young man. You must go your own way. Send for Lord Chelsford, if you will. But remember all that it will mean. Can't you see that such stern morality as yours is the most exquisite form of selfishness? Good-bye, Guy."

She glided away. I reached the "Brand" undisturbed.

CHAPTER XXXIX
THE TRAITOR

"I do not understand you, Ducaine," Lord Chelsford said slowly. "You have been a faithful and valuable servant to your country, and you know very well that your services are not likely to be forgotten. I want you only to be consistent. I must know from whom you received this packet."

"I cannot tell you, sir," I answered. "It was a terribly dark night, and it is not easy to identify a hand. Besides, it was snatched away almost at once."

"In your own mind, Ducaine," Chelsford said, "have you hazarded a guess as to who that unseen person might be?"

"It is too serious a matter to hazard guesses about, sir," I answered.

"Nevertheless," Lord Chelsford continued, eyeing me closely, "in your own mind you know very well who that person was. You are a bad liar, Ducaine. There was something about the hand which told you the truth—a ring, perhaps. At any rate, something."

"I had no time to feel for such things, sir," I answered.

"Ducaine," Lord Chelsford said, "I am forced to connect your refusal to hazard even a surmise as to the identity of that hand with your sudden desire to break off all connection with this matter. I am forced to come to a conclusion, Ducaine. You have discovered the truth. You know the traitor!"

"On the contrary, Lord Chelsford," I answered, "I know nothing.".

Later in the day he came to me again. I could see that he had made no fresh discovery.

"Ducaine," he said, "what time did you say that you left here last night?"

"At midnight, sir."

"And you were back?"

"Before one."

"That corresponds exactly with Grooton's statement," Lord Chelsford said. "And yet I have certain information that from a few minutes before eleven till two o'clock not one member of the Military Board quitted the library."

I bowed.

"That is conclusive," I remarked.

"It is remarkably inconclusive to me," Lord Chelsford remarked grimly. "Whom else save one of your friends who are all upon the Board could you possibly wish to shield?"

"That I even wish to do so," I answered, "is purely an assumption."

"You are fencing with me, young man," Lord Chelsford said grimly, "and it is not worth while. Hush!"

There was a rap at the door downstairs. We heard the Duke's measured tones.

"I understood that Lord Chelsford was here," he said.

"Lord Chelsford has left, your Grace," Grooton answered.

"And Mr. Hill?"

"He has been at the house all day, your Grace."

The Duke appeared to hesitate for a moment.

"Grooton," he said, "I rely upon you to see that Lord Chelsford has this note shortly. I am going for a little walk, and shall probably return this way. I wish you to understand that this note is for Lord Chelsford's own hand."

"Certainly, your Grace."

"Not only that, Grooton, but the fact that I called here and left a communication for Lord Chelsford is also—to be forgotten."

"I quite understand, your Grace," Grooton assured him.

The Duke struck a match, and a moment or two later we saw him strolling along the cliff side, smoking a cigarette, his hands behind him, prim, carefully dressed, walking with the measured ease of a man seeking an appetite for his dinner. He was scarcely out of sight, and Lord Chelsford was on the point of descending for his note, when my heart gave a great leap. Lady Angela emerged from the plantation and crossed the open space in front of the cottage with swift footsteps. Her hair was streaming in the breeze as though she had been running, but there was not a vestige of colour in her cheeks. Her eyes, too, were like the eyes of a frightened child.

Lord Chelsford descended the stairs and himself admitted her.

"Why, Angela," he exclaimed, "you look as though you had seen a ghost.
Is anything the matter?"

"Oh, I am afraid so," she answered. "Have you seen my father?"

"Why?" he asked, fingering the note which Grooton had silently laid upon the table.

"Something has happened!" she exclaimed. "I am sure of it. Last night he came to me before dinner. He told me that Blenavon was in trouble. It was necessary to send him money by a special messenger, by the only person who knew his whereabouts. He gave me a packet, and he told me that at a quarter-past twelve last night I was to be in my music-room, and directly the stable clock struck that I was to open the window, and some one would be there on the terrace and take the packet. I did exactly as he told me, and there was someone there; but I had just held out the packet when a third person snatches it away, and held my hand close to his eyes as though to try and guess who I was. I managed to get it away and close the window, but I think that the wrong person must have taken the packet. I told my father to-day, and — you know that terribly still look of his. I thought that he was never going to speak again. When I asked him if there was a good deal of money in it — he only groaned."

Upon the top of the stairs I was shaking with excitement. I heard Lord Chelsford speak, and his voice was hoarse.

"Since then," he asked, "what?"

"A man came to see father. He drove from Wells. He looked like a Frenchman, but he gave no name. He was in the library for an hour. When he left he walked straight out of the house and drove away again. I went into the library, and — you know how strong father is — he was crouching forward across the table, muttering to himself. It was like some sort of a fit. He did not know me when I spoke to him. Lord Chelsford, what does it all mean?"

"Go on!" he answered. "Tell me the rest."

"There is nothing else," she faltered. "He got better presently, and he kissed me. I have never known him to do such a thing before, except at morning or night. And then he locked himself in the study and wrote. About an hour afterwards I heard him — asking everywhere for you. The servants thought that you had come here. I saw him crossing the park, so I followed."

Lord Chelsford came to the bottom of the stairs and called me by name. I heard Lady Angela's little cry of surprise. I was downstairs in a moment, and she came straight into my arms. Her dear tear-stained little face buried itself upon my shoulder.

"I am so thankful, so thankful that you are here," she murmured.

And all the while, with the face of a man forced into the presence of tragedy, Lord Chelsford was reading that letter. When he had finished his hands were shaking and his face was grey. He moved over to the fireplace, and, without a moment's hesitation, he thrust the letter into the flames. Not content with that, he stood over it, poker in hand, and beat the ashes into powder. Then he turned to the door.

"Take care of Angela, Ducaine," he exclaimed, and hurried out.

But Lady Angela had taken alarm. She hastened after him, dragging me with her. Lord Chelsford was past middle age, but he was running along the cliff path like a boy. We followed. Lady Angela would have passed him, but I held her back. She did not speak a word. Some vague prescience of the truth even then, I think, had dawned upon her.

We must have gone a mile before we came in sight of him. He was strolling along, only dimly visible in the gathering twilight, still apparently smoking, and with the air of a man taking a leisurely promenade. He was toiling up the side of the highest cliff in the neighbourhood, and once we saw him turn seaward and take off his hat as though enjoying the breeze. Just as he neared the summit he looked round. Lord Chelsford waved his hand and shouted.

"Rowchester," he cried. "Hi! Wait for me."

The Duke waved his hand as though in salute, and turned apparently with the object of coming to meet us. But at that moment, without any apparent cause, he lurched over towards the cliff side, and we saw him fall. Lady Angela's cry of frenzied horror was the most awful thing I had ever heard. Lord Chelsford took her into his arms.

"Climb down, Ducaine," he gasped. "I'm done!"

I found the Duke on the shingles, curiously unmangled. He had the appearance of a man who had found death restful.

CHAPTER XL
THE THEORIES OF A NOVELIST

The novelist smiled. He had been buttonholed by a very great man, which pleased him. He raised his voice a little. There were others standing around. He fancied himself already the centre of the group. He forgot the greatness of the great man.

"In common with many other people, my dear Marquis," he said, "you labour under a great mistake. Human character is governed by as exact laws as the physical world. Give me a man's characteristics, and I will undertake to tell you exactly how he will act under any given circumstances. It is a question of mathematics. We all carry with us, inherited or acquired, a certain amount of resistance to evil influence, certain predilections towards good and vice versa, according as we are decent fellows or blackguards. Some natures are more complex than others, of course—that only means that the weighing up of the good and evil in them is a more difficult matter. There are experts who can tell you the weight of a haystack by looking at it, and there are others who are able at Christmas-time to indulge in an unquenchable thirst by accurately computing the weight, down to ounces, of the pig or turkey raffled for at their favourite public-house. So the trained student of his fellows can also diagnose his subjects and anticipate their actions."

The Marquis smiled.

"You analytical novelists would destroy for us the whole romance of life," he declared. "I will not listen to you any longer. I fear ignorance less than disillusion!"

He passed on, and the little group at once dispersed. The novelist was left alone. He went off in a huff. Lord Chelsford plucked me by the arm.

"Let us sit down, Ducaine," he said. "What rubbish these men of letters talk!"

I glanced towards the ballroom, but my companion shook his head.

"Angela is dancing with the Portuguese Ambassador," he said, "and he will never give up his ten minutes afterwards. You must pay the penalty of having — married the most beautiful woman in London, Guy, and sit out with the old fogies. What rubbish that fellow did talk!"

"You are thinking —" I murmured.

"Of the Duke! Yes! There was a man who to all appearance was a typical English gentleman, proud, sensitive of his honour, in every action which came before the world a right-dealing and a right-doing man. To do what seemed right to him from one point of view he stripped himself of lands and fortune, and when that was not enough he stooped to unutterable baseness. He was willing to betray his country to justify his own sense of personal honour."

"In justice to him," I said, "one must remember that he never for a moment believed in the possibility of a French invasion."

Lord Chelsford shook his head.

"It is too nice a point," he declared. "We may not reckon it in his favour. I wonder how our friends on the other side felt when they knew that they had paid fifty thousand pounds for false information? We ought to make you a peer, Ducaine. The Trogoldy money would stand it."

"For Heaven's sake, don't!" I cried. "What have I done that you should want to banish me into the pastures?"

"You talk too much," my companion murmured. "In the Lords it wouldn't matter, but in the Commons you are a nuisance. I suppose you want to be taken into the Cabinet."

"Quite true!" I admitted. "You want young men there, and I am ready any time."

"A man with a wife like yours," Lord Chelsford remarked, thoughtfully, "is bound to go anywhere he wants. Then he sits down and takes all the credit to himself."

Angela passed on the arm of the Ambassador. She waved her hand gaily to us, but her companion drew her firmly away. We both looked after her admiringly.

"Guy," Lord Chelsford said, "we have both of us done some good work in our time, but never anything better than the way we managed to hoodwink everybody—even herself, about her father. Amongst the middle classes he remains a canonized saint, the man who pauperized himself for their sakes. Ray was too full of Blenavon's little aberrations to suspect any one else, and our friends from across the water who might—I mean the woman—have been inclined for a little blackmail, were obliging enough to make a final disappearance in the unlucky Henriette. The woman was saved, though, by-the-bye."

"The woman is still alive," I told him, "but I will answer for her silence. I allow her a small pension—all she would accept. She is living in the south of France somewhere."

"And Blenavon," Lord Chelsford said, with a smile, "has married an American girl who has made a different man of him. What character those women have! She hasn't a penny, they tell me, until her father dies, and they work on their ranch from sunrise. She will be an ornament to our aristocracy when they do come back."

"They are coming next spring," I remarked, "if they can do it out of the profits of the ranch—not unless. Blenavon has carried out his father's wishes to the letter, and cut off the entail of everything that was necessary."

"What a silly ass that novelist was!" Lord Chelsford declared vigorously.